LETTERS TO MARINA

Letters to Marina

DACIA MARAINI

Translated by Dick Kitto and Elspeth Spottiswood

Camden Press

Published in 1987 by
Camden Press Ltd
43 Camden Passage, London N1 8EB, England

© 1981 Dacia Maraini
Translation © Dick Kitto and Elspeth Spottiswood

The translators wish to thank Dacia Maraini for her help
with the translation.

Set in Baskerville
by Photosetting & Secretarial Services
Yeovil and printed and bound by
Richard Clay Ltd, Bungay, Suffolk

British Library CIP Data

Maraini, Dacia
Letters to Marina. — (Women's fiction)
I. Title   II. Lettere a Marina. *English*
III. Series
853′.914[F] PQ4873.A69

ISBN 0-948491-12-4 Pbk

ABOUT THE AUTHOR

Dacia Maraini is one of Italy's best known women writers. Her novel The Age of Discontent ('L'Eta del Malessere') won the Prix Formentor in 1963 and has been translated into twelve languages. She has written nine novels, four volumes of poetry and nine plays.

OTHER WORKS BY DACIA MARAINI

Novels

La Vacanza (1962); published in Britain as 'The Holiday'
L'Eta del Malessere (1963): winner of the 'Prix Formentor' in 1963; published in Britain as 'The Age of Discontent'
A Memoria (1967)
Memorie di Una Ladra (1968); published in Britain as 'Memories of a Female Thief'
Donna in Guerra (1975); published in Britain as 'Woman at War'
Lettere a Marina (1981); published in Britain as 'Letters to Marina'
Il Treno per Helsinki (1984); to be published in Britain in 1988 as 'Train to Helsinki'
Isolina (1985)

Poetry

Crudelta all'aria aperta (1968)
Donne mie (1974)
Mangiami Pure (1980)
Dimenticato di Dimenticare (1983)

Theatre

Riccato a Teatro e Altre Commedie (1968)
Don Juan (1976)
La Donna Perfetta (1974)
Viva l'Italia (1976)
Dialogo di una Prostituta con un suo Cliente (1978)
I Sogni di Clitennestra (1981)
Suor Juana (1980)
Lezioni d'Amore (1982)
Mary Stuart (1984)

Dear Marina

At last I am settled here in this ugly flat. With my fingers on the keyboard of my typewriter I look out on the hazy green sea and I am filled with a sense of joyful anticipation only my neck still hurting from where you sank your teeth into it like a little girl.

Why am I here? To escape from you to finish the novel I've been working on half-heartedly for more than eighteen months to regain the strength I've lost not knowing how or why or whether it was because of the wrong direction I've taken over the last few years.

I shan't ring you up. I'll write to you and that will be enough. You refused to talk to me and now I'm doing the same to you. I'm writing these letters without your knowledge. I'm not even sure I'll post them. If you ever want us to become friends again we'll hang our sex outside the window like cherries in a basket and then we'll talk together.

But just now I want to tell you our story from the beginning since you seem to have forgotten it. Maybe I've forgotten it too. I feel a compulsion to tell you all those things about myself that you've never wanted to know. You were in love with a woman who came to you without a past new-born and naked out of the dark womb of time.

So here I am far away unburdening myself of everything you've always ignored – of the times we met and encountered each other and how I saw them with my short-sighted and distorted vision – that short-sightedness and vagueness which according to you makes all my accounts garbled and unrecognisable.

Giorgia told me you said I seduced you. That's true: an open seduction that was also a liberation and which set us both on fire and eventually drove us apart.

Just now I want to tell you how this painful love was born and grew

7

and all those comings and goings and me washing myself under my armpits with my thoughts far away. I have to begin right at the beginning because the recent story is too close to me and my legs have become immersed in a molten liquid that is as clinging as the moonshine's watery beams.

Dear Marina

Last night I dreamed I was with a girl who had no head. I took her by the hand and her fingers clung to mine affectionately. I talked to her even though I knew she had no ears and could not hear me. I was telling her about some plum jam that had turned out too bitter. She was not wounded but she was strangely mutilated. Round her chest she wore a piece of flowered organdie gathered roughly at the neck like the opening of a sack. Above it there was no neck – nothing – but this did not seem to disconcert either of us. She was a dark girl – not her hair of course because she did not have any but dark-skinned hands dark pubic hair a dark presence that disquieted and intrigued me and this child-like billowing dress clinging hands and pallid slender body from which I sensed her thoughts flowing into me as if she were communicating with me through the tips of her fingers.

I didn't know where we were going but we seemed to be approaching a house. But whose house? I can't recall any house that is both familiar and unfamiliar and has violet petunias on the window-sill.

I woke in a state of stupor and confusion. I was uncertain whether the girl with no head was you. You are all head: you have imprisoned your heart between the folds of your strong pitiless brain.

You say you want to hurt me because I've rejected you but perhaps it's I who reject you because I know you want to hurt me. Which comes first? Your wish to swallow me up followed by my flight or my flight followed by your determination to swallow me?

I had to escape from your stubborn mischievous wish to turn me into a mother against my every instinct – a bad violent mother unjust like all mothers who give their love where they should not and are indifferent to those who are really in need of it. With her dead son who died years ago still stirring uneasily in her womb she was all prepared to lavish care on her unhappy daughter but then suddenly reverted to the sad flute music of the boy child calling from within her.

Those lilies you sent me before you went away a great bunch of giant pale pink trumpets with powdery yellow pistils and a scent of such sweetness that it made my head swim and brought back long lost memories... a distant summer in Guatemala when my father took me on a visit to his lover a Danish girl with limpid eyes who lived in a garden full of lilies. The moment we arrived she led me under an airy colonnaded porch and sat me in a wicker chair in front of a plate of brown bread and honey. I stayed there for over an hour waiting for the two lovers who walked in the garden and then went together into the house.

That honey tasted of lilies and I was certain that the Danish girl had made it by treading the flowers in her garden with her feet like treading grapes. For an hour I stayed eating bread and honey happy with my imaginings but then I began to get bored. I did not get up because my father had told me not to. I imagined the two of them falling into a ravine being suffocated by quicksands or devoured by coyotes (at night they circle round like stray dogs scavenging the piles of rubbish behind the houses) and I saw my father's beautiful body covered in blood and I began to tremble all over.

But why did you send me those lilies? They're flowers I've never been able to appreciate. There's something about them that reminds me of hospitals so clean and polished and yet sensuous and carnal and the scent so insidious and sickening. It's true I've never once held a lily in my hands since those far-off days in Guatemala. Did you know this when you sent me those ten lilies their regal heads heavy with melting perfume? What was it you were saying to me? You never do anything without a meaning. Sending me those lilies means you want to tell me something but I can't imagine what it is. Perhaps you only want to remind me that even if you are somewhere far away you still

9

exist with your porcelain belly your perfumed arms and your senses keyed up and expectant.

Dear Marina

Shall I start with Marco or go right back to the beginning? Did you know that a few days before coming here I saw him again? He telephoned:
  'Can we see each other? I've so much to tell you.'
  'Where?'
  'The usual place.'
  He said it so charmingly. He could only mean the Piazza Sonnino in front of the Reale Cinema. You know how often I've stood there waiting for him and watched the people get off the bus. One used to arrive every minute and the doors would open and I'd stand there gaping at each man as he got off and moved in my direction: no not that one... not him... not him... Even though you don't know Marco's brown ribbed corduroy trousers you must remember the way he runs down steps so awkwardly and yet at such a speed looking both shy and cocksure as if to say 'Here I am twenty-five and handsome and randy and ready for anything. Love me and maybe I'll let you have a little bit of myself in exchange.'
  So there I was walking down the Piazza Sonnino and lo and behold he was there already waiting. Such a thing had never happened before! He was never punctual and it was always me who had to wait for him – 'Would you believe it we were held up because there was a fire!' – 'Would you believe it someone had his wallet stolen and the bus-driver refused to let anyone off the bus!' – 'Would you believe it there was an epilectic who started to scream! He may even have been a werewolf' – each time his excuses became more and more bizarre.
  He told me all about his latest lover a woman of fifty who has got him work with a new musical on the life of St Paul and he's going to sing and dance and get really good money. He was all excited about

it. He smiled so nicely and squeezed my hand and looked straight into my eyes all the time.

A year ago I would have been trembling all over with excitement. Now there's only a feeling of loss of emptiness of longing . . . The way he smiles no longer fills me with anguished love. Instead it gives me a rather painful and futile sensation of freedom – a freedom I don't really know how to take advantage of.

How fragile our memories are! I can hear you saying stop telling me about these men who don't interest me tell me about yourself. But I was in love with Marco so I have to tell you about him. Anyway that was when I met you – just at the time when that beautiful peacock's egg was in the process of being shattered. I have to begin from there from that fragile shell which somehow kept me drugged and numb encapsulated within its envelope for three whole years.

Dear Marina

I've been thinking of you in this solitary place I've fled to so as not to see you or be reminded of you. I left Rome secretly without saying a word to anyone. But I know you'll find me – you have the omniscience of a Sibyl. Although you shut yourself up in your house with cats and lavender and books and jars of jam and Indian cushions you have only to close your eyes for a moment to know where I am and what I am doing.

This flat is tiny and the smell of coffee percolates uninterruptedly right through the block. It's never absent. At about four in the morning it begins to die away only to return in full force at half past six. I am on the fourth floor and from my window I look out over a football ground that is strewn with rubbish. I can see a stretch of the road that goes to the South. The sea comes up between the houses but I only catch a glimpse of it the rest is cut off by an ugly eight-storey building. The bit I can see looks motionless and glassy. I can tell the time from its colour.

You know I don't wear a watch any more. Instead of wearing watches I give them away. Every time I fall in love I give a watch as a present. Symbolically this represents the female genitals.

I wrap the watchcase in gold paper tie it up with a red tassle and at the very moment when it's opened by loving hands I feel as if I've had an electric shock a sharp painful stab between my breasts. However much I'm thanked I am never satisfied. I don't want stupid thanks sham kisses and cries of joy. No I want something else – perhaps an instant of terror turning pale fainting the flesh shrivelling from fear – a moment frozen as if for eternity. Perhaps I want to create a sense of foreboding by the gift of this symbolic cunt: a woman's cunt its internal workings intricately jewelled cupped between the hands of a man. I want to force it on his astonished attention. There's a picture by Dali of a landscape with watches each attached to pieces of wood strewn limp and exhausted all over the soft sensual sand. That's my gift and he must never forget that it represents something quite different from ordinary social time – the eternal rhythm of the machine. A perilous profound rhythm which will become an integral part of the body of its wearer like a warning or a signal of danger.

I've arranged my things (very few to be honest): my books above the box of files and my swimming costume and towels in the cupboard on the wall that's stained with mildew. The kitchen cups are almost all chipped the spoons and cutlery tarnished. I spent this morning cleaning the bath with bleach. The landlady tells me that before I came a married couple lived here. They had an aquarium of exotic fish and sometimes I imagine them embracing in the middle of the bed where the mattress sags watched by the silver eyes of the spotted tropical fish. A rosary with large beads of pink mother-of-pearl hangs from the bedhead.

I've paid three months' rent in advance but I don't think I shall be able to put up with it here for more than a week.

Dear Marina

I said I would tell you our story but each time I begin I'm sidetracked by other things. Do you remember how you and I first met at Alda and Bice's place? You were sitting on a low divan facing me and I was aware you were looking at me with insistent curiosity. It was almost too blatant. From the beginning there was something compelling in your glance a shy delicate will to possess me.

I was at once struck by your gaiety. You were existing and yet not existing in a boundless reality without a shadow of fear. I immediately sensed that you possessed a courage close to frenzy.

Do you remember Alda's solid plates with red borders and the way her teeth would protrude in a quiet withdrawn smile as she offered you food? All the tiresome trivia of life – quarrels traffic money work used to fall away when I arrived at that table set so firmly on the ground with its white tablecloth shining plates and cut-glass decanter filled with water. And the way she cooks everything gently simmering it so that the food is transformed and all the flavours mingle together – the smell of pork fat fried bacon onions lemon verbena all dissolved in the steam rising from the pot. With the powerful hands of someone born and bred in the mountains Alda ladles the red-hot stew on to each plate asking 'More? More?' and her shy generous smile tells you that it's not just the stew that is being ladled on to your plate but the most vulnerable part of herself for you to savour appreciatively to the last morsel.

I like the way she and Bice live together. They are like an old married couple: she just a little masculine ready to undertake all the rough work in the house yet when you meet her protective and maternal and Bice picking up the wine glasses one by one as if they were flowers her eyebrows raised in perpetual detachment. Bice is moody and never tells the truth not because she revels in deception but because of the way she's been brought up: she would cut her throat rather than say anything hurtful. But her body says everything without her meaning it to. Her fine nervous hands her varnished nails her very white teeth her long slender legs her broad heavy lips her eyes that watch your every movement with scepticism and a fleeting

13

imperceptible distaste. She makes one want to provoke her: to put one's feet on the table and shout 'prick!' in her ear.

You were watching me with expectation and curiosity but I was obsessed by a stomach-ache and by the smell of food and by the starry ugliness of Alda and the loving tone of her voice.

Fiammetta's presence disturbed me too. It was she who brought you there do you remember? She'd told me such a lot about you about Marina and her Minerva-like intelligence Marina and her Persian cats Marina's grace and charm that made her seem like a Queen of Fate. I'd thought to myself – all that? And there you were in the flesh wearing sandals with your toes so sunburnt and such plump toes they were just like a baby's or like the fleshy spikey leaves of a cactus.

We didn't talk to each other much. But I was all the time aware of your devious smile following me as if to say: you won't escape me. I was already trapped in the magnetic constellation of your thoughts. Or was I mistaken? Was it I who circled around you holding out enticements like a net to ensnare you? Yet I have the impression that from the first moment we saw each other it was you who was determined to make me 'your love' as you put it. Or have I got it all wrong?

Dear Marina

It's five days since I came to this ugly flat and you haven't found me yet. Yesterday at about ten o'clock the doorbell rang. I went on tiptoe to answer it. I was sure it was you and I was already imagining our tender embrace. So many times you've rejected me and then come looking for me and rejected me again and come back for me again in this cruel and deathly game of cat and mouse. You've done this to me so often that in the end I never believed you really were rejecting me. But each time it seemed to be true – you used to say it's better that we don't see each other any more. Then for four or five days we'd go without missing each other and I'd get used to living without you. I forced myself not to think of you I tidied away the luggage in my head shut the cupboard doors and drew black curtains over the windows. On the sixth day I'd hear a long laugh heavy with sarcasm on the answer-phone. Then suddenly a telegram: 'The spring has gone dry' followed by a parcel of ginger biscuits and fresh pistachio nuts.

Then we'd go to the cinema together or to a restaurant two old friends happy to have found each other again. Long walks in the country picnics by the river near Orte sleeping under the oak tree in Fiammetta's garden drinking wine. I was so relieved to have you with me again. 'I don't want to possess you any more' you said. 'I am happy this way.'

We went to fringe theatre places where one had to go down three hundred steps and sit on a damp floor to see some play or other of sheer intellectual acrobatics. Afterwards we rushed to eat outsize ices smothered in fresh cream and then drink white wine to take away the sickly-sweet taste of raspberries. When you drink you pout your lips a little and half-close your eyes as if you were savouring some strange esoteric pleasure.

'Can I come down beside you?'

'But Marina we've decided not to make love any more.'

'I'm only coming to drink a glass of wine.'

'All right then.'

'You don't trust yourself.'

'Yes I do only I don't want to risk starting it up all over again.'

'No no we won't start again.'

In the kitchen drinking red wine nibbling pieces of fresh cheese. You take off your shoes.

'Come and lie down here I want to talk to you.'

Your eyes are shining your arms become serpents there are two dark moons in your eyes. I stretch out beside you. The glasses are still full. We drink. You reach out for the plate of cheese and dried plums. You eat greedily watching me from under half-closed eye-lids. What are you trying to tell me – why don't I take my boots off considering how hot it is?

You take off my boots. You take my foot in your hand. You fondle it.

'Be careful. I don't want to start anything again.'

'But I'm not starting anything.' I put my boots back on. 'Honestly – I'm not starting again. You don't trust me.'

'You know how bad it makes me feel this cat and mouse game.'

'Don't worry. I've become as wise and cautious as an old owl.'

Your hand caresses my ankle. My legs tingle all over. Heat rises up in my throat. Suddenly you bare one of my breasts and you take it in your mouth with awkward grace. I don't dare to breathe. I know that to refuse you at that moment would be like giving you poison.

'Marina please don't. Let's stop!'

But you aren't talking any more you are gulping down my milk like a glutton. You are becoming intoxicated.

'Marina please that's enough. Where has that wise old owl flown to?'

How can I escape from your embrace? We end up stretched out beside each other head to head kissing awkwardly. You pull my clothes off. You take possession of me so violently that it takes my breath away.

Then later you are shouting coarsely at me:

'You repel me with your lack of feeling. I hate you. You fill me with horror. You shut yourself away from me. You never give me one little bit of yourself. You want to repel me but it's you who's repulsive.'

I knew it would end up like this with you screaming in my ear. I told you it would. The owl has ruffled feathers and eyes overflowing with hate. You stare at me as if I were your worst enemy. You leave slamming the door. We don't see each other for a week but then you begin it all over again with an enigmatic laugh on the answer-phone or a poem in my ear or a box of sweets or a bunch of daffodils.

I think of all this while I'm on my way to open the door. I want to put my arms round you but at the same time I am wary of repeating this old game of seduction and rejection . . . and then it wasn't you!

It was the next door neighbour asking me to turn the radio down because her children were trying to get to sleep. She didn't seem at all resentful. In fact she looked at me with curiosity and sympathy. She

16

made no move to go – it was as if the radio had been a pretext for coming to see me. I asked her in. She is small and slender all skin and bone with red-rimmed eyes and a voice like a moth. I couldn't help wondering how on earth she'd managed to produce two large fat boys from this miniscule tormented body. I've seen them several times on the stairs. She sat down for a moment and drank a cup of coffee that I warmed up for her and told me about her husband who is a masseur working in a home for incurables.

Actually it wasn't the radio that was the pretext for her visit but the tape-recorder. I'd been listening to Verdi's Macbeth. She came in just as the waltz began.

'I love this music. It really speaks to me' she said. 'It reminds me of my father.'

Soon afterwards Mauro her eldest boy arrived charging into his mother with such force that it made her lose her balance. He stands there tottering on his two legs. He's almost two and he's eating up his mother bit by bit. There's something obscene about the way this boy devours his mother. His fat stomach is already full of shreds of maternal flesh. Satisfied and triumphant he thumps it with his two large hands.

Last night I dreamed that someone was throwing lead into the mouth of an old man. I had a strange feeling that it was something to do with my father when he had become as old as my grandfather. A sign of his refusal to speak perhaps. My grandfather and my uncle lived in the same house and never spoke to each other for twenty years – he would have cut off his tongue rather than communicate with his son. I was still only a child and I sat at mealtimes watching them. I wasn't afraid I even felt a certain irrational respect for them already foreseeing how this silence would take root in my unfledged mouth and would never leave me.

It wasn't a positive silence consisting of things that do not need to be expressed it wasn't one of those silences that transcend words. It was a disembodied silence made up of things left unsaid through too much anger and unhappiness a silence that expressed a sombre malevolent impotence an impotence of love.

Even if I never managed to talk to my father I held long lover's

17

discourses with my son. I loved the boy who floated in my womb his wayward blue eyes cheerful and churlish at the same time. I knew that even though I hadn't yet seen him. He clung impulsively to the umbilical cord with two powerful hands. I tried to guess whether he was a boy or a girl by suspending a ring from a hair. I'd been told that if it was a boy the ring would turn clockwise and so it did.

Perhaps another time and he would have made it. You can't imagine how this son stirred beneath the wide dome of my belly. He was an athlete with the muscles of a swimmer and all on his own he made headlong jumps that took my breath away each time falling back on the tender nourishing waters of his mother so that when I lay immobilised in bed with clots of blood slipping from my vagina he smiled in triumph.

Yes perhaps one more day would have been sufficient - a little more oxygen another twenty-four hours of exhausting assault on the cord and he would have come through. Instead he was already too large and he pressed down on the placenta until it was below him and so it was that the more he struggled for life the closer he came to death.

Towards the end I ceased to feel him jumping around. I was conscious of him moving and thrusting but he was doing it without any enjoyment as if he were in a paroxysm of rage. I could feel something wasn't right but I never imagined he was going to die. I held myself still as if I were trying to stop breathing. I ate like a pig. I stuffed myself with all the disgusting things that the hospital thrust at me to keep up my strength. I slept stretched out never turning on my side so as to give him a calm tranquil space. But he moved more and more feebly unable to find any peace.

Then one morning I stopped feeling him at all. I called the nurse. She said he was sleeping. Later I had to call the doctor. Both glued their ears to my belly exchanging secret looks from which I was excluded. Then they went away. Only when they brought a wheelchair to take me to the labour room was I told that he was dead and it was necessary to pull him out.

My legs were covered with two open sleeves of coarse cotton. I had to press my feet against two metal supports. But my son wouldn't come out. 'Push harder! Push harder!' But I didn't have any contractions at all. I just could not manage to push him out. The doctor tried to enlarge the opening of the uterus with his hands. I was transfixed by a violent stabbing pain. I fainted. My swimmer son my athlete stayed clinging to his mother's womb and refused to budge. He wanted to fester quietly away inside me to poison me with the venom of the eternal child. He wanted to capture me from within to absorb me and then to destroy me.

But I didn't want to let him go either. In my efforts to hold him back my muscles contracted and tautened like loving forceps closing round his body which I had so longed for. My belly clasped him and wanted him for itself.

I refused to surrender to the gloved hands of the obstetrician. I was determined not to go back home alone. Those healthy faces oozing politeness and practical intelligence and common sense filled me with horror. Together my son and I will go down into the darkness of the future – this was the only way I could feel after months of being confined to bed in this claustrophobic relationship that was silent pure overwhelming... and terrible. My body would not open and the child became heavy and frozen inside me and I prepared to die however meaninglessly in this hospital bed under an arc-light that blinded my eyes with these half-sleeves on my legs and the smell of surgical spirit and ether in my nostrils. Gross and clumsy with my much-beloved son whom I had chosen to imprison forever inside me I decided to abandon this world where we had walked together and walk with him in another world. I would forsake without a sigh all the good and beautiful things awaiting me outside where nothing mattered to me any more nothing at all. With my son I had fulfilled myself and now I could surrender myself to death. I did not feel the injections they were giving me and I could no longer distinguish what they were saying. I refused to breathe through the oxygen mask I wanted nothing but the pressure of my son's firm embrace inside my guts.

At that moment when I chose to die I let myself go and my uterus softened just enough to allow the head to slip out then the shoulders and then the body of a very beautiful baby with blue eyes wide open in death. The blood began to flow violently creating a torrent a cascade a river between the surfaces of my mangled flesh. Deprived of my son and all alone I was in danger of dying from loss of blood.

I didn't know anything more about myself until I was lifted up on pillows by two nurses and then undressed to the navel and bandaged tightly enough to suffocate me. It was 'to send the milk away' they told me. I took hold of my nipple and was able to make it spurt into the face of the nurse. I laughed at her as I did it and the woman scolded me in a motherly voice as if I had been a child. I was so weak and empty of blood that day after day they had to crucify me with two needles fixed into my wrists with sticking-plaster: dark blood descending drop by drop from two glass jars hung with two glistening tubes. As soon as one jar became empty they replaced it with another. Apparently out of three litres of blood I had lost two and a half.

Beneath the tight bandages I felt tiny athlete's feet pushing off to take a flying leap up! up! in the great blue vault of my numbed belly as my son did his acrobatic turns. I followed him with the interior eye that mothers have the warlike and watchful eye of a falcon and I held my breath when he poised himself for a moment in the vault before he seized the swinging cord to let himself fall gently on to the blood-stained floor of my womb. His somersaults went on for a long time especially at night making me giddy and giving me a sensation of nausea that twisted my mouth.

Still another two months of hospital reading novel after novel swollen now with words little black marks on paper. Crucified by those needles that nourished me so cruelly torturing my flesh blood foaming in the transparent jars white liquids slowly descending to fill my empty veins with sugar protein minerals salts.

I don't remember anything of that time except the nausea at night from the exasperated jumps of my phantom son inside my empty belly. It made me feverish to watch him but I could not stop myself.

Dear Marina

A short time before I left Rome the porter gave me a parcel with a note. I recognised the handwriting immediately: those 'ls' like buttonholes sewn in angry haste and the 'rs' which get confused with those speedy flying 'ns'. And your firm threatening signature 'M'. The note read 'Red Riding Hood has eaten the wolf' and even if you hadn't put your signature I would have known it was you.

Inside the parcel I found a pendant of black antique glass with a long teardrop to hang carefully round my tense white neck as a mark of my ingratitude.

I've asked you so often not to send me presents. I don't want them. The last time I picked up that ring you gave me I could feel your breath in my ears like a ferocious dragon. I felt the flames reaching right down my throat. It isn't presents you're giving me but little magic signs to imprison me inside the charmed circle of your will. The black glass teardrop on my throat the small crown of bleeding thorns on my finger the green enamel serpent encircling my wrist – I am nothing but a plaster madonna hung with votive offerings that will stay there for ever scintillating in the morning sunshine and in the evening lights as a memory of eternal promise.

Dear Marina

Another day of seclusion. Every morning I get up at half past seven. The alarum-clock goes off but my eyes are open even before it starts to ring. My sleepy gaze rests on the gasometer which stands at the far end of the football ground to the right of the sea. I look to see whether the large gray cylinder has risen or gone down during the night. On the distant horizon to the north I can make out the fiery plumes of the oil refinery in the morning mist. When the wind blows towards the south the flat is permeated by the heavy sickly-sweet smell of oil.

21

I get washed and dressed and go into the kitchen to make myself a cup of coffee. I hear my neighbour singing while she warms the milk for her boys. Later I hear her impetuously thumping the floor-cloth on to the floor as she drags it through the flat. The walls are made of paper and one can't avoid participating in the lives of one's neighbours. Signora Basilia has a loud hoarse voice and her tiny body is capable of the most incredible feats. Out of her miniscule belly she created and expelled two boys who weighed eleven pounds each at birth (she says with pride that 'they tore my body apart like two bulls'). And while she does the housework she bellows forth in a great deep voice full of cavernous echoes that you'd think belonged to a woman ten times her size.

I eat and drink slowly while I try to imagine the finger-nails of my characters. One can sometimes tell more from someone's fingers and nails than from their faces. Strange that with you I looked first at your feet rather than your hands. Perhaps it was because your cactus feet were so clearly visible beneath the table. From time to time you touched them as if you weren't quite sure of still finding them there all quiet and peaceful. After all feet talk like hands: yours told me that you were romantically and perversely in love with yourself.

After breakfast I go down to buy a paper and something for lunch – a thin slice of meat two tomatoes and a bunch of basil which I put in water in a glass jar to stand on the table where I work. I like to smell it while I'm writing.

The newsagent asks me 'Are you on your own?' I don't quite understand what he's getting at – on my own? Without children or husband or mother or father or sisters? He gives me an equivocal fatherly look whose implication is that if I am alone here without a man and without a family he will protect me – at least that's how I interpret it. The first time my neighbour came to see me on the excuse that her children were asleep she too asked me 'Are you all by yourself?' and from then on her curiosity has grown daily. A woman on holiday alone must be hiding something: some sort of grief or unrequited love or illness. Who knows what secret sorrow it might be?

For a moment I thought of telling her: 'I'm here to escape from a girl who wants to gobble me up.' But she wouldn't have understood.

And anyway that's not the whole truth. I'm also here to write my book. And to escape from the temptation of letting myself be destroyed by the child who has installed himself in my womb.

Towards midday I stop writing. I take my swimming costume and go down to the sea. I pass in front of the newsagent who greets me deferentially. I cross the Piazza Santa Caterina walk along the Corso Vittorio Emmanuelo cross the Via Liguria and I'm there. I go down some concrete steps on to the crowded dirty beach. I hire a beach umbrella and a deckchair and for a while I sit and read. Then as soon as I start to sweat I go into the water. I swim three hundred strokes as if I were undergoing a penance. I don't enjoy the smooth oily water that's littered with rubber canoes and screaming children and bits of plastic that cling to my body. I swim back to the shore and sit in the sun trying not to listen to other people's transistors. I read for about an hour and then I go home feeling hot and bad-tempered.

I've noticed some newly painted wooden boats which are for hire and tomorrow I think I'll hire one and go right out to sea.

At home I eat lunch listening to Rigoletto my eyes gazing vacantly out of the window on to an ancient landscape desecrated by the concrete tower blocks. From the kitchen window I can see white rocks that make sharp patterns on the green water small bushes bent by the wind and the steep coastline with mountains behind dominating the town.

After lunch I lie down for a rest on the big bed that's steeped in the familiar odours of conjugal life: sweet almond oil and urine cleaned over and over again with water and soap and talcum powder that smells of flowers. A huge bed with eighteenth-century brass bedheads a lumpy wool mattress which has witnessed God knows how many acts of copulation and birth and marriage and fights and rapes and deflowerings and abortions and death-agonies.

At four o'clock I start working again. At seven I go down for an ice-cream. At nine I have supper and then I read till eleven. Then I go to bed. This is my solitary day which is like all my other days and which I am determined to keep as monotonous and spartan as possible until I've finished this book and have freed myself from all those alien and unacknowledged ghosts from the past.

Dear Marina

I've written this letter over several days but I don't know when you'll read it. What I do know is that by the time you eventually hold it in your hands you'll already have found yourself a new mother to devour and you'll be happy with that ruthless happiness which only you know how to grasp without guilt or hesitation.

'I don't want your friendship or your affection. I want your body.' You've told me that so many times that I feel almost convinced – and yet not quite. I've been tempted to retaliate: like the time when I smeared your neck and tummy and thighs with honey – not of course the honey made from lilies that belonged to that Danish rival for my father's heart but another newer and heavier honey. I was trying to change your smell and taste . . . No – I wanted to cut you in pieces and then as a penance I would have drunk the familiar over-sweet honey of your blood.

One day Chantal cigarette in hand said in her angry compelling way: 'To love a man's body is to betray yourself to the enemy.' With her small dark sensual mouth and her large grey eyes she looked hard and cruel like a goddess of darkness – so full of gentleness and curiosity with women so cold and spiteful with men. But I knew her intention was to shock me rather than to put me down. Some part of her flowery intellect was laughing at herself and at me and at all the ferocity of women. Then she showed me a photo of her new lover a Rumanian girl with white square teeth narrow eyes and a soft clumsy body bound tightly in an unfashionable beige coat.

It was in the dead of night that the fifty Danaids with their lanterns flickering approached the fifty sons of Egypt who had raped them against their will and with matter-of-fact resolution had set about killing those unwanted and unloved husbands. But one of them Hypemnestra let the knife fall from her hand. She didn't have the heart to kill the handsome curly-headed man so fair and youthful who was sleeping beside her. Thus she betrayed her fifty sisters and from that time the fifty daughters of Danaus have been destined to carry on their heads water-jars pierced with holes.

This traitorous love this hand that failed to grasp the knife is an ancient blueprint of my own story as a woman. First my heart-breaking and defenceless love for my fair-haired athlete father with his slanting features who shunned me and whom I pursued over land and sea regardless of myself and my mother and my sisters. Then my all-consuming love for my lover sons.

A little girl seduced by her father a dark-eyed little girl seized in two fierce arms and clasped with all the delicacy in the world. A man who stepped out through the window into the night and returned next morning flushed drowsy relaxed and all smudged with lipstick.

I remember one hot day in August how much I wanted to get into his bed where he was lying naked reading a book. I was six or seven years old. He must have been about twenty-six. He was the most handsome of all the sons of Egypt with his skin the colour of amber and his stomach like a dry meadow set between the golden ridges of his muscles. It was the only time I saw him with his penis erect and swollen: a sail ready to set out on who knows what endless seas of seduction. He refused to let me come under the sheet with him. Cross and frowning he chased me away and I went off feeling hurt.

It wasn't that I wanted to make love with him. I didn't even know what sex was. I thought that babies were born out of the earth like plants picked up by their mother and cradled in a corner of her apron and put to the breast. This was what I had been led to believe.

So that sailing-ship all ready to embark had surprised me. I had often seen him naked but never like this so near to weighing anchor with all sails hoisted and bellying out in the wind. I did not think it was beautiful. I did not think anything. I only felt he was rejecting me and that was what upset me. And his erection was surely due to the thought of going to meet some lush girl whom he would soon be passionately embracing.

The second blueprint for my woman's story has to do with that fatal love for my son who still turns somersaults inside my belly.

First of all lover of the father and then lover of the son. Here is the betrayal as Chantal said about the Danaids who still make their journeys to the fountain carrying great terracotta jars on their shoulders. Chantal smiles showing her large widely-spaced teeth. She has a way of searching into your feelings by caressing you with her

25

hands. She is as indulgent and understanding in her actions as she is intolerant and harsh with words. I asked her if she had ever felt desire for a man's body. 'Never' she replied and as she said it she raised her upper lip like a spiteful snobbish kitten.

Dear Marina

I have almost grown used to this ugly place with its smells and its bad lighting. The trail of coffee that permeates it day and night keeps me company and makes me think of a house with families enclosed inside it like snails (I've always wanted to explore what lay at the bottom of a snail's shiny spirals) with each household lounging in pyjamas surrounded by all the smells of the night. At night too the windows are all lit up and sometimes my curiosity grows so strong that it almost suffocates me. What is it there under that lamp-shade edged with red? Inside those walls papered with flowers? Behind those brown shutters? I would like to extend my neck like a giraffe or turn myself into a bird and fly up to the eaves to look through the windows. I see a woman go by with a tray and I feel I know all about her life and her desires and her thoughts. I am her.

When I lived in Sicily I used to spend hours and hours in front of the window watching and wondering about other people's lives.

That little girl in a yellow dress who glides along the balcony? What is she thinking? That old woman picking basil leaves from a pot hanging on her window-sill? And that young man wearing a vest who uses the window as a mirror to shave in? I invent stories and I imagine complicated entanglements with undercurrents of hatred and hidden jealousies and passionate emotions and secret pangs.

While I am making myself a slice of toast I am overcome by the smell of coffee as it wafts through the building. The thought of the emotional involvements of all the families in the block stirs me with a feeling of excitement and alarm. Then there is the cry of a new-born baby and everything seems once more a foregone conclusion predictable stale already lived through a thousand times and no longer of interest. But it only takes a banging shutter or a hand stretched out from a balcony or the edge of a dress appearing from behind a half-shut window to reawaken the excitement of my imagination.

Starting again on the novel that I've allowed to lie fallow for so long has become a burden. I feel that the structure doesn't work and I shall have to begin all over again. I have come to hate the characters. The plot seems to revolve round and round in inconclusive circles. I don't really know if it's worth the effort of continuing to work on it but if I stop I'm overcome by a feeling of emptiness. I lack the perseverance to sort out the tangle I've created. I seem quite incapable of extricating myself from it. Perhaps it's all a trick to keep me occupied and give me a sense of importance and make me feel I'm not absolutely useless.

Dear Marina

Marco was making love to Bruna for eight months and he never told me. Handsome Marco! On some days when he wore that red handkerchief round his neck (the revolutionary red blood that symbolises peace and hope for the future) with his bouncing black curls framing his forehead his narrow smiling lips his broad muscular chest I thought of him as a young irreverent Neptune greedy for life and satiated with self-satisfaction.

Marco is gentle and gracious and he has the artfulness to be completely compliant in a way that captivates women. He never imposes himself he doesn't give orders and he isn't aggressive. Instead he speaks gently smiles sweetly and ingratiates himself with caresses. He knows how to listen to your problems and then he takes your aching head between his broad beautiful hands and sucks out your anguish with a tender intoxicating kiss.

27

He lives for women. And women court him and love him and protect him and help him and satisfy him entirely. For him work isn't all that important. He has no ambition. He has no anxieties. He hasn't ever wanted a child. He himself is the happiest child of all the women he's loved.

Marco kept assuring me he loved me. Yet for eight months he'd been making love to Bruna and had never told me. Occasionally I'd sensed a weariness when he made love to me a feeling that he was far away when he embraced me. It worried me but I never cottoned on to the reason for it.

Then one evening when we were eating pizzas set on a dazzling white tablecloth and he was crumbling bread between his fingers he told me slowly cautiously trying not to hurt me that he had made love to Bruna. He didn't tell me that he had been doing it for eight months he only talked about it having happened twice during the previous week. And while he was telling me he held my hand and kissed my fingers one by one as if he were making the tenderest advances.

What could I say? I reverted to my old childhood habit of dissimulation. After all it had been of some use during all those years of silence at mealtimes with my grandfather: the lowering of the voice to a whisper to ask for the salt or the water from a pompous old man who hadn't talked to his own son for twenty years.

Only when I'd left Marco near his home – round the corner from the house so that his wife wouldn't see – was I shaken by fits of retching and sobbing that I'd kept back till then. But what we had said to each other? You know for days I just couldn't recall a word of it. After that revelation I'd understood immediately that it meant the end of our love and I stayed in bed like an idiot unable to eat or drink or do anything and my head a complete blank without a thought in it.

Day after day I turned over in my mind the discussion that had followed his confession repeating it to myself again and again in disbelief.

'What do you want to do?' I'd asked him.

'How do you feel about going with me while I'm going with her as well?'

'It all depends... but do you still love me?'

'I love you so much Bianca I always want you.'

'Then how come you made love to her?'

'I don't know. She's my wife's best friend she's always dropping in to see us. Then the other day in the country we all three got undressed to sunbathe and she was between us and we began playing a game of touching each other without Miriam seeing us. It was stupid if you like – but exciting. Anyway I began to touch her breast ever so lightly and then her ankle all in front of Miriam but she was thinking about something else and not paying us any attention. Can you see? It was a sort of challenge to the taboos of friendship and trust. Later in the night I lay waiting because Miriam couldn't sleep and when I saw she'd at last dozed off I went down to the kitchen. I swear I wasn't thinking about Bruna being there. It just happened I found her in the kitchen because she hadn't managed to get to sleep either and we went out on to the terrace to look at the stars and by then it was too late...'

'And does she know about me?'

'Of course she does. I'm always talking about you and she's very jealous.'

'And she wants to have an affair with you while I'm still around?'

'No. She says she can't put up with the three of us: it's either you or her.'

'So you see there isn't much choice.'

'But we could make love without her knowing...'

'So that was your two-faced proposal when you said you loved me so much?'

'My darling I only know that I'm all fucked-up. I'm a loathsome hateful egotist. I know that but I swear to God I love you very much and I can't say more than that.'

'Have you told your wife about her?'

'You must be mad – her best friend.'

'So what do you want to do?'

'Nothing that's all. I want Miriam and I want Bruna and I want you because I love all three of you in different ways and I love you and need you all.'

'But why don't you talk about it calmly to them like you've talked to me? If we all three of us agreed it might be possible to carry on but this way with so many deceptions and mysteries and lies I don't know how long it could last.'

I was calm and reasonable: the good little girl in the shabby dress playing the part she had learned at mealtimes with her grandfather: to divide herself into two to chirp like a bird to separate her heart from her head never to show her real feelings never to let herself go never to lose control never to make a scene for fear of other people taking me over and forcing themselves on me and wrenching my guts and trampling on me with nailed boots.

We stayed late talking it over together in the car like two people full of concern and regard for each other. I was asking him what he wanted to do and he kept insisting that he was selfish and 'all fucked-up'. He must have repeated the word 'fucked-up' a thousand times. While he was kissing my fingers I tried to understand what it was that made me go on loving him. I could see all his weak spots so clearly. But then Marco doesn't really express himself through words it's the way he moves it's his fresh-scented breath his sensitive sensuous fingers probing into the life of things with the instinct of a panther that watches through the night for the footprints of a gazelle and follows it with loving patience until he has caught and devoured it and then lies stretched out along a leafy branch with half-closed eyes replete and happy diligently licking his paws.

Marco's eroticism doesn't come from his penis which is frail and delicate like a small baby's. It is more in the way he surrenders himself and gives himself in the way he responds to the sugary glances women bestow on him so that he's always immersed in a honeyed present in which desire can flower.

The first time I made love to him I thought he was impotent. His athlete's body with its brawny chest and the flags in his eyes – and then his miniature wrinkled penis incapable of standing up on its own. Later I came to learn that although it was shy it was not lacking in power providing it was not watched too closely and so long as the demands made on it weren't too exacting. Before it could spring into life it needed soft amber lights somnolent kisses sheets damp with the drowsy embrace of bodies entwined in prolonged and indolent caresses... then it could enter with its little head quivering timidly like a glow-worm which slips secretly into its niche.

But Marco himself the proud possessor of this infant penis didn't suffer from inhibitions: he would laugh and make fun of it. Like all men for whom womanising is a way of life he knew that pleasure is not dependent on size. That is an age-old myth created by men and belonging to them: the sword the club the sceptre the spade the gun the cannon the terrible executioner loaded with projectiles to be discharged into women with punitive fury.

Marco lives off women like a butterfly dipping its proboscis into the hearts of flowers to suck up their pollen and he knows very well that women are not obsessed with dreams of a giant penis. So far as they are concerned this is a male projection which bores them to tears.

Marco rests his soft lips on a woman's sex and plays upon it with a tender delicacy to bring out of her clitoris festive joyful melodies. As for his new-born infant he takes it between two fingers and slides it into his lover and makes it dance on tiptoe with a delicate grace that does not wound or assault but responds to her rhythms until she explodes into an orgasm that comes from deep within her.

Dear Marina

Even before I met you when Fiammetta used to talk about you your name Marina - marine - sea - water - made me think of a cobbled pavement half submerged in fresh clear water over which waves rippled and fell softly on to its stony bottom.

Ever since I've known you disconcerting shadows have emerged from this deep sea-bed. I remember once I was swimming underwater trying to separate a sea-urchin from the rock it was attached to when suddenly I was confronted by a gigantic eel which slipped threateningly out of a dark cleft. I only got away just in time. I expect you know that sea eels have big mouths full of powerful teeth and can bite ferociously.

Then that evening at Alda and Bice's place we talked about love and about loving another woman and Alda related how she'd fallen in love with Bice during a visit to England when they found they hadn't much money and had to sleep in a youth hostel. Then Fiammetta told us how she had been in love with that man Valerio for ten years and all of a sudden right out of the blue fell in love with Wanda whom she knew at work.

You stayed silent. You gazed at me – or rather you fixed your eyes on me as if you were trying to find out if I were good to eat. I don't know whether you were looking for love but certainly your eyes were predatory. Later you told me how after two anguished years with Rita and six months of abstinence you were searching for a body in which you could nest.

I too was in a state of limbo. Marco with his silent innocent smile still inhabited my internal space. At night sometimes I woke up desperately wanting to hold him in my arms a desire so strong it gave me cramps in my belly. He had left Miriam and gone off to live with Bruna so I wasn't seeing him any more. But every so often he'd ring me up to tell me he loved me. I don't know why – perhaps to keep me dangling on a string in the hope that he might come back to me one of these days. That's his technique: the expectation the titillation the uncertainty that makes a death agony out of every love affair and finally the betrayal the lies the sincerity all mixed up together – he always needed to feel a pair of adoring eyes fixed dotingly on him.

For months I'd ceased to have any ties. I had begun to enjoy waking up in the morning without commitments or promises free for new encounters. I could go where I liked when I liked or I could shut myself up at home and sleep or go out dressed to kill and look round in search of adventure. I didn't have to account for my movements to anyone.

I was in that state when I saw your eyes tiptoeing over my naked arms. Did I foresee a storm? Possibly not. I was attracted to the clear transparent sea evoked by your name. Then as chance would have it Fiammetta said that on Saturday she was going to the country and she invited us to come. We both said yes and felt happy to part – knowing that later we could resume our game of exchanging provocative glances.

You came to my place to pick me up in your ramshackle Renault Four that was the colour of stale egg yolk and we set out. We weren't in any hurry to arrive and we stopped twice: once to buy cigarettes and then off the road to park down a muddy lane because you said the engine was overheating and burning oil.

Daisies caught by the frost smelling like medicinal herbs the tepid warmth of the sun the sheep scattered over the hillside the big flies with green wings that flew round our heads... I remember it all so clearly. You told me about Rita about your husband the quiet and gentle Ivan about your mother who always rejects you and always wins you back with such artful cunning. We never stopped talking and I thought your intelligence was just like your name Marina transparent and clear with a stone-hard rationality criss-crossed by currents of intuition and imagination.

We arrived at Fiammetta's at eight o'clock. We ate vegetables broiled on skewers over the fire in her freezing house. Then Fiammetta went upstairs to bed and we made ourselves up a mattress on the floor with cushions from the sofa and an open sleeping bag on top. It was cold but we each kept to our own side of the bed without touching. We put out the light and you talked but I don't remember what about. I answered though my thoughts were elsewhere. I was sleepy but you intrigued me and an idea wandered like a wilful serpent twisting inside my head – the idea of starting the game myself and seducing you.

So I stretched out my hand towards your hand. In my ears and eyes a surge of blood overwhelmed me with a flood of emotion. The darkness our makeshift bed the feeling of warmth in the middle of that icy room... your body cocooned in its Moroccan dressing-gown was a mystery I had to uncover.

To break the tension I determined that whatever the cost I would strike the first spark to get to the bottom of my tumultuous feelings.

I have always enjoyed the moment of seduction the moment in which everything is possible when one word is enough to create a bond or to destroy it. It exhilarates me to break through the last resistance in spite of knowing that I will find myself face to face with overpowering terror.

In that dark torpor amongst dressing-gowns and night-dresses woollen socks scarves and cushions I explored your body bit by bit with a perverse sacreligious pleasure. Your delicate skin your breath held in suspense your hair that fell over my cheeks and down my neck. It was a strangely pure experience.

Only when I find myself face to face with your sex melted by sensation and by desire do I have that moment of panic. Now the last resistance has given way and what do I find myself confronting? My own self. A dark primeval self which I do not know and perhaps do not want to know. From inside that arcane darkness my mother's blind despairing eyes gaze out at me and I am overcome by an acute anxiety that makes my senses reel. I must do it I said to myself I must go deep into this marvellous discovery I must plunge down into this marine anemone even if I have to wake the sleeping serpent. I shut my eyes and stopped thinking and I cradled you with my tongue. 'To be a woman means this' says Chantal. 'Loving knowing acknowledging penetrating other women with love and tenderness as if they were oneself.'

From that moment I entered an ocean filled with opposite currents. I had to know you in order to love you but I had to love you in order to know you. I experienced both freely and happily. I undertook this exploit like St George on his winged horse and I set out with helmet breastplate sword and banner to enter the world of women's love. You were the resplendent sea in which I could bathe and be purified. You were generous and ardent. You had an intelligence like coral that fascinated me.

We had the same tastes for Russian novels for the poetry of Emily Dickinson and Verdi's operas for talking right through the night for home-made cakes mixed salads birds and cats. From that moment we did everything together – talking reading walking eating: we were inseparable... the strangeness of a breast under my hand... the strangeness of a smooth cheek under my lips... the strangeness of your long black hair cascading over my eyes and nose at each

34

embrace. It was beautiful to put my leg between yours and to push my head into your armpit to bite your breast to stroke your bottom. But then ... the moment when I found myself face to face with your sex. How sweet was that small rose-coloured anemone dredged from the depths of the sea opening out under my exploring fingers. A moon-like spectre emerged from that innocent sea-flower and made my heart throb. Your sex was no longer a sea-fruit no longer an anemone opening and shutting inside a shaded hollow but something more elusive: the debris in the ruined house of my childhood the statue in the garden of one of my father's lovers the damp encrusted chapel in my boarding-school the host tasting of paper which I turned round under my tongue transforming it into the living flesh of Christ's body the voluptuous hand of my mother an unmade bed a lilac dress patterned with round leaves I wore when I was three years old a tap that dripped when I was half awake and I don't know what other turmoil of lost forgotten things that return and return to haunt me.

But there at the very bottom of your open sex was my mother ... and I was filled with all the terror recalled by a forgotten temptation of incest. Your body was different recognisably separate from mine and I could embrace and caress it – at least that's what I told myself. Yet when I found your sex confronting me I couldn't help knowing that it was also the lacerated flesh of my mother's heart – a mother I had loved and lost in some far-away dream – and this awareness annihilated me.

And so I rebelled against what Chantal called 'the father's prohibitions that make us abject and compliant'. I rebelled – kissing you there where I felt most negated and lost as if I had shattered into a thousand fragments.

Dear Marina

Last night I dreamt that the house I was living in was on fire. It was more like a barn than a house. It had a low roof which gave on to another house. My house was on fire but I reassured myself: 'It doesn't matter because it won't burn the whole house down.' So I started to eat some apple cores but then I felt a tremendous heat and I saw the inside walls beginning to bulge out and tilt sideways. I realised that the house was about to collapse. I rushed towards the door but it was already ablaze and I wasn't able to get out. So I climbed up to the window and managed to escape by pulling myself up on totthe roof. A moment later the whole house went up in flames and I watched the timbers burning and the black ash flying into the air. But I didn't feel frightened or upset. I was just pleased that I'd been able to save myself in time.

Was the dream associated with my letter of yesterday? I don't know. I woke up with a sensation of burning heat and went into the kitchen to get a drink of water. The tap water tasted of chlorine. I had a tepid shower. I tried to fix my thoughts on the smell of coffee that pervades the flat at this time of the morning.

In the language of dreams a house signifies death or so they say. In that house some of my feelings were exploding and my thoughts turning to ashes forcing me out of the daily routine of quiet domesticity in which I've been simmering. They are all nonsense I told myself they are nothing but dreams after all and dreams are only garbled images of the day. And when the images speak they make use of such enigmatic language that you can only assimilate it. You can't analyse it. Either there's nothing or out of the blue one's mind is illuminated like a flashlight.

It seems absurd to think that I came here to escape from you and then feel the need to write to you every day. I've got into the habit of talking to you about what I've been thinking or dreaming or writing and it's not easy to stop. You are 'a sister who has marched in step with me' as Chantal would say. I'm quite unable to talk to my own sister or mother though I love them very much. Even when I was a child it seemed like incest to talk about myself. The least intimacy

36

with them ran the risk of becoming physical – an outrage which immediately created a wall of silence.

Unlike me Roberta could tell me everything about herself quite freely – all about the husband from whom she was separated and her two daughters and her latest lover. I used to listen to her feeling slightly embarrassed. It was as if she was showing me the inside of her navel. The family navel in which old scandals stagnate and are never appeased but remain in everyone's memories as terrible griefs and agonising losses.

Roberta... sweet Roberta... I can't forget how she looked that day in a distant Sicilian summer her body brown from the sun her blonde hair hanging dishevelled on her shoulders her open confident expression her face as always a little chubby and crumpled. She was accompanied by a black and brown dog called Regina. My father as usual was away on his travels – 'We only love the one who isn't there – the absent one' as Chantal would say. My mother had a new lover who sang very well but was ingratiating and dull. My brother Teodoro was staying with my grandmother.

I am outside looking in through the window. I see Roberta come in with her swaying walk I watch her go up to the sideboard and reach out to a big dish with a blue border on which there is a piece of apple tart. She looks round furtively and then takes it and puts it inside her blouse and immediately walks off towards the sea followed by her dog... An apricot tree a billowing tent the taste of apples in the kitchen flaking off the tongue...

My memory of Roberta's beauty remains fixed in that summer of poverty and turbulent growth when she was sixteen and we were living in the desolate Sicilian countryside. Later on over the years her body gradually got out of hand. It became all flabby and started to get wrinkled. She had grown up sensible and mature but then she seemed to lose her balance. She became ill with recurrent feelings of neurotic self-rejection lying in bed for years without the will to live. Cigarettes propped against wine glasses cups balanced on top of pillows dirty sheets gaping slippers dusty hair stained and decaying teeth eyes heavy with black murky water.

When she telephoned me to say 'I've just taken fifty sleeping pills.

Please help me' I rushed over to find her in her dressing-gown making herself a cup of coffee. She looked happy and smiling. Then she collapsed. I took her to hospital where they pumped her out. I wanted to stay with her so they shut me inside a small room lined with white tiles. I was holding her things in my arms – a pair of shoes with down-trodden heels a green woollen skirt a baggy white jumper and a small shapeless purse. I waited there for an hour gazing at these meagre belongings. When they brought her out on a stretcher I couldn't manage to say even one word of comfort to her. I was dumb and blind as if I'd been turned to stone.

In my mind I try to recapture the memory of that indolent beautiful seductive girl. I still see her as she was when she reached out for the tart and slipped it secretively inside her blouse: she was so sure of herself. It is stupid of me to fix my mind on this remembered image. Even you've told me what a fool I am to be always trying to immobilise people wanting them to stay anchored for ever in their vanished past.

But from the day she took the apple tart my whole world was turned upside down. I really don't know how or why this was. Up to that day she and I shared a faith in fantastic happenings and enchantments. After it everything became separated – predictable and mundane.

Roberta and I had planned to stage a play in which she would sing and I would dance. We would build a proscenium on the sea-bed and the audience would sway to and fro among the fishes protected by a great box of crystal. She would let loose her long blonde hair and it would cover us while we lay asleep at the bottom of the sea in our room of glass.

We had decided to sail away on a large light raft taking with us fresh water to last a year light clothes vases of flowers and of course Regina. We would live off the fish we caught and seaweed. At night like whales we would gulp down the shining plankton that floats on the surface of the water.

Then we would each have five children and we'd exchange them with each other. We'd set off for Africa and there we'd collect coral and catch snakes. We would be inseparable one of us dressed in blue

38

and the other in orange one with short ash-blonde hair the other with fair curls tied in a pony-tail.

At that moment when she took the apple tart and thrust it into her blouse I realised with absolute certainty that all this was finished. Unknown to her I continued to watch her through the window. With a sideways look into the mirror on the wall she went out swinging her green skirt followed by the black and brown dog. Afterwards I didn't think any more about it but the spell that had linked us was broken. I knew that I was no longer me and she was no longer her. Bit by bit our enchanted unit was splitting apart. We continued to plan journeys and grandiose adventures but I did it with clenched teeth as if I were only doing it to avert some catastrophe. That window through which I had seen her pass with such self-assurance came between us – from then on it seemed to me that her image would always be distorted . . . till the day of her suicide attempt and her refuge in a hospital ward.

Next day I went to the hospital to find her but she was not in her bed. I went round asking everyone where she was. No one seemed to know anything. After two hours of searching they told me she had been taken to the psychiatric hospital. Why? They didn't know. I rushed there in the car. When at last I found her she was shut behind a door that had panes of glass like the window – but in this case one-way glass which was only transparent from my side. She was standing together with a crowd of other women wearing a long white gown fastened at the back with ties. Her face was ravaged and devastated and she looked totally alone.

Dear Marina

It's two weeks now since I arrived in this place. I've written two more chapters of my novel. At times it seems as if I am sailing in a small boat on the open sea. Then when I come to read it again it all seems meaningless. 'The eloquent diffidence of women' as Chantal would say. With her shrill resonant voice and her dark gesturing hands Chantal could have been a Sybil. In ancient times she would have worn threadbare garments accumulated over a lifetime and sat at the entrance to a cave cluttered with urns small jars plants and cooking pots her hands covered in ashes and strongly perfumed unguents. 'How strange that after forty years one is still wearing the same shoes one was born with. How stupid that without one even being aware of it or concerned about it they've always been a size too narrow. Look at your own feet and you'll see: they're covered with corns because of the way your shoes pinch you and restrict your circulation. Haven't you ever noticed that walking has always been painful even when it seemed quick and easy. But then – take off your shoes and you'll find you can't walk because the way you walk has become part of your whole life-style and perception of the world. So we women live our lives in a world that has been created without us and acts against us. But we also have a sadistic love-hate attitude towards this culture as we always have towards those who tyrannise over us.'

Chantal . . . always in love with an older woman and always ready to sacrifice herself so as to take care of her and wait on her. The last time I saw her she was being taken over by a very thin woman with a beautiful mouth and bright frightened eyes and a face that was covered in fine wrinkles. Her husband had tried to kill her and she'd run away. She'd been unable to find work and so she was forced to live off her friends. Until she met Chantal and miraculously became a little girl again through Chantal's patient love.

'To write is to isolate and separate oneself from other women and to adopt the mental attitudes of a man's prick.'

'But Chantal you must admit that women have always written memoirs confessions diaries and letters.'

'If a woman uses man's language I'd say that's an appalling contradiction.'

'But I don't know any other language Chantal.'

On that street of the foxes with silver tails what can one say without making an idiotic exhibition of oneself? Chantal holds her lover's hands between hers and with all the energy of her body she communicates strength and encouragement. Marion looks at her with gratitude but also a little fearfully as if she were asking herself how long this exalted devotion can last.

I know you don't like Chantal very much. You say she's too fanatical. But that's not quite true. It's the way she talks with her spear poised ready to strike that's alarming but don't forget she's holding that spear in a hand that's so gentle and caressing and is always ready to come to anyone's rescue.

Dear Marina

Last night I dreamed I was amongst a small group of people with Annangela Violetta Rita and Pina. We were eating a big cream trifle and Violetta was telling us about how to shave pubic hair so as not to catch an infection.

I woke up with such an acute nostalgia for our weekly meetings – in spite of the irritant of Violetta's egotism which made her always want to talk about herself and in spite of Rita's aggression. It was a time when all the energy and hostility of the group was building up round Rita's head like clouds turning to rain and dissolving the tightly-knit web of her ideas. She laid out her experiences as if they were precious tablets incised in marble for everyone to look at. Then it all got turned inside out and shaken up until eventually things resolved themselves.

More than anyone I miss Annangela for her suppressed laughter and her long exploratory hands and for the wonder of her short-sighted eyes. Even amongst a group of five people there are different degrees of understanding. Pina and her problems with men and the way she always falls in love with the wrong person. Rita with her married lover over whom she loses sleep and weaves fantasies. Violetta's first love affair while she was pregnant with her second child.

Annangela and I want to start the meetings again in October but the others are hesitant. Rita is the only one to have reached the

41

conclusion that the experience is over and to say that this is no longer the right time for self-analysis.

I've talked to them about you so often that they must feel they know you even though they've never met you: Marina the beautiful sea with red and brown seaweed rising and falling on the tide. But for you my weekly meetings to 'chatter' with my friends were a source of irritation. When you talked about them you used to twist up your mouth. You were annoyed when I escaped every Wednesday to surround myself with an attentive circle of women you didn't know. Huddling together inside Leviathan's belly our hands joined our feelings aflame all set to overthrow the cluttered houses of our pasts: the love for a mother all but impenetrable in its complexity the invasion by the father the first experience of sex – all five of us had been first approached by men within the family circle – relationships with friends fiancés sons and husbands.

Dear Marina

Last night I took sleeping pills and I woke this morning after a short heavy sleep in such a daze that I couldn't recognise things in the market. I stood in front of some lettuces for five minutes thinking What on earth are those objects? 'Chicory endive radishes' I kept repeating the words to myself without being able to associate the object in front of my eyes with the name I had in my mind.

Red mullet whiting trout eels scorpion-fish swordfish. For a moment I become aware that I am looking at the fish through the eyes of a woman who lived centuries ago: a woman whose hands were covered in shining scales and who had all her life been familiar with this dead white fish the smell of entrails and putrescence the faint scent of carnations. I do not actually see the fish I recognise them by touch. They are part of my experience of the world perceived through fingers that open snatch knead dip stuff and baste and through hands impregnated with rich overpowering smells.

I got talking to the old woman in a flowered apron who was selling fish and shouting rude jokes to the passers by. But she didn't seem very eager to talk to me. She looked at me suspiciously. What was I doing there chatting away while she was working? Why wasn't I buying anything? So in order to ingratiate myself with her I filled my shopping basket with fish: squids that were bruised and slippery 'genuine' clams and even an octopus with long pinkish-grey tentacles.

All at once it dawned on me that this was probably the same woman through whose eyes I'd just been looking from a distance of a thousand years. I watched her more closely and almost unawares I felt myself slipping into the greedy exuberance of her dark wrinkled body. I could tell she lived on her own from the way she handled money: her fingers closed round the notes with casual yet voracious haste like the quick graceful cunning of a fox as it lays hold of a chicken.

The swing of her coral ear-rings helped me to lose myself in her: two long narrow pendants widening out at the bottom with a small flower of tiny yellow petals fastened on to the ear-lobes. They swung lightly to and fro as her shoulders rose and fell following the movements of her hefty arms. Her large wrinkled hands grasped the fish flung it down on the table and took hold of the knife – less a knife than a hatchet with a massive handle – letting it fall precisely where the clean flesh meets the backbone. From time to time she used her wrist to shove back a wisp of grey hair that had slipped out of her bun.

I sensed the cheerful disdain she felt towards her customers who came up gave her the once-over sniffed at her fish felt like having a good snigger behind her back started to make some comment but were never quite quick enough for her. I sensed her irritation at a political argument going on between two market stallholders. I feel as if nothing matters any more neither politics nor the market nor the fish nor anything at all. All my attention seems to be concentrated on a few small sensuous pleasures: the raw taste of home-made grappa which fills me with the burning certainty that I am still alive the sensation of coolness in my genitals as I sit for ages on the lavatory while my eyes follow the image of a fly dying on the wall opposite the

43

feeling of clean sheets against my bare feet the crisp dry consistency of a new thousand-lira note the weight of hundred and two-hundred lira coins in the palm of my hand the sour milky smell of my new-born nephew as I secretly offer him my wrinkled breast and he sucks from it a few drops of fluid the last residue of my unfulfilled womanhood.

Dear Marina

Yesterday I came back home with two kilos of fish which I hadn't an idea what to do with. I cleaned them mechanically forcing myself back into some sort of familiar routine. I put them all into an earthenware dish and took it round to my neighbour. Basilia looked at me with astonishment. Suddenly little Mauro climbed on my back pulling himself up by my hair. He and his brother have a habit of attacking the bodies of grown-ups biting pulling shouting smelling shoving in a way that makes them invincible. One can tell that when they grow up and have money they'll be adored by women and will give them a bad deal just the same as they are robbing their mother now. Big strong and lively with their curly heads acting as cushions they throw themselves against the walls and make them tremble. Woe betide all those who find themselves in the invaders' path! I said this to their mother and she gave me a beatific smile happy to think of her sons growing up to be winners. She has watery eyes and sparse dry hair and when she smiles she shows her black decayed teeth.

She is delighted to see me. She makes me sit down and forces me to eat stale baby rusks and drink some vinegary wine that smells of strawberries. Then in her supple voice so unexpectedly and mysteriously powerful she tells me about herself. How she was raped by her father when she was nine – 'I was a woman already. Just imagine! I was having periods so I got pregnant and my mother aborted me with a litre of Epsom salts. That gave me an ulcer and it's still there. When I was twenty-five I got pregnant through the Holy

44

Ghost – that's the only way I can explain it. I didn't want that second child so I went to a neighbour and she lent me a probe and showed me how to push it in. After struggling with it for three days the miscarriage started and I couldn't stand the pain so I said 'That's it! I'm going to the hospital.' But I never said a word to Toniano I wasn't going to tell him. So I went to hospital and they scraped me out. Then they asked me 'Who got you an abortion?' I said 'What? I don't know anything about that. It just happened.' They said they knew that wasn't true but they'd let it go this time. They kept me in hospital for three days but they couldn't stop all the blood I was losing not even with all their big pipes and tubes. And so it went on – after Mauro there was an ugly girl who was born dead and then the last.'

I tell her about my miscarriage at seven months. She listens attentively and sympathetically. From now on we are friends. We have both suffered the same things: miscarriages haemorrhages unwanted pregnancies. We are equal. But we are also very different and I use the dish of fresh fish to efface these differences created on my side by privilege and on hers by premature ageing. She thanks me warmly. Her eyes don't display any envy but even a little compassion. 'Poor thing all on her own' is what she is thinking and she sees herself as being luckier than me because she has a husband who screws her every night and sons who eat her alive.

Dear Marina

I haven't managed to write a thing today. Each time I've struggled to find a word I've had to cross it out. By the end I had a small cemetery of black crosses in front of me. I stretched out on the bed but I couldn't keep my legs still. I ran some very hot water into the bath. I sank into that womb of boiling liquid and stayed there for half an hour quite still thinking of nothing. I wanted to masturbate but my fingers felt too heavy and they lay inert at the bottom of the bath. I dried myself and got dressed. I went out and walked along the promenade by the sea. It was crowded. The unexpected sound of horses' hooves on the pavement gave me a feeling of peace. I stopped at the smallest most run-down bar along the front: the Neptune Bar an old-fashioned place rather unimaginatively converted into a café – ugly shabby tables covered in checked oil-cloth and stained with wine four plastic chairs flung round each table a big coffee-machine above a massive bar counter of old wood grown dark with use homemade shelves along the wall and a row of half-empty bottles.

I sat down. I ordered a glass of milk flavoured with mint. Facing me on the opposite side of the road a girl was standing in the doorway of a shop. She was almost a child. She had a sulky expression dark violet lips and blue circles under her eyes. She stayed there quite motionless on the doorstep looking out on to the street with a sullen stare not seeming to see it. She epitomised the state of my being though I am certain that I would never have expressed such an absolute sense of desolation however much I was feeling it in my veins. I would have liked to be her and to show the world my angry childish face with the indifference and innocence of someone who has managed to stay alive through sheer inertia.

The waiter brought me my glass of milk. Looking up I met his sparkling blue eyes. A boy of eighteen or nineteen his face pitted his white teeth broken in front his hands red from washing-up water. I asked him what I owed. He made a sign with his fingers and gave me a teasing smile.

I paid and he went off behind the counter to dry cups. I watched his thin drooping shoulders rising and falling gently beneath his white jacket. While he was working the coffee machine he stared at me with an expression of childlike defiance.

I wished I was the girl standing upright in the doorway. Then I would have returned the boy's stare with a look of sulky disdain. Instead I sat there with my drawn face my awkward gestures my badly-fitting clothes my weary thoughts. I don't know why but at certain moments I'm overcome by a desperate urge to be someone other than myself. I would like to be anyone – that old gouty woman who's just passing by – that pregnant lady dragging herself along in high-heeled clogs of pink wood – that little girl with two colourless plaits bound tightly at the nape of her neck – even that terrier bitch that's crossing the street with her head down and her teats swinging under her belly . . . anybody except this person who is so predictable and boring to me and whom I have carried round with me for too many years.

You intrigued me because you had never suffered from this habit of rejecting yourself at every opportunity. You are your own best friend in love with your own princess's feet your proud sturdy legs and your tumultuous breasts!

I looked down at the mint turning my milk green and thought 'I don't care much for this drink but its colour cheers me up: it reminds me of the colour of the barman's eyes the colour the sea has on some mornings when I look out of my window the colour of grass dissolved in a mist at night when the green merges into the white and melts so delicately at the first light of dawn. Anyway – drinking it will relax my contracted guts.'

I got up. I bought the daily papers and went home to read them. Then I grilled myself a piece of steak and boiled some rice. I ate listening to Rigoletto and immediately afterwards I settled down to write.

Dear Marina

Last night I dreamed I was with a group of women in a large light room. We were cooking and gossiping cheerfully. Outside on the other side of the street some men were sheltering together from the sun under a sheet. While she was chopping parsley one of the women used the word 'fag'. I asked her what it meant and she replied that it meant 'faggot' but I guessed she was telling a lie.

I wrote earlier saying that I wanted to tell you all about you and me. But I've never stuck to this because I keep wanting to talk to you about other things about what's going on inside my head about my dreams about what I'm doing. But I can't do that either because in the end you're only interested in my body. You don't really pay any attention and that inhibits me from expressing myself and makes it impossible for me to think or talk. What gives me a kick when I'm with you is the satisfaction of putting you down and rejecting you and humiliating you until you're left with nothing. You want something to hang on to and I get a perverse pleasure in cutting the ground from under your feet so as to see if you can succeed in loving a perfect idiot like me.

At first I used to talk to you a lot I even told you about my fear of a woman's sex. I told you how once when I was little I saw my nurse lying asleep on the bed with her legs wide apart and how I crept stealthily up to her to look at that bearded face between her thighs – for me it was a strange face with a hairy mouth and no eyes. I knew it was forbidden but I stood and stared at it until she woke up and gave me a slap across my mouth.

What did I see in that face? Why did it frighten me so? Was it because it was shut away under skirts and aprons and inside steaming kitchens? Did it convey to me a repetition of gestures that were always the same an unexpressed revolt that festers in the wounds of the flesh? Was it an awareness that the soft face fringed with curls would one day be mine also?

'If you refuse to submerge yourself in the cunt of the mother – if you refuse to devour it and be devoured by it then you are a traitor and an ignoble *fag*.' Now I know where the word 'fag' in my dream came from. It was Chantal who had used it and I know very well what it means: a fag is the little boy at school who is bullied by the big boys the servant in a single-sex community where anyone who does not use violence is violated. In my dream I pretended not to understand it – perhaps because I suspect myself of being a fag just as Chantal said.

I haven't told you about the time when my mother gave me a package and told me to go and throw it down the lavatory. We were staying at a hotel in the mountains and she was in bed with a temperature. Obediently I carried it to the bathroom but then it came apart in my hands and I found two pads soaked with blood. I immediately thought of murder: my mother must have murdered someone – could it have been a baby? I thought she must have cut its throat and now she was sending me to get rid of the evidence of her crime.

I threw everything away and I took care to hide every trace of what I had done. I cleaned the lavatory bowl which was splashed with red I washed my hands again and again and before leaving the bathroom I looked up and down the corridor holding my breath. I went back to the bedroom with the idea of helping my mother to conceal her crime. I found her asleep in the dark. I sat down on the floor beside the bed and watched her shyly waiting for her to wake up. This happened when I was about five.

I felt no horror at my mother's crime. Only a determination to protect her. Without knowing how children were born I had instinctively associated the blood with a baby. But I never thought about my mother's sex. That remained a face that was still an unknown enigma to me.

There is a story about a little girl who has to pass through a wood to get back home. She is frightened but summons up the courage to return to her mother who is waiting for her. Suddenly she sees someone coming towards her out of the thick of the wood. She is seized with such panic that she is unable to breathe but she decides to go on with her head bent down. So she walks along bent forward until she comes up to a man. Then when she lifts her eyes she sees that he hasn't got a face. He has a body clothes arms legs and hair but instead of his face there is only a smooth egg.

Terrified the girl runs away. She runs and runs her heart beating in her throat. She comes to a clearing. She sees a small cart going slowly along the lane towards her house. She comes up to it and jumps in. Terrified and out of breath she tells the driver what has happened to her. 'I saw someone without a face' she says. And the man turns round and says 'Like me?'

As I've tried to tell you when I was a child the female genitals seemed to me like a face that wasn't a face. And I've just at this very moment remembered that it was my father who told me this story when I was about seven. How was it I had linked the story with my mother's sex? Was it at his suggestion? I don't know. The strange thing is that in the story the people without any sex are men – first the pilgrim and then the driver of the cart. Men with a face but without either eyes or nose. But how did a man's face turn into a woman's sex? I don't seem able to get to the bottom of this riddle. Sitting rigidly on its paws the sphinx watches me with stony eyes.

My father leans over and displays his face covered with a smooth white handkerchief and says 'Like me?' He laughs delightedly at himself for having given me a fright.

Those were the years of seduction the years when my handsome young father – aged twenty-five with the body of an athlete and spell-binding sensual eyes the colour of black coffee – seized my heart with two broad delicate hands. He took me with him to the mountains to the sea to the river. He took me swimming and catching tadpoles. He took me on his motor-bike and he took me with him on the train. Most of all the train was a source of wonder and anguish. We always arrived two seconds before it was due to leave and with last rushed steps he swept me flying on his arm into the end carriage. Sometimes I fell and he would pull me along like an empty bag lacerating my knees on the asphalt platform.

When the train stopped he would get out saying 'I'm going off for a minute to get something to drink.' I would plead with him not to go because I was so frightened the train would leave without him. But the handsome athlete would shrug his shoulders and run off laughing as if to say that my worries were ridiculous: he could play a game of chance with the train whenever he liked. He was free. He could run the risk. He would disappear from the window and I would stand waiting for him with my head leaning out of it anxiety gnawing at my guts. Often the train would leave without him and I would sit in my seat totally dumbfounded overwhelmed by a bottomless despair and not daring to utter a word. Once the train had regained its carefree tip-tap rhythm I would suddenly see him appear at the end of the corridor carrying a bottle of fizzy lemonade in his hand. He would hold it out offering it to me with an engaging gesture as if I were his travelling companion. At the same time he would be watching me to see if my courage had forsaken me and I was in tears. I played his

50

game by making nothing of it. I would drink the lemonade boldly looking him straight in the eyes.

It was a silent seduction. He never spoke about himself. Everything I knew about him came from my mother who talked of him with a mixture of admiration and rancour. It was she who told me about his love for his mother and how when he was in Guatemala he had known the day of her death in spite of not having had any news of it. At the exact moment she died he had been overwhelmed by a shattering melancholy. It was six months before he learned the reason for this sudden and inexplicable grief.

It was she too who told me how he had engaged in mortal combat with my grandfather before he was able to leave home. Those were the early years of fascism and my grandfather had been won over by the spirit of bold adventure which he identified with the new ideology. So one day in the belief that it would be a nice surprise he brought my father a beautiful Party membership card and the promise of a magnificent job. My father tore up the card without saying a word and left the house. From that day they never spoke and right up to the end of the war they were like two enemies. He and my mother went hungry and eventually left for Guatemala that today is torn by the savagery of 'private armies' whose soldiers torture loot and rape. He had a scholarship in Central American studies and they stayed there until the end of 1946.

Between me and my father words were unnecessary. He never used to tell me stories. Except for the one about the man without a face but that was in a moment of boredom to console me for having upset me. It was my mother who carried on the oral traditions of our family. With my father I could only be myself – nothing more. To demonstrate his love he'd take hold of me and put me astride the front of his motor bike and set off like lightning. I could feel the warmth of his chest against my backbone. The wind blustered into my mouth and cut my face. I never protested. Physical pain didn't matter: it was a sign of life. Even death didn't matter – one held one's head high and confronted it coldly. In life one had to take risks and leap into the dark just for the fun of it – but only for sublime and exalted reasons. One must never fall into smallmindedness. For him that was the

51

greatest sin: pettiness avarice calculating cunning. Pettiness was everything that bound the individual to his own paltry concerns and interests and profits. He hated any kind of narrow-mindedness or intrigue. He liked to behave like St Martin – if he saw someone in difficulties to cut his cloak in two and make him a present of one half. But then at other times he would laugh at other people's misfortune and despise them for it.

With me he never acted the teacher or the protector. He treated me like an equal the companion of his games his journeys his adventures and if I wasn't up to it that was my look-out. Once he made me walk ten kilometres in the snow and when I got back to the house my fingers were half frozen and I had a temperature. My mother was furious and accused him of being selfish and mad. In reply he hit her and for that she never forgave him. I think it was the only time in his life that he did hit her.

With him poverty was never something unendurable. He was always able to invent new distractions: once he painted all the stones in the garden another time he made me a puppet out of wood and once we went hunting for wild roots and wild figs.

He never talked about money. He never complained if we only ate meat once a month. He would eat dry bread and tomatoes as if he were being regaled with the most exquisite dish in the world. Meanwhile my mother was always there to hold up a wall that was crumbling to deal with the creditors the bills the rent the household expenses schoolbooks the price of milk shoes and meat. Every month there was a recurrent nightmare of demands for money that wasn't there. And when it was time to pay my father was always absent. He would be away travelling on projects that were ever wilder and more extravagant and more extraordinary. So in despair my mother contracted further debts in order to get straight for the next month.

It was my mother who pointed out that after being re-soled eight times my shoes wouldn't last any longer. It was she who showed me how threadbare my overcoat was and how my socks were full of holes. I followed my father's example and thought all such things unimportant. He was capable of spending the equivalent of three days' housekeeping money to buy some expensive book and then he would laugh when my mother got angry at the prospect of being forced into new debts.

I had to turn to her if I wanted to know anything about his family and my grandparents. It was she who taught me wonderful songs which she had learned from her own mother and it was through songs and fairy-stories that she taught me to read and draw and think.

Action adventures taking risks surprises travelling the pursuit of love enchantment the race to be won silence all belonged to my father. Domestic things words stories about the family money eating sleeping friendships and songs were associated with my mother.

Yet she was not just a housewife. She had run away from home at eighteen to travel through Italy with a rucksack on her back. She had started to do sculpture. She had scandalised her parents by getting married in a registry office without a wedding dress or flowers or a reception. She struggled against poverty like Don Quixote tilting at windmills she took lovers when she wanted to she read lots of books she was free from social prejudices and anxieties. But in my imagination it was my father who was my favourite. I was entranced by his mystery his impregnability and his gaiety so different from all the other fathers I knew: simultaneously so profoundly childlike and so primordial – a Peter Pan with shining hair always in flight through an open window.

Dear Marina

Last night I had another dream about a house on fire. It wasn't my house this time I was in the Piazza del Duomo in Milan and I was watching the top floor of a row of flats burning. The fire flared out through the windows with long angry flames. People were throwing themselves out holding their noses as if they were diving into water but instead their bodies shattered on to the pavement. They made no noise as they fell and there was no blood nor anything of that sort.

Some people threw themselves down with open arms as if they were trying to fly. Others turned somersaults before they reached the ground. The corpses piled up on the pavement but everyone just went on looking up above their heads. It was like a theatrical performance menacing and unrelenting. But strangely enough there was nothing really sinister about it.

Suddenly my attention and that of the other passers-by was caught by something strange: a girl leapt out of a window holding a parachute of red umbrellas. She sat in her armchair suspended beneath the umbrellas but instead of carrying her down to earth the parachute billowed upwards in the breeze and floated away into the sky while she sat calmly in the red armchair with an amused smile on her face.

I don't know why I go on telling you my dreams in this absurd way. Or perhaps yes I do know – because I used to enjoy the way you listened and tried to interpret them. I remember one night in Orvieto after a storm had overtaken us in the street and we had gone back to the hotel wet through and laughing. We'd dried our hair with a big white bath-towel that smelled of bleach. We were hungry and there wasn't a thing to eat. The night porter kept on repeating that the kitchen was closed and he couldn't give us anything and you insisted saying: 'I'll go into the kitchen myself and find a bit of bread I can fry up.' But he was even more icy: 'I'm sorry signora but it's impossible. I haven't got the key.' Actually he was furious because we'd woken him up at two in the morning and he was determined not to stir himself.

'Can I drink your milk?' You were lying curled up in my arms and you began to suck my breast. It was the mother and daughter game. You told me how it was such good sweet creamy milk and it seemed as if you were really swallowing it. You said it was like condensed milk but even better. And I stroked your hair as if I were fondling a little child.

We went to sleep clasped together our damp hair sticking to our cheeks a faint smell of mother's milk and skin dusted with talcum powder. That night too I dreamed about devastating fires and spectacular jumps on to the empty pavement below.

I remember how next morning your face was all puffy as you asked me attentively for details of the dream. And then while I stuffed myself with new bread and fresh butter and marmalade you chose your words slowly and carefully as you explained: 'The burning house is your desire for change . . . it's got something to do with your relationship with your family which has broken down irretrievably. You're setting fire to your own inertia and blindness so that you'll be forced to make a change and go away.'

You were like a beautiful sleeping sibyl in your Moroccan dressing-gown your eyes very dark and wide-open your sun-tanned hands crumbling bread on the bedcover.

When I was at boarding-school I used to dream about fires too. But more often I'd dream of flying. I would stand on tiptoe and begin to fly so as to escape from a fire or from someone who wanted to kill me. It was tiring especially to begin with when it seemed as if I would never be able to lift myself off the ground. Every time it was like a bet with myself. But then I succeeded and I'd hang on to a branch or a parapet and I'd look down and be paralysed with giddiness my head would spin and I'd be unable to move. Then I'd pluck up courage and throw myself into space with my arms spread wide and I'd start flying again letting my body stretch out in the wind and I'd experience an excruciating pleasure.

Often I would wake up with a start to find the muddy-eyed housemistress ordering me to 'keep your hands above the blankets'. I hated her and I'd protest by coughing painfully a convulsive cough that woke my neighbours in the dormitory and brought the matron running in to ask 'What is it child?' I wouldn't answer. I began to really cough with a lacerating sore throat swollen eyes and purple face. Then the little matron ran to fetch an infusion of lime-flowers. Dipping a small delicately-pointed brush into it and thrusting her fat fingers into my mouth she dabbed it on my throat.

Dear Marina

I want to tell you about myself because the person you were in love with was a lifeless statue without a past. You never used to ask me anything about myself except what immediately concerned you. You weren't interested in the things I used to talk about – perhaps because I would have given you quite a different picture from the one you wanted to have of me.

I've never told you how they used to slap my hands at school when I said the words 'bum' and 'shit'. They were forbidden words which we repeated to each other in whispers fearful of prying ears. Instead of 'foot' we used to have to say 'extremity' instead of 'bottom' 'sit-upon' and as for 'shit' we weren't even supposed to have ever heard of it. We used to say 'I need to go' but only in a whisper never out loud. Talking about money was thought to be vulgar. A well-brought-up girl should speak as little as possible. She should smile a lot but not in a provocative way: her smile must be shy and submissive. She must be demure. She must keep her eyes lowered and only look straight at people who were less well-bred than herself. She must never ask for anything but wait until it was offered never laugh coarsely never show her body never touch herself never touch other people's bodies and so it went on a never-ending list of commandments.

Every week there were credits. A pink credit for those who had been well-behaved and worked hard a white credit for those who had only been so-so and a grey one for girls who had been bad. I never managed to get a white one. I was no good at school subjects I was too absent-minded and too interested in other things. My behaviour was rated as bad in spite of my shyness which was seen as 'very feminine'. I played ball games too impetuously I read forbidden books in secret I had difficulty getting to sleep and every time the mistress passed me on her night-rounds she'd find me with my hands under the blankets and not above them.

My hands stayed underneath because they were touching what must not be touched for any reason whatsoever. I masturbated incorrigibly at least three times a night. Then I'd ask forgiveness from the tormented body of Christ hanging above my bed. I even touched

56

it with my fingers still wet and the feeling of its cold limbs filled me with remorse.

Sometimes the mistress caught me just as I was about to come. 'Put your hands outside' she would order me in an indignant whisper but I would be slow to respond and I'd look at her with dull obstinacy. Then she would pull my hands out roughly leaving me feeling tense and crushed and unable to continue.

To prevent us touching our bodies they made us bathe quickly curry-combing our flesh as if we were horses. Once a week we all went down to the cellar where the baths were. Everyone carried clean socks and knickers and had their own towel with their name sewn in red at one corner. On the floor there were big iron tubs with lions' feet all painted a uniform grey.

Each girl came in and undressed and got into the hot water. Then the mistress arrived with soap and a coarse flannel. In two minutes she soaped and washed you without even looking at you. Naturally the genitals were left untouched. Sometimes the mistress passed a bristly washing glove above them carelessly scratching the skin.

It was forbidden to dawdle or to soap oneself or to lie and soak in the hot water even when it was freezing outside. We had to get straight in and out and dry ourselves on our rough bath-towels that smelt of bleach and hurry to go and join the queue up to the dining-hall with our hair still plastered down with steam.

Bathing became one of my masturbation fantasies: I would imagine a bath that lasted a whole hour slowly dissolving my limbs in a tub full of steaming hot water.

We were all in love – some with a housemistress some with a classmate and others with one of the teachers. The teachers did not live in the school they came in daily from outside and they were treated as if they were outsiders bringing in dangerous contagion from the town. In that feminine world only love between women could exist. The only man was the priest who came every day to say Mass and on Saturdays to hear confessions. He was about sixty he had stained teeth and he was bigoted and boring. The only other male we ever saw was the gardener and he was forbidden to speak to us even from a distance. When we were let loose among the flower-beds at break-time he disappeared. He was a thin bloodless youth with something wooden and unattractive about him.

Those of us who shared the same dormitory were enmeshed in passionate love affairs. Every secret was known to everyone else: Rosaria loved Bettina and tormented us all because she didn't feel she was appreciated as much as she ought to be. Nina loved Giulietta and no one could separate them for a minute not even the headmistress. They were always together always yoked to each other gossiping mysteriously and if anyone scolded them they would cry so noisily that they were left alone.

There were tales of seduction and amorous adventures involving dangerous journeys between one dormitory and another in the dead of night. There was also violence and physical abuse. One night three of the big girls got hold of Beatrice who was just eight years old and attacked her. They left her all bruised and scratched but everyone was too scared to give them away. One of the three was called Evelina. She was a very tall dark girl with hands like a boxer and we all knew that when she decided to beat you up she would do it and leave you half-dead.

Beatrice was in the same class as me. I remember that the morning after this had happened to her she sat on her chair without speaking and wouldn't eat. Her deep black eyes were speckled with yellow and she sat motionless and gazed fixedly at the wall.

'Come on Beatrice eat something! What's the matter?'

But Beatrice wouldn't eat a thing. Sitting at a nearby table the three friends kept her under close observation.

Another time it was the turn of Licia who was only six. They stripped her and made her lie face downwards and forced all sorts of things up her bottom: pieces of screwed-up paper and olives stolen from the kitchen and egg-shells and cherries and even a spoon. For three days she lay on her stomach sore and bleeding. But even then she didn't say a word. The matron treated her for a form of diarrhoea and after a few days she was back in her place serious and composed but not daring to look the three friends in the face.

But most of these love affairs were chaste particularly those between girls in the junior and middle school where I was. The older girls were more sophisticated over their desires and organised dangerous erotic games. However even they took care not to risk their 'virginity'. To take away 'a girl's most treasured asset' as the headmistress put it would have been unpardonable and probably none of the girls would have kept quiet – a scandal would have been inevitable.

Instead we younger ones fell in love with each other but paralysed with shame and ignorance we kept our loves secret. Being all together in the dining-hall or in chapel or at the wash-basins before going to bed we were submerged without realising it in a kind of collective sensuality. A glance or a gesture or a smile was enough to make one happy or unhappy under the watchful longing eyes of the others.

Like Lilla and Gianna and Domitilla I was in love with a girl who was older than me. She was sixteen and I was eight. Her name was Sara and she was short and fair-haired with hazel eyes. She wasn't beautiful but she had a way with her that held me spellbound. She was very small and dainty and she seemed to glide along with a quiet grace like water. The white starched collars which encircled her neck opened out like two wings. She was studious and very good at everything especially at music: she could play the piano and she improvised songs. I would stay for hours watching her long fingers with their bitten nails rippling over the keys. She had a loud infectious laugh which could be heard all over the school. But she was composed and gentle and shy and except for those outbursts of laughter she was not someone who ever called attention to herself.

I can't have spoken to her more than twenty times. She wasn't in my class and I only saw her occasionally in the dining-hall or the chapel or the garden. But to catch a glimpse of her fair curly head in chapel even from a distance put me in a good mood for the rest of the day. Every morning I waited for her to come into the dining-hall and I couldn't eat until she'd sat down at her table only a few yards from where I was sitting. She knew I loved her although I'd never said anything and every now and then she sent me a long provocative glance. We never touched each other. I was content with this distant love consisting of glances and expectations and intimations of desire. I felt elated just to watch her spread the dubious tomato jam that was provided on her fresh bread every morning. The others grumbled and made grimaces of disgust every time that jam appeared but she didn't. She spread the red mush on her bread as if it were the most exquisite delicacy and she raised it to her mouth with a slightly gawky grace.

A girl called Rolanda was in love with me. She was tall and had bandy legs lots of hair very long arms and a beautiful face with irregular features and golden-brown eyes fringed by long eyelashes. Rolanda was in the same class as me and always managed to sit on my bench. She lent me pens and pencils and helped me with arithmetic and she shared the cake her father brought her every month. Unlike me who never had the courage to declare my love she was always sending me a series of abrupt little notes that risked bringing the authority of the housemistresses down on our heads.

I thought her infantile and I never deigned to give her a glance. And then she was so lacking in grace so brash, so boisterously extrovert. When I surprised her gazing spellbound at my hands while I was plaiting my hair my reaction was a feeling of irritation.

It was a female world full of torments and joys. The older girls could not tolerate the lack of freedom and every once in a while they would escape to go to dancehalls with rather dreary lascivious young men. I only suffered from some of the petty restrictions like having to eat horrible burnt food always having to bath in a rush having to go to mass every morning having to go to confession once a week having to speak in a low voice having to go to bed when I didn't feel like it having to keep my hands on top of the bedcover having to wake up every morning at six having to queue for everything. But I didn't really mind living in this female community that swarmed with conflicting emotions and was awash with heedless sensuality.

Dear Marina

I slept well last night thinking about my boarding school. Thousands of details I thought I'd completely forgotten floated into my mind. In my attempts to reveal myself to you I'm finding all sorts of far-away things which I thought were dead for ever. I come upon small mysterious objects perfectly preserved in some part of my emotions. They make me feel quite drunk.

Into my mind drift images of the housemistresses who alternated between playing with us and lacerating us with their tongues. I remember Maria Gonzales who was nicknamed 'The Bolshevik'. It was rumoured that under her blouse instead of the Madonna hanging between her breasts she wore a medallion of Lenin. This was looked on as a scandal but it also aroused a kind of fascination in us. They said that her father had been an anarchist murdered by the Fascists in 1937. She never talked about herself. She used to watch us playing rounders with her wide-open eyes fixed on the ball. Every so often she would take a little girl aside and tell her 'Well done! But put a bit more muscle into it!' She was the most lenient over giving marks and doling out punishments and the least demanding over our being polite and learning our lessons. Her strong ugly face expressed a dark sadness that sometimes made me feel I loved her.

The others were more predictable. They were like the aunts and mothers that we had all left behind at home. They were practising Catholics and they spoke carefully in words of polished elegance. They did their job well enough but without much enthusiasm.

La Vecchioni was tall and shapely with tinted hair and finger-nails varnished bright red. It was said that she had two lovers at once and kept both their photographs in her handbag. She was a woman who seldom spoke. At mealtimes she sat quietly holding her fork tightly in her hand. She had thin lips which ended unexpectedly with two commas turning upwards. Although she was very kind I didn't like her because I felt she was two-faced.

Then there was Pasetti who was nicknamed 'iron-fist' because she was so quick to anger and so strong. She really enjoyed punishing anyone who was disobedient. When she took you by the arm she became red and breathless and dug her nails into you.

Then there was 'The Whale' though I never knew why she was called that. Perhaps it was because she was fat – although she wasn't all that fat. Perhaps it was because she really did look like a whale with her smooth olive skin always a little oily as if she were emerging from the depths of the ocean. And when she sneezed it was just like a whale spouting. She was slow-moving placid and not very interesting but she was kind and honest and everyone liked her.

The most surprising teacher was Sister Esterina who was the only nun in the school apart from the head cook. Sister Esterina judged everyone by their hair. To her we were all Medusas with serpents coming out of our heads. Eventually she lighted on a girl with just the right hair: that was Priscilla a little blonde girl who wore ear-rings and was always tidy and neat with a slightly sulky mouth and big blue eyes. A doll in fact.

Sister Esterina used to comb Priscilla's hair with a small silver comb she'd been given when she took her vows. She would sit her down in front of the mirror and divide her hair into lots of strands and then wind each strand of hair round a roll of silver foil. Then she pinned each little roll to her scalp with a small hair-grip. In half an hour Priscilla's head would look like a little cluster of shooting-stars. Sister Esterina would gaze at her with half-closed eyes admiring her masterpiece. Then she sent her to bed.

Next morning she would arrive in the dormitory rubbing her hands in anticipation her rosary jingling at her hips. She would seize hold of Priscilla's head and unroll all the little bundles of hair. Then she would brush it and comb it and say 'Doesn't she look like a little angel?' Priscilla would look at her radiant reflection in the mirror: the soft blonde curls framing her pink and white face looking like the enormous angel whose wings were spread in flight in the picture next to the statue of the Virgin Mary in the school chapel.

Priscilla was Sister Esterina's masterpiece. We were all fascinated by the perfection of her beauty. Priscilla didn't play rounders like the rest of us. She didn't eat spaghetti or meat rissoles or drink milky coffee for breakfast or any common things like that. Her palate was accustomed to rose-petal tea delicate vegetable soup consommé fruit syrups barley sugar raspberry conserve. She suffered from nightmares and used to wake up screaming and be unable to get to sleep until Sister Esterina had brought her some camomile tea and cradled her in her arms.

It was her parents who gave most to the poor. Once a week in the dining-hall the headmistress used to read out a list of donations made to the neediest families. There were gifts of money for the poor and for the school and for those pupils who were badly off. The names of Priscilla's parents occurred most often alongside sums of money that sounded to me like a fortune. Each time Sister Esterina's face would take on an ecstatic expression though occasionally she would become a little confused as if this largesse were something unbecoming which she was responsible for. Priscilla on the other hand never seemed to be aware of anything not even the approbation bestowed upon her in the middle of the crowded dining-hall by the headmistress.

For me the weekly reading out of these lists was torture. Not only did my parents never donate 'gifts' but I was among those who depended on others for their contributions. I was one of the pupils whose fees were always in arrears a fact which was brought politely but punctually to my notice each week.

The headmistress was very cordial to the donors. Towards those who were behind with the fees she was distant even if outwardly amiable and polite. She never made outspoken comments but in one way or another she let her displeasure be apparent. And then the punishments: if your parents were donors you would hardly ever be punished at all even if you'd done really badly whereas if you were behind with the fees no occasion was lost for making you go without your supper.

Rolanda said that the announcements in the dining-hall were absolutely ridiculous and that I shouldn't take it to heart: it was just a way of getting more money out of the parents. But it remained something that filled me with shame. I told her it was all very well for her to talk because her parents were among the donors. But she shrugged her shoulders and said: 'When I'm grown-up I'll leave my shit of a father and I'll go round the world with a ruck-sack on my back.'

Rolanda's father was a good-looking young man who came to visit her once a month bringing silk handkerchiefs acacia honey toasted almonds and once even a big pretentious-looking teddy bear which Rolanda immediately threw into the dustbin. The headmistress talked at length to Rolanda's father telling him about all the difficulties the school had to face and how the girls nowadays were demanding rude and immodest. Rolanda retired to the corner to eat the fondants her father had brought her from Paris but she didn't seem to enjoy them very much and her eyes flashed with indigation.

I liked her elegant carefree father with his short-sighted blue eyes but Rolanda said such terrible things about him that I was also a little afraid of him. According to her this fair young man had driven his wife to death and when she was scarcely in her grave he began to squander all her money. He didn't give a damn about anything: he pushed Rolanda off to boarding-school so that he could steal from her in turn and now his daughter's bed was occupied by young men who wore elegant trousers and who sucked his blood like leeches and it wouldn't be long before he'd got through all her money as well and they'd be driven to penury. Thus spoke Rolanda spitting on the ground.

The headmistress had a soft spot for him because she said he was well-bred and upright. 'Upright my arse!' said Rolanda and was immediately sent to bed without any supper.

Heaven knows why I'm telling you all this Marina. But once I'd begun I couldn't stop and now it's two in the morning and I can't keep my eyes open any longer. Good-night.

Dear Marina

Three weeks have gone by and you still haven't found me. I am relieved. But perhaps you've given up looking. In which case I wonder what you have been doing?

When I am close to you I long to escape. When I am far away I think of you all the time.

This morning Marco rang me. He said he needed to talk to me. His voice sounded full of anxiety. I told him I've no intention of budging from here and no wish for him to come looking for me. I said we'll meet and talk when I get back to Rome.

'But I must talk to you now.'

'What about Marco?'

'I can't tell you on the phone.'

'Try.'

'I can't.'

'All right then let it wait.'

'I can't wait I need to talk to you urgently.'

'Who gave you my number?'

'Fiammetta.'

There's Fiammetta for you! Too disorganised to be able to keep a promise. I'd asked her not to give my telephone number to anyone and off she goes and gives it to Marco of all people. However with any luck he won't know the address and in any case he probably won't want the bother of coming all this way to see me. To think that a year ago I would have leapt ten yards in the air only to hear his voice. I would have swallowed down all my bitterness and gone anywhere just to hear him talk about his wife about Bruna about his problems. I would have done anything to see him to smell his smell to feel the touch of his arm for a moment. Now alas even his cheekbones wouldn't turn me on!

We'd known each other for three years and never thought of making love. Then one day I offered him a slice of bread and butter after a night in a camp-site on the Dalmatian coast where we were plagued with mosquitoes. I felt his eyes roving over my face and cheeks and I began to feel hot and my belly to contract. That afternoon we kissed inside the shower hut.

When after three years of loving me he told me he'd slept with Bruna the first thing that came into my head was to go and talk to her. I knew that she was very friendly with Miriam but I hardly knew Miriam at all. The first time I'd seen her was at the circus. I was sitting eating sugar-lumps when I saw Marco hand in hand with this lovely girl with dark hair and white skin and firm sensible appearance – it was Miriam. I immediately wanted to get to know her to talk to her. But the first time she answered the phone and I tried to chat she sounded very distant.

With Bruna it was different. I looked up her number in the telephone directory. I didn't want Marco to know I was contacting her. I made an appointment to meet her outside her office. I didn't know what she looked like although Marco had shown me a photo of her and Miriam on a beach: her hair was tied back and she had an angry smile and fleshy calves. It was strange the way they both looked alike even though Miriam was better-looking.

One thing I did know was that Bruna wore glasses. I scrutinised the women coming out of the Research Institute intently. They all wore glasses! But she must be different I knew that – she was a research worker and not an office worker like all these women who all had the vacant down-trodden look of office girls.

As soon as I saw her I knew it was her. She came to meet me with the absent look of someone who'd had too much to drink. She had on a white organdie blouse and a skirt of light material which fluttered round her legs. Suddenly my senses tuned in to the flavour of her.

Dear Marina

I haven't been out shopping for three days. I got so exhausted the last time I went to the market. But today I must go again. I haven't got a thing left in the fridge. While I was working yesterday evening I finished off the last two eggs with some stale bread and rolls that tasted all musty.

Yesterday after supper I went to the cinema. The cashier gave me two tickets. I told her I only wanted one. She looked at me suspiciously and continued to push two towards me. I grabbed one paid for it and went in. I felt her inquisitive look following me. Women who go to the cinema alone in the evening must be unusual in this small town.

The hall was full of boys between thirteen and sixteen. I don't remember what the film was called – it was a brutal American film in which everything was shown in close-up: huge brash images which assaulted my eyes in a sequence of rapid jerks and convulsions – enormous feet emerging from the screen noses hanging over your head breasts and bottoms of outsize dimensions blown up and protruding. The story: a youth from Little Italy in New York who works in a paint-shop becomes a dance champion falls in love with little rich girl is beaten up by Puerto Ricans acts the hero on Verrazzano Bridge goes in for a dance competition wins it quarrels with his mother because he won't go to church loses his job because of the dancing and in the end gets it back again. Altogether an honest working-class lad who lives in a racist ghetto conceited and over-bearing but also generous and loyal and tender-hearted (he gives up his title in favour of a Puerto Rican couple who are better than him but who were excluded on racist grounds). He's in love but with the wrong girl at any rate in the eyes of his mother and his family and also of course in the eyes of the audience because she is full of ambitious dreams and anxieties because she's a few years older than him and because she needs to be the dominant partner. In other words she's the worst example of the future American mother who acts out her frustrations through her sons and ends up by sending them to Vietnam to 'voluptuously' kill the poor homeless natives.

After the cinema I was walking up the street towards my flat when I was approached by a man dressed in a light blue suit who asked me for a light. I don't smoke. Pig eyes and a smooth sly expression. Insisted on accompanying me. 'No thanks.' 'But what are you doing all alone like this?' Voice sardonic insinuating. 'I'm quite all right.'

'I'll see you back home you never know what sort of people you might run into it's dangerous for a woman to be out alone at night.' 'I don't want to be seen home thank you.' He walked a few steps behind me for a hundred yards then suddenly came up close and pressed his open hand on my bottom. 'You ugly pig!' I shouted at him and he raised his arm to hit me. I started to run and luckily he didn't follow me.

Just recently I've been having insomnia. One night I made myself camomile tea like Sister Esterina used to make for Priscilla with a lot of sugar and a pinch of cinnamon. But it didn't work. I switched on the light. I picked up a book of poems by Emily Dickinson.

There is a solitude of space
A solitude of sea
A solitude of death, but these
Society shall be
Compared with that profounder site
That polar privacy
A soul admitted to itself –
Finite infinity

Emily dressed all in white imprisoned inside a room for thirty years shutting herself away protected by her younger sister Lavinia her guardian and nurse.

Once there was a fire and Emily woke up terrified and her sister forbade her to look out of the window so that she shouldn't be upset by what she saw. She accepted her sister's tyranny to save herself from being upset. A sphinx all dressed in white choosing to shut herself away inside the family tomb.

As I lay there between sleeping and waking I saw her sitting beside the window holding an exercise book in her hand. She was dressed in milk-white and her lips were curled in a pallid half-smile.

'Do you shut yourself away to protect yourself or what?'

'History is made up of spittle.'

'But history is the road that leads towards you. Why did you make it so difficult?'

'Have you never drunk hot wine spiced with bitter ginger?'

'You talk in riddles.'

'Try drinking it.'

'What are you afraid of?'

'I used to sleep with my feet covered.'

'When you wrote you were covered right up to your neck.'

'Like going naked into the market-place.'

'Why did you choose the life of a recluse enslaved in the house?'

'Servitude is like attar of roses.'

'Do you believe there is pleasure in servitude?'

'I had bracelets on my ankles.'

'Did you never want to travel?'

'The spider has lost her children.'

'You never had children. You were never even married. Is it true you were in love with a woman called Kate?'

'If I look in the mirror I see a woman who has hair the same colour as mine.'

'Why did you never want children?'

'I have brittle nails.'

'Even now you make people lose track of you.'

'Do you like my dress of Dutch lace?'

'You are afraid.'

'It is you who is afraid of me.'

I woke up with a feeling of anguish. I was sweating and short of breath and felt as if I had been buried alive.

Through the open window came a gust of hot air. The book of poems had fallen open to the floor. Angry voices came up from the street below. I went to the window. Some youths were arguing about a motor-bike. I shut the window. I swallowed a sleeping-pill and in no time I fell asleep.

Dear Marina

Here I am and I can't help feeling that I escaped from you only so as to come back to you. With my hostile mariner's heart I escaped from Marina to the marine-blue sea and a desperate longing to be anywhere but here. That intense labyrinthine way you live your life the way you have of burying yourself with your own two hands and rising again more vibrant and more dazzling than ever. As if one's eyes were blinded from watching the morning star before embarking on another long day of troubles.

About midday I went for a long swim out towards the rocks of San Biagio. The water was cold and clear. I'd put on my fins and I let myself be carried along by the waves. I was cold and I kicked my legs hard to keep warm. After a hundred yards I felt exhausted and I stopped. My head was going round and round and I was out of breath.

Right there in the middle of the open sea a hundred yards from the shore I met up with a brand new rubber canoe blazing with two middle-aged desperadoes who lay straddled across it their gross brazen bodies suntanned and self-satisfied. Having made certain I was alone they idly began to chat me up: 'Hey let's have a look at those lovely tits.' 'What's your arse like?' I started to swim with my head bent purposefully down into the water. How I hated those over-grown bodies devoid of decency those lords of the world hunters from habit bent upon hunting wherever they find a prey so that they can feel alive without even the thrill of real brutality or the excitement of real violence but only a kind of dead spurious self-gratification.

How well I recognised that look they had that look of being good family men affectionate with their children hail-fellow-well-met with their buddies full of love for the mother who has been wiping their bums for over forty years convinced they are being polite because they let you go first into a restaurant full of rancour towards any woman who isn't attractive and available. I know those flabby bellies bunged up with undigested food chock full of hidden avarice and fear camouflaged as cynicism – a devouring fear of everything feminine which they carry around inside them.

Guffawing derisively they shout 'Come on then let's have a look at that beautiful arse' and thrash the water with their feet. I keep my eyes shut and my thoughts concentrated elsewhere. But I can't escape from the noise of their laughter. The harsh throaty voices of smokers in which you can recognise so much: family rows office jokes the lies they tell their wives spitefulness with colleagues vulgarity and petty meannesses all of which have left traces like indelible scars. Men of middle class middle income middle heart middle soul middle prick but they are all the millions of fucked-up people who make up the world lacking any vitality or wickedness or savage greatness. With sub-human feebleness and faint-heartedness and obscenity and indecency they swallow the soft vulnerable bodies of their mothers their sisters their wives and the daughters with whom they are in love.

But why why my Marina do I tell you about this early morning anger? When I got back home I threw up the sandwich of bread and honey I'd eaten before going out.

Dear Marina

At this moment I'm lying stretched out on the big bed in front of the open window thinking about your secret laughter and how you were so beautiful with your dark irregular features and how you always wanted to be me even when you remained most deeply yourself.

The image of your fleshy feet and your thick ankles comes into my mind and that way you have of walking as if you were treading grapes to make wine for us. Inside your head your thoughts are choking with grey prickly thistles the kind that mules like eating all rough and hairy and shot through with periwinkle blue. The mules take arrogant possession of their space and I know there's something mulish in you too the way you stamp with your hard hooves and nothing can shift you.

There were lots of mules in Sicily during my childhood and they all had a passion for those thistles the colour of smoke tinged with blue.

Five o'clock in the morning and it was time to wake up. It was midsummer's day and the banging of fireworks rattled open the windows. Yes it was summer and I was sleeping inside a hot dark tower haunted by the ghost of my grandfather. I woke up with the sweat running down my spine. I was lying next to Rosalia who was six years older than me. I was about twelve or thirteen. She had taught me all about the world of men and the world of women initiating me into a labyrinth of rules and hierarchies that had been passed down to her through generations of grandparents and great-grandparents. Rosalia was in love with a cousin who played the accordion and worked as a mason's apprentice. When she was fifteen she was seduced by an uncle and gave birth to a mongol child who had been put away in an institution. Since then she'd known everything there was to know and I drank in her words like a sweet liqueur.

By seven o'clock we'd got dressed and we breakfasted off bread and black olives. I told her how my dead grandfather had woken me up in th middle of the night to tell me something I couldn't understand. Rosalia was on familiar terms with the dead: her mother had died when she was three and every month she came to visit her and sit on her bed and give her advice about the housekeeping. Sometimes too she advised her what numbers to play on the national lottery. But the numbers she gave her never came up and Rosalia thought her mother was taking her for a ride. 'My bitch of a mother who's now choking in hell tells me to bet on 16 and 28 and 32 and she says: "Keep cool keep cool those numbers are all right." So I go and play them and then the numbers come up three weeks later!'

At nine o'clock there was mass which the whole village attended but more out of social duty than religious feeling: it was mainly an opportunity to display the latest fashion in clothes and hair-styles. Rosalia would wear a pink dress with organdie frills which came down to her ankles... I can still taste its flavour of crushed strawberries and face powder on my tongue... I wore my usual brown skirt and the yellow blouse that I hated. It smelt of over-ripe melons that were already partly spoiled and beginning to go rotten. But there wasn't any money for new clothes. Luckily I didn't have to wear the shoes I wore in the winter which had been repaired time and time again because I had a pair of shiny red sandals of which I was very proud.

At eleven o'clock there was a horse race and at twelve there was a big family lunch. My mother and father were away on their travels. I had been entrusted to Rosalia who took me to her house to eat Sicilian pizzas. The house seemed to be inhabited by swarms of worker bees – sisters aunts grand-parents great-aunts and great-great-aunts. Inside it there was a constant chatter of voices and a continuous frantic stamping of bare feet.

Four of these women were in their eighties and dressed in long black skirts that stank of stale frying-oil. Their heads were small and sleek their hair perfectly coiffured and pinned back at the nape of the neck with tortoiseshell hairpins. Each of them was fully occupied in preparing something for the feast that was to take place in the evening: ricotta cream – tomato sauce – anchovy pizzas – boiled eggs – and for the tart chopped parsley and basil and toasted almonds and fried celery and aubergines. The kitchen was not large enough to prepare a really important meal so every room in the house was invaded by earthenware dishes bowls little jars of copper or china – plastic had not yet supplanted the familiar sound of spoons being beaten against crockery – and there was a multitude of women running hither and thither all excited and happy.

While Rosalia and I were resting in the big bed between sheets – a privilege accorded to me because I was a child and a guest and to her because she was looking after me – the others worked unceasingly till nightfall. Every so often there would be a scuffle: I would hear a niece scolding her aunt for having spilled flour on to the clean floor and the aunt scolding her niece for putting too much salt in the pasta. They would hurl a thousand insults and scream and shout 'bitch' at each other. Then they would return to working together quite peaceably. I found it impossible to sleep in all this uproar but I shut my eyes and enjoyed a somnolent sensation of peace and quiet as I listened to the sound of eggs being beaten in an enamel bowl and milk being strained into a basin.

At five in the afternoon the *passiata* would begin. During the *passiata* matches are made and unrequited love affairs and passions

73

and hatreds are born. Groups of men and groups of women strolled separately up and down between the two rows of stalls selling roast almonds sunflower seeds and marzipan. They eyed each other with feigned indifference. Rosalia used to meet her cousin to whom she wasn't allowed to address a word. They smiled at each other from a distance he standing in a circle of his friends all wearing blue suits with pink and white ties and she surrounded by her friends dressed in elegant filmy dresses.

Rosalia was addicted to reading adult comics. She used to read 'Dream' and once persuaded me to write a letter to a famous comics star with the exotic name of Ramil Noran. The letter was to be signed by both of us. I didn't for a moment expect to get a reply whereas she was quite convinced that he would write to her and went to the Post Office every day to ask for news. Sometimes she kept me awake till two in the morning talking about the romantic Ramil of her dreams. She was to marry Cousin Tano and she would have his children and remain faithful to him 'unto death'. But Ramil Noran would stay in her thoughts as an unfulfilled desire and ever-recurring fantasy. Ramil represented the wide world beyond our smalltown life a radiance we never questioned because it was unattainable like that of the film stars we watched some evenings in the one and only shabby cinema the place boasted of: he descended the stairs like a bird of prey he slipped into a big red convertible lightly grasped the steering-wheel with two fingers and kissed a ravishing blonde whose face took on a look of ecstasy as he pressed her to his manly chest. He laughed revealing a row of pearl-white teeth and then drove off towards some unknown enchanted destination.

One morning Rosalia woke me up by jumping on the bed and shouting: 'He's written! He's written!' She held up the letter addressed to her and kissed it without daring to open it.

'When are you going to open the letter then?' I asked. But she waited till the evening when we were alone together and then she opened it with trembling fingers. Inside was a photograph of Ramil Noran smiling an artificial pampered smile and beneath it a flourishing signature.

She was disappointed. She felt let down. She had been expecting a love letter or an assignation or heaven knows what. She burst into floods of tears and I stroked her hair in an attempt to console her. She fell asleep in my arms like a child with her wet mouth against my breast. You see – I was already playing the role of mother. Even at that age I had this perverse obsession with motherhood. And as it grew dark she cuddled up close to me even though she was much more grown-up than I was. She chose the part of daughter because she wanted to be loved and caressed in my arms just like you did.

At eight there was a sumptuous supper. Since a saint's feast-day only comes once a year it has to be celebrated in grand style with roast kid steaming hot potatoes flavoured with rosemary sparkling red wine stewed rabbit ricotta cream strong coffee and liqueurs.

At ten o'clock there was a street procession by the light of acetylene lamps. Then at half-past eleven a grand firework display – two families competing for the admiration of the crowd. The first put on a display of catherine wheels green flames opening out into red flowers and domes of golden yellow. The second followed with wreaths of silver showers and jets of liquid fire and shooting stars. Then a jury decided which was the best display.

After the fireworks there was dancing in the Piazza del Trinità. But it was not thought proper for a woman on her own to join in. Instead only married couples and little girls who hadn't reached the age of puberty took part. Girls of marriageable age stayed together in groups and watched the men dancing with each other. Rosalia leaned on my thin child's shoulders and dug her nails into my flesh at having to hold back her desire to dance. On a platform knocked together from large badly planed planks of wood her Tano was playing his accordion like a man possessed.

All over the place were small powerful donkeys tied to stakes and left there to munch hay. They had drawn the peasants' carts from as far away as twenty kilometres bringing food tents stalls and people. The mules were left untethered and uncared for and they wandered around with their eyes agog. I liked going up to them unobserved and stroking their muzzles and feeling the smooth skin on their noses under my hand. They would allow themselves to be touched almost as if they didn't feel it. But sometimes they would raise their lips to show their teeth like a dog snarling. At other times they would stick out a long rough tongue and lick my hand. Occasionally one would become excited and exhibit a gigantic livid penis which dangled down between its legs.

You can see how that mule inside your head stirs up memories as I drift into the forgotten places of those distant years of my Sicilian childhood when I was so shy and ingenuous that I must have seemed like a half-wit trapped between the smells of dresses and the smells of people so unaware of myself that I became absorbed in everything I saw without distinction.

Later Rosalia got married. She had four children. Her husband Tano became ill with a chronic skin disease and she moved to Palermo to take a job as a waitress so that she could support him and her children.

She was the first daughter in my life. Or perhaps not. Perhaps my first daughter was Roberta who loved me and then rejected me just as one loves and then rejects one's mother. But even that isn't quite the truth: I believe that my first daughter even before Roberta was my own mother. She was more ingenuous and resigned towards life than I was. She was the tender rose-coloured star that shone upon me night after night when I lay in bed unable to sleep deluding myself that I had given birth to it.

Dear Marina

Last night I dreamed that you were aiming poisoned arrows at me. I took shelter behind a rock which turned into a tub of milk and then I found myself immersed inside it waiting for the last arrow – the one which would find its mark and kill me.

I'm aware how frightened I am of your violent side. I've experienced it so often – like when you flung me savagely onto the floor just because I'd talked at supper with a woman friend from France or that time you swept your arms across my work-table and scattered all my papers into the air or when you arrived with Fiammetta's portrait of me slashed through with a nail. You threw it down in the doorway and went off without saying a word. You wanted to wound me. No – it was more than that it was a savage primæval attempt to destroy me. I rang you up and told you this. You laughed and replied that on the contrary it was I who had wounded your image inside myself so it was I who had destroyed you. That's what you said but it wasn't true. It wasn't my death-wish it was yours and you'd expressed it like a witch.

That's another reason why I've come here Marina to extricate myself from your witch's spells. To escape from being imprisoned between your harsh black wings.

> *Witchcraft was hung, in History,*
> *But History and I*
> *Find all the Witchcraft that we need*
> *Around us, every Day –*

Emily Dickinson in her skirt of white piqué the little starched collar and the snow-white muslin with red polka dots.

> *Sweet is the swamp with its secrets,*
> *Until we meet a snake;*
> *'Tis then we sigh for houses,*
> *And our departure take*
>
> *At that enthralling gallop*
> *That only childhood knows.*
> *A snake is summer's treason,*
> *And guile is where it goes.*

Which of us was it who met the snake the betrayer of eternal summer as we ran barefoot through the fresh grass humming that joyous refrain *'Le donne sono dolci Le donne sono miti'?* You or I? I or you?

> *The trace of untamed feet*
> *Your body of celestial flesh*
> *The moons of your defeated eyes*

How frail our friendship
We can no longer speak
Of women's harmony
Instead we bite each other's necks in truth
You suck my eyes like eggs
And probe my belly with your claw-like hands . . .

This poem was written by a woman I see as both friend and enemy
– some kind of a ghost. I know her because she and I have butted each
other's faces in a mirror.

Chantal would say that we are perpetuating 'the negative
characteristics of male violence' but whose daughter is our violence
and why does it easily become the mother? I don't know if it comes
from those mulish thoughts which browse in your head or from the
tensions in my own lungs – I just don't know. The fact is we are both
infected by it.

Dear Marina

Last night it rained. It cleared the air. This morning my neighbour
came in to see me. She was wearing slippers and a black dressing-
gown wrapped tightly round her waist. Without heels she's no taller
than a child. If it weren't for her ravaged face her stained and broken
teeth and her hair already streaked with grey she'd look like a little
girl.

She brought me some wine made by her relations in the country.
She sat down in the kitchen and we drank a toast to our friendship.
She tells me she has no friends and doesn't talk to anyone except for
her sister-in-law when she helps her with her kitchen-garden.

'My sister-in-law keeps pigs and chickens. She depends on me
because she doesn't really trust anyone else not even to do her
darning. 'Who knows what sort of a botch they'd make of it?' she says.
So when I go there she gives me a whole basket of things to mend and

while I'm doing it we talk. Her husband – that's my brother – has it off with the next-door neighbour's daughter but she can't say anything to him because he gets violent. Once he took a pot-shot at a cousin because he'd told him off for getting rid of a new-born piglet. Another time he tried to throttle Marisella because he was jealous of an old friend who used to come and see her – but there wasn't anything wrong about it he only used to come and gossip. Then the other day he tried to put it in her mouth but she wouldn't do such a thing not even for our Heavenly Father and so he knocked her about.'

I asked her how it is possible for her brother to be so different from her when she's so sweet and gentle. She said God had willed it so and she laughed – but it was as if she were crying because she was ashamed of her mouth with its lack of teeth and her thin sparse hair and her emaciated body. She concealed herself as much as she could behind this sad laughter begging pardon for being in the world.

'He spent three years with the friars my brother did and then he wanted to become a monk. He always said his prayers and behaved right and his one and only passion was to go off and set traps for small birds. He used to put out a net for them and as soon as the birds got caught in it he'd beat them to death with a stick and then string them up on a nylon cord like a necklace. Then he fell in love with a woman who's a lot bigger than him called Vespertina. She was about forty and black as pitch and to get him to leave the monastery she put a spell on him and made him drink a drop of menstrual blood and from that time he lost his head and he couldn't be trusted – nobody could withstand that blood nobody. Then Vespertina left him for the local tailor and he went completely to pieces and swallowed a whole litre of bleach because he wanted to do himself in. But he managed to recover even though he was left with a great hole in his stomach and then he seemed calmer again and he got married to Marisella but he never loved her. The only woman he could think of was Vespertina because of that magic spell she put on him. Marisella has tried to use counter-spells lots of times but they've never worked.'

For more than an hour I stayed listening held by her deep resonant voice. While she was telling the story she became transformed: taller and more ethereal with her eyes burning so that they held you spellbound. I drank another glass of her wine: it was immature acidulous and cloudy. I felt stimulated. In another century Basilia would have been a story teller sitting in the middle of a group of neighbours all working with their hands and recounting marvellous sagas and romances.

Anything she describes becomes an epic. There's a rhythm in her voice which comes from the deepest and most profound part of her being. I see her sitting inside a circle of women of all ages wearing coifs tightly fastened under their chins little girls with clogs and billowing sleeves mothers with milk-stained undervests all listening to this small woman with her strong powerful voice. And I too would be sitting there drinking in her words. The spell was broken by a scream from Mauro demanding his mother. Basilia ran out anxiously excusing herself for having wasted my time and guilty at having neglected her sons and her domestic chores and her cooking for even a few minutes.

I went back to my typewriter. I can't help thinking that if Basilia had been luckier and had had a bit more education she might have written stories and novels. She would certainly have been more skilful – more interesting and compelling – than me. But would she have been able to transfer onto paper the tempestuous yearning rhythms of her speech?

I'm writing badly. I've come to hate this novel for which I've chosen to segregate myself and live all alone. The characters are weak and contrived. The casual fragmented style of writing which attracted me to begin with now leaves me cold.

Dear Marina

I woke up thinking of you. In my imagination I can see you sitting at your rose-coloured table of polished cherry-wood with four sheets of white paper in front of you and your dark fingers pressing down on the pen as you write. Your head is bent to one side your eyes are attentive your lips pressed tight and those dark fingers of yours spread a net out of which spring all the bright discordant ribbons and translucent pebbles that are your poems.

On the walls all your books are arranged in order and there's your collection of little shells and the small Chinese cupboard of black lacquer with gold dragons and carved branches at each corner and hanging almost over your head the wooden cage with the stuffed bird in it that sways at every breath of wind. The windows are wide open and the cat is sleeping on the step that leads down to the terrace with its green curling plants which thrust their branches into the house.

I bent down to give you a kiss and you vanished. But I could still smell your hair fragrant with sandalwood mixed with the sour smell of sleep and of saliva.

I drank a cup of very hot coffee as I contemplated the crescent of the sea which today is a smooth desolate grey. I ate a slice of bread and honey and settled down to write.

But Gaetano's petulant voice came floating into my ears: 'What the hell do you think you're doing?'

'I'm enjoying myself Gaetano.'

'It's absolutely impossible to write novels.' He said this with the assurance of someone who is quite disinterested but who knows the truth because he has dipped into it with his fingers.

'But you said some nice things about that book of Melo's.'

'That wasn't a novel it was a personal reflection on his own impotence.'

'It still reads like a novel.'

'Writing is an act of obscenity. Even my friend Artand says that.'

'Yes and all the time he's writing poetry plays essays even a historical novel.'

'Music has been dead for a century. Painting died during the last twenty years with Duchamps. The novel died with Joyce. All that's left is to masturbate in solitude. How utterly squalid it all is!'

'You're a moralist and a necrophiliac.'

'And you're a masturbator. Yes... even you.'

Gaetano is that Sicilian friend of mine I've talked to you about sometimes. I think you may have met him last year at my house.

We've been close friends ever since we were young. He had a great passion for literature deciphered ancient texts and wrote some good criticism. He read a great deal and he knew the whole history of Sicily. He kept a poem by Ciullo d'Alcamo hanging over his bed with the inscription 'to Gaetano 1235 A.D.' He used to claim that Ciullo had written that poem for him and he'd look straight at me with his large challenging eyes.

Then just when he was offered the post of junior lecturer at Urbino University he dropped out and went to work on the land. All the time he was studying at University he never went with women he devoted his time to books and to his research. He'd talk very freely about sex and give advice to his friends along Freudian and Reichian lines but he never got around to making love himself. He seemed to prefer to live through the love-affairs of his friends – particularly when these were painful and complicated. He was never so close to me as when I was hopelessly in love with a cold enigmatic man who would be warm and caring towards me one moment and the next would suddenly withdraw. Gaetano used to come with me when we met and he would escort me home and stay till two in the morning holding forth and dissecting my feelings as if they were small corpses devoid of any trace of mystery.

He expatiated on every possible reason for my being in love every reason for Antonio's ambiguous behaviour the reason for our agonising encounters the reason for our moments of happiness the reason for his sudden coldness and the reason for my weakness. He knew it all!

He would explain every detail to me with the patience of a true scientist. Sometimes he'd get angry when I didn't agree with him. For example I didn't find it much help when I was suffering from the pangs of love to be told that Antonio was looking for the father I carried within me. It wasn't much consolation when I could get neither yes nor no from the sophisticated lips of my unloving lover to be told that I was defending myself against my secret sadistic fantasies about my mother by disguising myself as 'a sacrificial lamb' (as Gaetano put it). Like the stone woman in Dante or the restless probings of memory inside the cabinet of the past.

When he went to take up farming he had to work for someone else because he was broke. From that moment his life suddenly changed. Up till then he had been an extrovert generous and always ready to give himself to his friends. Now all of a sudden he became solitary and taciturn and miserly with himself. He broke off lots of friendships he gave up his work on ancient texts in Aramaic he no longer listened to music no longer gave his time to people no longer went for walks no longer offered advice.

He also discovered sex or rather the practice of it: falling in love making love the play of bodies the fires of passion the escapes the promises the betrayals the langours of the flesh the anguish. Greedy and silent he lived entirely for himself.

Now I hardly ever see him. He stayed in Sicily. I live in Rome. Occasionally I would catch sight of him making it with yet another woman – often he has three or four of them on the go at once and he claims that they all love each other dearly. He keeps getting them pregnant and he's delighted with each new baby when it's born. He's always getting into trouble with these complicated and intricate relationships of which he is the succulent kernel.

Now he must be almost forty but instead of growing older he seems to be getting younger every day. His hollowed-out face is lit up by a restless smile like rippling water lightly ruffled by the wind. His magnetic hazel eyes are like those of a young boy. When I see him I feel good though he still takes me to task for my obstinacy in writing novels and accuses me of abusing myself shamefully instead of letting myself flow in the 'orgiastic currents of life.'

I remember him when we used to play table tennis on the ramshackle garden table at his house. It was a decaying seventeenth century villa with crumbling ceilings dilapidated balconies and mouldering walls and they were living in the three rooms which had miraculously remained standing. He would give me advice and bully me because he was trying to teach me to play with 'flair'. Once he was shouting 'not like that! Hold the bat more naturally. Throw yourself forwards with your knees in line with your chest. For heaven's sake let's have a bit more style. Bend that arm a bit more gracefully' and he took a jump backwards to serve and fell on his bottom in a

83

mulberry bush. I couldn't stop laughing and he looked at me angrily as he extricated himself. There was something about him of an unshakeable Don Quixote in love with the truth and also in love with himself.

Another memory I have is of sitting with him on the steps of my house eating some cakes that were made by the nuns. They had a cream filling – that flavour of citron and bergamot and violets ... I've never managed to find it again even though I've been round all the best cake-shops in Palermo.

I'd like to write a book that would be a 'painful reflection of one's own impotence' just to gain Gaetano's approval for once. But I know I'll never be able to do it. The truth is that he has never approved of me either when I was in love with those uncouth characters whom he used to say I must have picked up out of the rubbish bin or when I wrote stories and poetry and even less when I wrote novels. For him I remain and probably always will the heedless little girl: I fall in love with people I'd far better have nothing to do with. I'm infatuated with my infantile father who always rejected me. I prefer the darkness of the emotions to the clear light of reason. I read so many books in such a confused way that I get nowhere in the direction of 'having a good cultural background' – as he once put it protruding his lips which were always a little discoloured.

Dear Marina

More confused and disturbing dreams last night: I was shut in a smoky kitchen that wasn't my own but reminded me of that abandoned house I discovered on my walks in the woods at C. a kitchen that had reawakened after a slumber of two hundred years. Huge cooking pans a wood-burning stove a hearth with saucepans hanging against the black smoke-grimed walls.

In my hand I was holding an egg lightly speckled with brown. I skimmed the cream off the milk into an earthenware dish and mixed it with sugar and flour to make fritters. Something was worrying me but I didn't know whether it was the smoke-grimed walls making everything look so dark or the feeling of being in a strange unidentifiable time. I broke the egg cleanly and felt the yolk running down through my fingers. Then I woke up.

You'd have to be exceptionally clever to extract all the hidden meanings from that dream. I can imagine you saying 'You're afraid of centering on your self you're trying to establish an identity by constructing images from the past which compensate you for the void in which you're actually living. Eggs are the offspring that emerge from your negative ways of thinking. Milk is the nourishment you are denying me.'

Marina you've got something in common with Gaetano in your compulsive obsession with revealing me to myself and analysing me and possessing me. 'I am an incestuous daughter' you said to me once in a letter 'and this is something that will never change. Your milk is only a part of you it's only the nourishment and affection that you give but you are not only your milk you are also your breast and it's that breast I love and desire and want you to love and desire in me too.'

I remember so well your handwriting with all its loops and lunges. 'We are identical yet different – identical like two daughters of a father and different like the daughters of a mother.' But then in another letter you left for me wrapped in silver paper with a packet of aniseed-flavoured biscuits you wrote: 'For me you are different like a daughter of a father is different and identical like the daughter of a mother. If you want something from me even if it's only affection you insist on me giving it to you like the daughter of a mother and certainly not like the daughter of a father. But if I have to be a daughter it is not an incestuous daughter and if I have to be a mother it is not an incestuous mother and this won't ever change either. We pursue each other because we are different from each other and yet we are also alike. Above all we want our mutual identity (and here identity means both of us being daughters of the same mother) which we never succeed in finding because of that first initial difference which fascinated both of us. You give me your milk and that's

85

marvellous – don't think I don't appreciate it – but in the end you are only fulfilling an obligation if you don't also enjoy giving me your breast.'

In the face of that precarious and yet very powerful taboo the question is: should I shoot the apple balanced on the head of the son or not? Should I grasp his penis in my hand and swallow his semen or not? Confronted with that choice I cannot simply be indifferent. To do it would be a transgression and therefore an even profounder recognition of the taboo. Not to do it would be an almost conscious acceptance of censorship. You would not have these incestuous desires if you did not believe blindly in the taboos of the mother-daughter relationship. Which tree the apple comes from isn't very important: I don't know – and anyway it's not significant – how much the conditions for transmitting cultural taboos matter in comparison with the exquisite and tender kernel of the human condition. (My sister's dog Regina had children from the strongest and most handsome of her sons who was called Rospo.) The fact is you carry this kind of censorship inside yourself and you delight in denying it satisfaction and turning it inside out like a glove.

Don't the Greek myths tell us that there were originally three kinds of hermaphrodite beings? Man-man woman-woman and man-woman. These creatures offended Zeus and so he divided them into two opposites each of which was destined to search for the other all their lives. Each sought his or her original counterpart: the man-man will only love men the woman-woman will only love women and the man-woman and woman-man will love their opposites. So Plato his head crowned with brown curly hair walked up and down back and forth spouting out saliva and filling space with his geometrical explanations of the universe. And yet one must be richer and freer to express one's sexuality without hiding oneself under a blueprint of convention. 'It is a well-known fact that many little girls prefer to climb trees and play violent games out-of-doors rather than play with dolls and help their mothers' wrote Charlotte Wolff dropping wise bricks on the cover of her book *Love Between Women*. I believe it was you who gave me that book – or perhaps it was Chantal.

This book was written in 1936 from the particular slant of Vassar

86

College where Mary McCarthy and other lanky middle-class girls had begun to question the whole concept of the family as it was understood by doctors and psychiatrists (breast-feeding as a mother's duty femininity as a sacrifice homosexuality as a deviation) in favour of contraception and free love. There they were standing in line with long gowns down to their ankles dark blue mortar-boards perched on top of their blonde hair clutching their degrees in their hands. How often have we seen them in films like *Life is a Splendid Thing*?

Did you climbs trees and play war-games? Then you are a homosexual. Did you play with dolls and imitate your mother in the kitchen? Then you are heterosexual... Charlotte Wolff is like so many other psycho-analysts with long stringy necks who look down on the fray with a paternalistic smile and lose sight of their feet and their feelings.

Marina you never behaved like a boy. You never brandished guns or refused to wear organdie dresses. You played with dolls and at cooking till quite late – you told me so yourself. Fiammetta on the other hand was always rivalling the boys. As the only girl among so many boys she dived thirty feet from a rock swam naked in rivers climbed trees carried a sheath-knife always wore trousers and wasn't afraid of anything.

As for me I was mad about dolls. I played at looking after babies and at cooking. But I did know how to swim as well and I used to go and hunt for sea-urchins and limpets. I flung myself down steep slopes on my bicycle that hadn't any brakes I climbed roofs I stole fruit from orchards – but I also spent hours bent over books reading especially in bed by the light of a small pocket torch. And I knitted. And made jam and toffee. And all my friends behaved in much the same way they played war games and acted in plays and then shut themselves indoors to feed their lifeless baby dolls with morsels of food. One game comes into my mind – would it have been masculine or feminine? We used to stand on one side of the road waiting for a car or lorry to come by and at the last minute when it was almost on top of us we'd dash across the road. The winner was the one who came nearest to being hit by the car. It was a silly game. The expression on the faces of the poor drivers who suddenly found themselves having to brake with a child right under their wheels was comical. How we laughed at their panic!

But Charlotte Wolff – one of the few psycho-analysts ever to have written a whole book around this subject – can't see beyond the idea of 'illness'. In spite of all the affection and support she gave her patients her research was aimed at 'curing' anyone who could not play the social game and who therefore needed to be led back to a standardised 'normality'. Yet in her heart she loved those patients who were suffering from so much pride and such distress.

Dear Marina

My mother with her beautiful face ageing and bleary-eyed gazed at me for a long time with a perplexed look and then said: 'It's you growing up that's making me grow old. It's your fault if I'm sinking down towards death.' This is the distressing dream I had last night after reading the Diaries of Anaïs Nin till three in the morning. I hugged my mother I kissed her I told her I didn't want her to grow old. But she was angry: 'It's no good your hugging me it's your young feet that are pushing me into my grave.' I was devastated by these words and wept desperately. I woke up sobbing.

Something in me obstinately refuses to accept the break-up of my original family even though all of them communicated to me unacknowledged feelings of guilt and destructiveness. In its happier moments this sense of the family is enshrined in a photograph of all five of us. My mother so fair so lovely her long wavy hair her short-sighted blue eyes with a sort of beatific yet troubled look. My father his chestnut brown curls cut very short his long narrow eyes his seductive mouth. Brother Teodoro his face round and white. My sister Roberta her delicate lips her gentle eyes her look of inner wonder. And me – with my long ash-blonde hair sitting right in the centre looking calm and thoughtful one hand in my mother's and the other in my father's.

From then onwards everything started to go downhill. Up till then I believed the family would go on and on forever just as it always had done. I felt confident and safe. But then my sense of security began to decay like a cavity in my lung. I grew up. I became acquainted with suffering.

From the moment when that photograph was taken the unthinking and unquestioned happiness of our life together began to leak like a boat filled with sunlight through whose planks murky and threatening rivulets are trickling – rivulets which will eventually become torrents until the boat is swamped and carried away into a dark abyss.

All that happened later only confirmed my worst fears: my father's girl-friends his ever-lengthening journeys and absences from our daily life my mother's lovers the mounting debts the house-hunting the furniture removals the quarrels the illnesses the deepening furrows on my mother's face her heart trouble my father's devastating silences our unending moves from one town to another having to beg friends and relations for a roof the sudden departure of Teodoro and finally Roberta's illness. How can I ever come to terms with such a disintegration?

'I don't want to grow up' I shouted at my mother. 'I'd rather have maggots in my feet than push you into your grave.' But I know that's impossible and I catch my breath and cry out with the pain of it. There's the photograph and I can't get away from it however much I hate it for expressing all that happiness that is lost for ever.

I remember once I was moaning in my sleep and I felt two hands gently shaking and caressing and fondling me. It was my mother all made up and perfumed and ready to go out with one of her lovers. He was a small middle-aged man with nervous predatory eyes and I hated him. Before I had raised my eyelids I could smell her jasmine scent with its suffocating sweetness. Then I opened my eyes and saw her: she was wearing a filmy dress of white and blue crêpe-de-chine with a leather belt fastened tightly round her waist. Her mouth was painted a glistening geranium red. I was enchanted by this marvellous vision but at the same time I experienced a horrible feeling of loss. I was already seventeen and she was forty. To see her

89

like this her whole being so beautiful and throbbing with life produced a violent emotion in me. That dazzling white flower painted geranium red would soon be stripped of its petals and would only last for a brief moment. And this brief moment would be passed with that dark curly-haired creature with his vulgar smile. Only a few days ago when she had gone out for a minute he had tried to take down my knickers. I wanted to tell her not to trust him. But that would have spoiled everything for her. I asked her to stay with me. She smiled gratefully but she did not give in. She blew me a kiss and went off.

Dear Marina

For days and days I just eat sandwiches because I don't feel like cooking. But yesterday evening I made a decision: I invited Basilia and her husband to supper. Today I bought some squid I cooked spaghetti with a shell-fish sauce. I made a tomato salad flavoured with basil and a peach tart. I don't like cooking for myself but I enjoy it when I have visitors. Only without meaning to I had caused Basilia to get into a state of agitation. She was busy ironing her own and her husband's things from five o'clock in the afternoon onwards. I heard her go downstairs to ask the woman who lives on the floor below to look after the children for a couple of hours. She rushed out to get her shoes re-soled and then she washed her hair – altogether a big to-do over this invitation which she had accepted enthusiastically but which made her feel she had to doll herself up as neat as a new pin. I told her it didn't matter she was to come just as she was. I'd be glad to see her and that was enough. But she didn't think that was right. At one moment I even heard her giving Mauro a slap because he was whining and this really made me laugh.

I spent the afternoon preparing the food. I didn't get tired. I really enjoyed the pleasure of working entirely with my hands: chopping tomatoes and feeling the juice run down the palm of my hand enjoying the sharp pungent smell as I peeled a beautiful white onion prising the shellfish open by pressing my nails against the smooth compactness of their shells breaking an egg against the rim of an earthenware bowl and letting it slip down into the dish heaping up flour on the table making a hole in the middle of it into which I pour the milk and sugar kneading it so that it becomes as elastic as clay. When I am able to do this quite slowly and carefully without any feeling of pressure it creates in me a clarity of mind that heightens my senses.

I enjoy the smell of pastry cooking in the oven the smell of the water in which the spaghetti is boiling the smell of crushed basil the smell of garlic on the lettuce leaves the smell of ripe peaches of milk of raw tomatoes. I know I am going to feel really hungry.

Yet I am nauseated by the smells of communal cooking in hospitals schools and cafeterias and even in restaurants. When I was in the maternity hospital I could never eat a thing. I gave it all away to the woman in the next bed in exchange for one or two figs or a fresh-picked apple which her husband had brought her from the country. At school I was as thin as a rake because I ate so little. Signora Gonzales used to say: 'Why aren't you eating Bianca? You'll never grow like that. You'll end up suffering from starvation. Aren't you hungry?' Every time I would promise her that at the next supper or breakfast I would try to eat more. But when I was faced with the milk smelling of the earthenware bowl it had been kept in or the soup with its layer of stale fat floating on the surface or when I sniffed my spoon that stank of egg-yolk or when the sister deposited a slice of overdone meat on to my plate my stomach would heave. I would scrape my fork on the plate and cut the meat into little bits and leave it or give it to my neighbours in return for a lettuce leaf or a cherry.

There used to be a competition between us as to who had the narrowest waist. We measured each other with a piece of string. I always won because I was the thinnest but it was a victory that didn't bring me much credit: our ideal figure was modelled on the narrow waist wide hips and big breasts of film stars like Rosalind Russell or Elizabeth Taylor and slim legs like Esther Williams. These paragons of beauty really did have good figures and incredible bodies that could do everything from dancing to swimming and could move equally gracefully in the kitchen on the diving board on the dance floor or in the bed. They had eyes like dolls and when they smiled they revealed an absolutely perfect row of teeth they danced for hours without perspiring or getting a hair out of place their skirts were never too long or too short and never showed a hole or a darn. We pinned colour photographs of them above our beds although we knew for sure the sister would pull them down within an hour.

My waist band was tightened so many times that my waist could be encircled by two outstretched hands. My skirt hung straight from my hips and my blouse hung down over my thin shoulders on to my flat chest. Every now and then the headmistress would look at me with a commiserating glance and say: 'Bianca you're so slovenly you go round looking like a ragamuffin. You should learn to be tidier and you should eat more.'

This headmistress Signora Diamante Bagnato was a strange unpredictable sort of woman. Sometimes she could be very friendly and warm and stop to talk to the ugliest and most awkward little girls at other times she would behave very distantly. She would treat the poorest pupils most harshly and publicly humiliate them she'd be peevish with the teachers and highhanded with the nuns. We would never know what mood she'd be in. Rolanda used to say that she was divided into two halves like the Madonna who was enthroned in the chapel. You could see that the Madonna was made of two plaster casts joined along the nose and chin because there was a ridge down the centre where they met. The two pieces did not match exactly: it looked as if one of them had been disfigured with a sharp finger nail. The rich silk vestments and the blue velvet mantle did not manage to conceal the original division beneath.

Rolanda explained how Signora Diamante was made up of two casts one good and one bad that fitted into a whole. The good part was uppermost when she was at peace with herself when she had slept well when she had been able to pray without interruption and when she had noted down all the imperfections of the pupils and teachers in her special exercise book with the waxed cover. But when she had got up in too much of a rush and hurried down into the kitchen to find the soup burnt and when instead of praying she had begun the day thinking of chicken livers or of a pupil who had answered her back or a teacher who had shown too much 'independence' then her bad part came to the fore. This was Rolanda's theory and I had to admit she was right.

I didn't dislike Signora Diamante but I avoided her. She frightened me a little because I never knew what to expect from her. Once when I was ill in bed she was very kind to me: she brought me a tray with bread and cheese and mortadella sausage and talked to me for a long time about the angels. Then I almost felt I was in love with her with her long regal nose her pale slender hands and her irresolute way of walking.

Then a few days later she sent me a note on grey paper with the one word 'undisciplined' written on it and underlined several times. On the same day at dinner-time in the dining-hall she was reading out the list of 'charity girls' in front of all two hundred pupils and when she got to my name she stopped and said something that took my breath away. I don't remember her exact words but they referred to my parents' lack of money and my shabby clothes.

Another time during the night I suddenly found her beside my bed with her feet bare and her eyes wide open but looking almost as if she were still asleep. I don't remember whether I was masturbating or whether I'd just finished but I pulled my hands out guiltily and placed them above the bed-clothes according to the rules and lay waiting for the expected scolding. But she didn't say a word. She looked down at me with a vacant troubled look. I was too scared to ask her anything or even speak to her. With a tender gesture she uncovered me and gazed for a long time at my bare belly which I didn't dare try to cover up. Then she went off without making a sound shut away inside her long white nightdress heavy with lace and frills.

I was thinking about all these things during supper while I went to and fro between the kitchen stove and the dining table feeling a little embarrassed by my two guests. Basilia wasn't saying a word. She seems to be another person when she's with her husband: her body becomes hunched and old and her eyes disappear into their sockets.

He too was ill at ease. He was dressed in a blue suit with a gaudy silver tie printed with black dots. He ate voraciously never looking at me once. He seemed incapable of carrying on a connected thread of conversation: every few words became lost in lakes of silence.

Finally after supper I had the idea of asking him about his sons. Then he came to life and after that I couldn't stop him talking. He boasted of their exploits as if they were the prodigious deeds of mythical heroes – the enterprises of the great Mauro – the inventions of little Cesaro – what one had said and what the other had done. He is inordinately proud of them but has obviously been bringing them up in the worst possible way filling them with the notion that it's essential to diddle everybody to stamp on the weak to think only of money and not give a damn about people's feelings or anything of that sort. The only time he looked at his wife was to say 'Isn't that so Basilia?' and she agreed gravely and happily.

Dear Marina

This morning I woke up with my eyes all swollen and a bitter taste in my mouth. I think I must have drunk too much wine last night. I swallowed down some boiling hot coffee and went out to buy the papers. It was about eight o'clock and the sun was not too hot. It felt good. I also bought a large water-melon attracted by its vibrant green colour and its perfect spherical shape.

'A little girl was raped by a man of thirty-two. The police have arrested the girl's uncle Umberto Bosco. He raped her last Saturday in his workshop.' A small item at the bottom of the crime page. 'The girl had not told anyone. When she got home she had gone straight to bed with a fever and only a violent haemorrhage had exposed the truth.'

The women in our little consciousness-raising group had all behaved in the same way – me with them. You are five years old and a man sits you on his lap with your legs apart and he starts to stretch the elastic of your knickers with his two fingers. And you? You remain trapped and speechless. You are forced into being his accomplice because the five years of your upbringing have taught you that little girls should always be silent and submissive.

One woman had been seduced by her uncle another by her brother another had been approached by a priest who was a friend of the family. And no one had been brave enough to tell their parents. Some women talked about it for the first time in our group.

I remember sitting waiting for my mother to put on my new shoes. A man came in and all I can remember about him is his delicate hands like a woman's and his big hairy wrists. He thrust his fingers inside my vagina. I was only just five and I didn't even understand what he was doing. I felt a painful tearing sensation and then his hot hands touching my face. I intuitively sensed his fear and experienced it as my own. By this small brutal act he forced me into an inescapable complicity: for years and years I entirely forgot it until one day I talked about it with a feeling of shame to a boy I was in love with. He shouted that he would have killed the rat if he had met him and this plunged me into feeling that I was already a 'damaged object' even before my encounter with those intrusive hands.

Dear Marina

It seems as if I've been here for months. Yesterday was the first time I've been able to write with any enjoyment. At ten o'clock in the evening I got up from my writing table feeling so hungry that I couldn't see straight. I fried myself two eggs and demolished them with two big slices of brown bread.

Then I went out for a breath of air. The Neptune Bar was open. I sat down to have a glass of milk flavoured with peppermint. Once again I saw the barman with blue eyes and broken teeth. He smiled invitingly. I watched him as he moved between the chairs and tables with the blundering grace of a peacock. He was showing off his tall slim body and his curly hair and his handsome smile as if he didn't quite believe in them himself.

At midnight the bar closed and I returned home feeling chilled from having the sea breeze on my back for over an hour. But first I waited to watch the boy as he closed the iron shutters got into his white baby Fiat and left accelerating in the direction of the mountains. I stayed sitting behind the corner of a big urn with a cactus plant in it my bottom resting on the bare earth strewn with cigarette ends. I didn't want him to see me watching him and he didn't.

In bed I couldn't get to sleep. I remembered how I had once had a doll called Marina like you. A proud haughty doll who was missing an arm. She had powdery curls and dark impenetrable eyes. She was a rag doll my mother had made for me at a time when we didn't have any money to buy toys.

Marina was my theatre doll. With her I enacted complicated plays on a rug spread out on the floor. Marina was a disabled girl who lived all by herself in an enchanted castle where everything happened by magic: doors opened of their own accord food was prepared without human intervention and arrived at the table already dished up and was eaten with spoons which did not have to be held. The bed made itself and the bath was filled with boiling hot water without anyone turning on the taps and the bath towel appeared by magic to cover her shoulders. In the garden the roses leaned forward so that passers-by could smell their scent.

Marina lost her arm in battle. Mounted on a white charger with a breastplate of silver she had gone forth to conquer an enormous dragon who was devouring all the women in the neighbourhood. She vanquished him but in the course of the battle she lost an arm. Her sweetheart her father and her mother had all been eaten by the dragon and she lived alone in an enchanted castle waiting for she knew not what while she enjoyed the delights of the magical garden blooming with flowers of amethyst and crystal.

She was called Marina because her father was a fisherman and he had found her in his net along with his catch. At the time he had mistaken her for a fish and he was about to throw her into the frying-pan when she began to sing. He realised it was no fish he had caught and he carried her in triumph to his wife who decided to adopt her. Then when she grew older and was preparing to become the bride of an honest woodcutter called Pertica the countryside was thrown into confusion by the arrival of this dragon who threatened to destroy the town completely unless he was provided daily with a woman or a little girl for his dinner. Her betrothed went out with the other young men of the town to do battle with the dragon but they were all eaten up. So she decided to try herself with the help of the magic trident she had brought with her from the depths of the sea. With its aid she slew the dragon and as a reward she was given the enchanted castle in which frankly she was a little bored.

Marina wasn't the doll I used to take to bed with me. She was called Lilla and her cheeks were eaten with leprosy. I felt very motherly towards her and I used to cuddle her against my chest. Slipping her between the sheets I suffocated her with kisses and fed her with milk. Marina wasn't so lucky – she spent the night sitting on the chest of drawers with her beautiful dusty head always set bolt upright on her neck her shining eyes looking out bravely into the darkness. Marina never slept. She was the sentinel against ghosts and the terrible creatures of the night. Like Bradamante she was always ready to jump on her horse and gallop through the woods drinking from magic fountains. She was without friends or lovers and had only the memory of her dead betrothed to whom she would remain faithful for the rest of her life.

This enthusiasm for fidelity came from my Aunt Giordana who was the sister of my grandfather Giacomo. I used to go with my mother to see them in the small untidy room they inhabited on the first floor of our old family house which is now completely in ruins. She had a happy monkey-like face that fascinated me. She used to offer us little sweetcakes with nuts and cold tea and then she'd show us her latest watercolours of quartered oxen tempestuous seas cats skinned alive and men torn to pieces.

I used to look at the small paintings with feelings of horror but I never said a word. She would laugh and ask me: 'Would you like this one or that one?' and I didn't know how to say 'no' without offending

97

her. But she didn't wait for a reply. She would pile the picture on the top of the others and pick up her paint brushes. She had a severe distinctive style of painting. She had painted pictures all her life without ever thinking of herself as an artist. She called them 'my pastimes' or 'my hobbies' and when the pile of paintings became too high she would throw them away into the dustbin.

I heard from my mother that when she was young Aunt Giordana had been engaged to a sea captain who had gone down with his ship and from that time she'd never been able to look a man in the face. She lived in poverty off the tiny allowance my grandfather gave her. She existed in one room eating nothing but boiled potatoes and painting these violent little pictures which looked as if they came from the naive hand of some crazy Flemish monk.

From her Marina had acquired an exalted pride and fidelity. Her adventures were inspired by stories from King Arthur all of which I had learned from puppet plays. Bradamante Angelica and Alcina the witch were my heroines.

Old Aunt Giordana died two years ago at the age of ninety leaving a hundred paintings and an armchair with a broken seat. The paintings were thrown away. Her fat body was buried in a vault under thirteen feet of concrete among thousands of other bodies in one of the most crowded cemeteries in the city. The fame of her exceptional fidelity was much extolled in the family until it faded away as the family itself declined.

Dear Marina

I have not always been
So idly talking of myself
To sullen refractory listeners

writes Daria Menicanti in that book of luminous poems entitled *Via Pré*.

Marina I haven't always talked to you about myself with such abandon and with so much pleasure at penetrating into you through your eyes and ears. Nor have I ever revealed so much of myself to such a distant and refractory recipient.

This is a time when a whole lot of things seem to have got broken. In less than a week I've broken a tooth my watch stopped I broke the gold chain that held your tear-drop of black glass a capillary burst inside my nose (I lost enough blood to fill a small wine-skin) and finally after having too cold a swim my period stopped.

This morning I woke up at five o'clock with a sense of some loss or breakdown taking place at that exact moment. I opened my window. Outside all was quiet. Crickets trilled softly among the acacia trees outside the building. The street lights were still on. The little town looked calm and friendly. During the day it becomes noisy and chaotic. I had to take a Valium to get back to sleep.

I've just opened the book of poems by Emily Dickinson the woman always dressed in white.

> *The day came slow till – Five o'clock –*
> *Then Spring before the Hills*
> *Like Hindered Rubies – or the Light*
> *A Sudden Musket – spills –*

That pompous old Mr Higginson thought the poems of the young Emily 'lacked structure' even though he did recognise her as having 'an incomparable lyrical gift an audacity of ideological associations and verbal assurance.' In other words women have passionate ideas but don't know how to write. Form and structure are beyond them. When Emily asked old Mr Higginson (whom she idolised) whether he advised her to publish a few verses he told her bluntly that it was not worth the trouble.

> *'Tis Iris, Sir, and Aster –*
> *Anemone, and Bell –*
> *Bartsia in the blanket red*
> *And chubby Daffodil!*

When Mr Higginson that illustrious man of letters came to visit

Emily for the first time Emily presented him with two lilies holding in her hands these two perfumed candelabra to proclaim and solemnise her state of living death in life.

I had a Terror since September – I could tell to none –
and so I sing as the Boy does by the Burying Ground –
because I am afraid.

Emily was in love with her sister-in-law Sue who was the young wife of her brother. It was Sue she talked to and confided in. Two wise brown heads two starched mob-caps coming close to each other and touching each other lightly.

Her sweet weight on my Heart at Night
Had scarcely deigned to be
When, stirring, for Belief's delight
My Bride had slipped away

If 'twas a Dream – made solid – just
The Heaven to confirm –
Or if Myself I dreamed of Her –
The power to presume . . .

The caps and skirts getting close to each other and it becomes an enigma a fiction. No one knows whether Emily loved anyone and if so who it was: Susan . . . Kate . . . ?

When Katie walks, this simple pair accompany her side,
When Katie runs unwearied they follow on the road,
When Katie kneels, their loving hands still clasp her pious knee –
Ah! Katie! Smile at Fortune, with two so knit to thee!

Or was she in love with young Edward Hunt as they said – or was it Leonard Humphrey?

Once again I went to sleep with the book of poems open upside down on my chest. I dreamed of a window and of dogs eating lilies.

Dear Marina

It doesn't make much sense writing to you about myself while I'm shut away inside this ugly anonymous flat trying to force myself to construct a novel which refuses to have a structure. I escape in every possible way. I build up bricks or what I think are bricks and I find them crumbling away eaten by some disease that devours stone. I put frames into windows and discover they are holes in the void.

There is a painting by Magritte of a window and in place of the landscape there's a picture of a painted sky. That's my novel. Incoherent. Meaningless. In place of the house there's a canvas with a house painted on it. In place of the characters there's a sheet of paper describing them. A game of question and answer that ends in nothing.

I've been here for a long time now. I've even become fond of this ugly little town of Southern Italy this squalid flat and this dirty sea that holds me clumsily afloat. Soon the summer will be over. Many families have left already. Folded beach umbrellas lean propped against the empty bathing huts. It's the beginning of mellowness and relaxation of unexpected rainstorms of tepid raindrops bringing with them the heavy smell of asphalt. In Palmero I remember long suspended afternoons spent waiting on the pavement for my lover. That too was for me the beginning of a time of ambiguity and passionate longing a most troubled sensual time when winter intrudes into summer so gently that you become uneasy and corrupted and it is such a joy making love while outside there is mud and rain and the water smells of chlorine and familiar things become distant and vaguely menacing.

I've never told you about the Owl my impatient and irresponsible lover husband who for so many years played the role of father for me – my father always escaping always in flight seducing and seduced by a succession of women with angelic faces. I know you like the Owl. You've never been jealous of him. Perhaps because you knew that we hadn't made love together for so long. Your jealousy was never roused by emotions only by the flesh.

You hated Angelo even though you knew I wasn't in love with him but merely went to bed with him so as to stop myself thinking about Marco any more. Becoming involved with someone else is the only way I know to take my mind off an unhappy love affair. Having an affair with Angelo was a way of distracting myself from Marco after I'd made that pact with Bruna and before you appeared on my horizon like a storm at sea.

The Owl took the place of my father with his flights and adventures and betrayals and seductions and tenderness and fickleness. During the early years I felt I was going to die every time he flirted with a girl. The same wounds and torments then as when my heart first tasted bitterness.

Three of us sitting at a table under a pergola with wasps circling slowly round us. In front of us a plate with slices of ham and pieces of melon. The girl is the friend of a friend. She sits lifting her long coloured skirt with an awkward gesture like peasant girls do. Her pretty transparent face leaning on her open palm offered itself to him like a flower. I watched his transformation as he sat beside me – his eyes moving provocatively his lips opening all ready to smile his whole body leaning forward stirred by gusts of excitement. Sensual and predatory he threw himself shamelessly into the conquest of this fresh unknown flower. He avoided my eyes just like my father used to do – my father so tender and lovable yet quite prepared to break any object he encountered with two pitiless fingers in order to pursue his own pleasure.

So the game of seduction begins. It will run its appointed course in the usual way: the next day the girl will telephone him saying she would like to see him and he will hurry to their assignation wearing a crumpled pink shirt and a white linen jacket. My ever-so-elegant father-husband with his insatiable desires.

I very soon gave up all expectations of fidelity. After the first cyclones of jealousy that tore my roots from the earth and carried me away on their deathly whirlwinds it became clear to me that either I must rid myself of this compulsive need to possess or I would die from it. And I began to think of myself as separate from him and to have love affairs and to cultivate my own friendships.

The Owl grew older sleeping in bed beside me. He grew white feathers. But he still couldn't resist the attraction of a woman's pretty face. How many nights did he come in late reeking of heavy alien smells. How many nights did I wait for him with the anxiety of a loving mother and the grief of a betrayed daughter. He was never a real father for me never protected me never gave me any real security. He was just like my own father with a sensuality that stripped him of authority – needing to escape from me so that he could love me from a safe distance. Neither my first nor my second father could ever provide me with the peace of mind and trust that would reassure me that their love was real. They never wanted to teach me anything even if they actually taught me everything they never wanted to possess even if they possessed me body and soul they never wanted to bind and mutilate me even if they bound and mutilated me again and again they never wanted to forbid me anything even if they forbade me everything against my will.

By the time I was fourteen I was already having love affairs. I went out with whoever took my fancy I came home at midnight I brought friends back to the house I travelled everywhere on my own I did exactly what I wanted. My father never suspected me never reproached me and never forbade me anything. I must have seemed like a tramp always in love with some handsome boy. But the trouble was it was him only him I loved. I only had to smell a shirt he'd been wearing for my heart to miss a beat. His voice on the telephone brought a lump to my throat.

My two vagabond fathers stalked through my heart leaving the fleeting imprint of their wolf-like footsteps. I had committed the sin of idolatry. But sometimes God dies simply because he has swallowed some stupid rat-poison. For all his omnipotence he is helpless against something of such little account as maternal love.

When I gave birth to my dead son I was overwhelmed by another kind of sensuality: the dead son put his mouth in the place where the father had suckled the milk.

It took thirty years to achieve this transformation. Now my body has taken different paths my little girl body has been leavened and has displayed its awnings and its oil-lamps and its cradles. Now there are other little girls drifting here and there with delicate footsteps wanting to be loved.

Dear Marina

Last night I dreamed about a woman. She took me by the hand. The woman was me. When I saw myself close to I was afraid. It unnerved me to be both myself and someone else. I decided to run away. But further on I met another woman. I said to myself it's just as well I don't know her. She won't ask me to be her. But then when she came close I realised that once again it was myself.

Heaven knows how and where this self-rejection has its origins. All of a sudden I remember myself at the age of ten in love with the Madonna. It was when I was at boarding-school. I made an altar out of paper decorated with gold lilies and put it in my desk. Secretly I brought her things to eat sugar and cinnamon and dried figs and nuts. Kneeling in the chapel I looked up at her and I was intoxicated by her sweetness. I felt her heavenly blue entering my throat and lungs. The azure of her mantle her eyes her temples her breasts. Every sin was an offence against the purity of that celestial blue.

The Madonna never complained never sat in judgement never gave orders. She always stood there motionless in a state of mystical stillness that fascinated me. She was more than a mother or a daughter she encompassed the majesty of the whole universe. My love for her coincided with a time of inward dissolution. I longed to vanish out of sight and cease to exist. I was transported by the statues of icy marble on the tombs in empty churches the smell of incense the corpse-like lassitude embodied in the dusty blue drapery of the eternal mother... O Holy Virgin how I loved you for your silent stillness for your demented passivity for the deadly poison of your azure depths for the way you stood so chastely absent without thoughts or wishes without doubts or desires in a gentle twilight inertia...

104

I could not identify with her in everything because then I would have had to become another person. In the deepest part of my being I wanted to stay in the real world with its desires anxieties curiosity and rebellion. But I worshipped her. I was drawn to her by everything I experienced of the serene tranquillity which she communicated to me. I didn't love her as I loved Christ who confronted me with thoughts of disobedience and heroism. I went to her for consolation as if I were going out into the night to be swallowed up and lose myself in the darkness. That was a time when I became obsessed with the idea of self-destruction. I couldn't see any reason for being alive and I rejected this world which seemed to me so stupid and banal. That celestial blueness held me spellbound. I wanted to feel myself encircled within the folds of her azure mantle. I longed to become absorbed into her inhuman peace.

In the chapel in the chill of early morning she breathed as if she were being fed slowly and softly with something tangible. I took morsels of food from out of my mouth and brought them to her. I wanted to nourish her to placate her to satiate her so that she wouldn't consume me – even though I had a passionate desire to be consumed.

Dear Marina

I've got into the habit of going every morning to read the papers in the Neptune Bar. I lean back against the red plastic seat my knees resting against the big table stained with wine. I like looking up to see the sharp angular face of the barman. I like to watch his comings and goings from out of the corner of my eye. From time to time I encounter his bright gaze.

This morning I rang Giorgia to have some news of you. She told me you'd found work with a publisher. It won't last. You're just like my father seeing every job as a contemptible compromise with the world a betrayal of our deepest dreams of innocence. You'll work to earn just enough money to enable you to get by but then inevitably you'll behave in some way that creates an awkward situation and an irreparable breakdown between you and your employer or between you and the people who are close to you. You'll hate them. They'll be aware of your hatred and will reject you. You'll go back home and shut yourself away your beautiful dark head bent over your books in your light bright room full of objects surrounded by hand-blown glasses little wooden statues stuffed birds rose-coloured shells Chinese baskets Persian rugs succulent plants Indian bedcovers.

There are always some people who work and have to compromise themselves for the sake of those who opt out. My mother for my father your mother for you. You can despise reality you can find it petty and reject it but if you do you are forcing someone else to thrust their hands into this reality of shit and dirty themselves right up to their necks and they'll do it lovingly and courageously because they love you.

Giorgia told me she'd met you for supper. You had spaghetti and fried aubergines. Then you drank a barley coffee and afterwards you went to the cinema to see a horror film. So you see that in one way or another I spy on you and follow you from a distance filled with apprehension. I want to know what you are doing and what you are thinking and where you are going to in your crystal-clear darkness. I so wish I had been there with you eating fried aubergines and drinking bad wine! Giorgia is broke and so are you yet you both drink wine with your meals – those heavy sulphurous wines from Frascati which bring on a headache or that red wine from Albano at six hundred liras a bottle which leaves a bitter taste and tinges your mouth with violet.

Although I don't drink I've begun to browse in wine shops. I like the smell of new wine coming from the bottom of the racks and I like looking at the rows of bottles arrayed along the shelves to find something you would enjoy.

Giorgia guessed I was telephoning her to talk about you. She took it rather badly. She's right but I can't pretend. I think she knows I love her for herself even if at that moment I was more interested in you than in her.

I asked her about her love affair with Ivan that exiled Russian living in Milan.

'He rings me up every day but I think I'm bored with him already' she said.

'Is there someone else then?'

'There could be.'

'Who is it?'

'You don't know him.'

'Tell me all the same.'

'You don't give a damn. You're only ringing up about Marina.'

'Hell! Tell me who it is.'

'He's a ham actor but he's got a marvellous body. He's a blond type with a dark swarthy look. I don't think he loves me a bit. He turns me on and if he carries on like this I'll fall madly in love with him. You know how I always run after anyone who's trying to get away from me.'

The difficulty is that Giorgia and I are too alike to attract one another. There's no curiosity about each other in our friendship. Whereas you have the power to surprise me all the time. I'll never really get to know you and it's this that makes me interested in you – I want to search deep down inside you with my submarine eyes. Perhaps the relationship between Giorgia and I would never have existed if you had not acted as a catalyst while we were both intent on exploring the enigmas of your disconcerting face.

Dear Marina

Last night I woke up with a burning sensation. I felt between my legs. It was blood. I got out of bed and cupping my hands between my legs went into the bathroom. I dried myself with a piece of cotton wool and then left it there on the edge of the basin. I slipped a sanitary pad into my pants and went back to bed.

In the morning I found the bathroom had been invaded by ants.

They were all meticulously eating my blood. Swollen with plasma they were scurrying to and fro forming a brown chain that connected the wash-basin to the window. I threw the piece of cotton-wool down the lavatory and sprayed insecticide along the edge of the basin. I waited a moment before going back to my writing. I stayed there quite still fascinated with horror. Death was overtaking the ants as they ran causing them to spin round and round in agonised convulsions and end up on their backs desperately waving their legs in the air. Some went to sniff their dead companions and raise them with their feet and laboriously drag them away. Others came up close to an ant that was dying gave it a slight shove with their heads and then turned in the opposite direction. Blind and lost they collided with each other then started out again in the same direction fell down got up for a moment and finally fell down again trembling and quivering.

Many had died but the line remained unbroken. There was confusion but no panic. The living continued their hurried journeys loaded with heavy corpses. I didn't have the courage to spray any more insecticide and they are still there dragging away dead bodies and tracing a black snake-like path across the bathroom floor.

Between the discovery of my blood in the night and the discovery of the ants in the morning I had a strange dream. A plaster dove came and alighted on my window-sill. Looking at it closely I realised it was harnessed with a metal framework that completely encased it. While I was watching it emitted a grey puff of smoke from its bottom. Then the metal framework opened outwards and from the creature's small claw emerged a little roll of paper. I unrolled it and found it was blank.

I stroked the dove which seemed exhausted by its journey and I saw it was made in a strange way: on its head was a helmet that looked like some of those heads that surmount Egyptian tombs – a helmet of hair as stiff and compressed as marble. The body all white and soft with the head of a warrior. I was seized with a feeling of overwhelming tenderness and melancholy for that fragile white body as if I knew it would soon be dead.

In the dream I thought it was my son coming back. And that

108

strange dove with the smoke coming from its bottom and its helmet head motionless while I caressed it? And the note? You would certainly have found an explanation Marina. It was beyond me.

A man with pig's ears stood between me and the window. He was probing my uterus. A steel instrument slipped out of his hand and dropped on the floor. He picked it up and pushed it inside me. I wanted to say something but I couldn't manage it. My tongue was glued to the roof of my mouth with the pain.

The pig with the red transparent ears probed inside me with his arm. It was covered with black bristly hairs. I told him I was going to be sick. He made a sign with his head and a nurse with a stomach like a barrel handed me a small basin that smelled of egg.

My second abortion – but this time it was from a better class of doctor. I had been told I would have a difficult pregnancy and it wasn't certain that the child would be all right. So I made my own decision.

I was lying under the blanket with red and black checks. I couldn't see my hands. They had cut them off. I thought the woman with the stomach like a barrel must have thrown them away. I felt feverish. I think I must have fainted. The woman brought me round with a slap. 'Now dear I'll get you a taxi. How are you? Are you feeling all right?' She grasped my hand firmly. Her expression was blank but friendly. At last I was able to feel my hands again. I smiled at her gratefully.

She brought her dark swollen lips close to my face. She had pointed yellow teeth. Tell me grandma why do you have such big teeth? All the better to eat you with my little girl. 'Would you like more water?' There was a dead fly at the bottom of the glass. The teeth glinted menacingly. Don't look at me like that. It'll all go away and then I'll feel all right. She implanted her teeth in my neck. I was about to scream when I saw that she was dissolving calmly and quietly beside me. Only her apron remained. I got up. I put on my shoes and my coat and skirt. Once again I felt her close behind me solicitously pressing her barrel stomach against my back and pushing me gently through the door. I realised she was the pig's wife from the way she shifted the doormat with her feet.

Dear Marina

Why do I tell you all this about myself so painfully? Perhaps because I've got stuck in the quicksands of my arid novel and I long for someone to distract me. Or perhaps you are the person I see balanced precariously inside my head. I see your face leaning out – your dark melting eyes and the soft dark down which makes a sensual shadow over your mouth. That shadow is the most primaeval thing about you: it makes me think of the long black skirts of peasant women sweetmeats made of wheat and honey misshapen feet inside hard leather shoes odours of incense and cacciocavallo cheese flavoured with pepper something that dies without dying . . . the mother of the mother of the mother of the mother of my mother who opens the door into a darkened room. Is Concetta there? Now she is coming.

A dark skin that has never seen the sun. Veins all blue and yellow as if they had been painted with iodine. Beneath those skirts black stockings held up by shapeless suspenders. A smooth blond plait hanging over one shoulder. Gigliola and I go to see the goats being slaughtered. We pass by Aunt Genca's shop to buy sugar drops coloured a shrill pink that illuminates the whole shop. Then we go down to the cave with the concrete floor where the goats stand with wide open eyes. Gigliola's uncle cuts their throats . . . an agonised bleating that ends in a death-rattle.

I am aghast. I want to run away. 'No stay and I'll come back home with you.' I stayed. The blood collected in the grooves of the floor and ran into a hole where it gurgled as if it were boiling and sent up purple bubbles along its surface. I watched it fascinated.

That afternoon in Gigliola's house she wanted me to lie down with her for a rest in the big double bed. Her mother and her grandmother her aunt and her sister were all in the kitchen bottling tomatoes. Gigliola lay with her head on my knees. 'Now let's pretend I'm the goat that's going to be killed.' I had to feel her round the neck and waist to see if she was sound just like her uncle did before thrusting his knife into the animal's throat.

'Now take everything off me so that I die naked.'

I began with her organdie blouse which had metal buttons. It slid

110

through my fingers like a light froth and I could sense the taste of it in my mouth. Then the pea green skirt that smelled musty and had been washed and washed and put out to dry in the tiny courtyard alongside the mule and the chickens. Then the vest her mother made her wear even in summer. Gigliola had no breasts and neither had I. We were only eight or nine years old. And our shoes – yes I'd almost forgotten our shoes encrusted with dried blood. A pair of sandals that had once been a lovely blue and were now grey with rusty buckles.

I took her feet in my hands. 'Aren't my feet beautiful?' Yes they were beautiful: very small tender feet. 'You must take everything off me' she said in a whisper. She had long white cotton knickers with broken elastic held by a safety-pin. But she wasn't ashamed of it. I knew about her poverty just as she knew about mine. We had the arrogant indifference that only children and mad people know. It didn't worry us going around looking a bit ragged and dirty not having enough proper food to eat. There were so many other much more fascinating things to absorb us and take our breath away.

I pulled down the elastic with two fingers – a timid embarrassed gesture. Stark naked she jumped excitedly up and down on the bed with her bony legs and a dark smudge between her anaemic thighs and her bottom sticking out. 'Now kill me! Kill me!' She lay down with her head resting on my knees. Her eyes rolled upwards and her body was perspiring. She offered me her white throat drawn backwards with the look of a sacrificial victim. I was overcome with ecstasy and I killed her with my copper bracelet pressing the metal into her innocent flesh.

'Now I'm dead cut me in pieces.' She stretched out her white body on the bed. She offered me her torso with its prominent ribs and narrow hips. With mounting excitement I painstakingly dis-membered her by pressing the bracelet between her ribs round her waist and at her elbow and knee joints.

She was convulsed with tremors. 'Now cut my legs off.' She was trembling. The knife had to sink into her groin and rip the flesh from her bones. For a second I felt the taste of blood in my mouth and I was seized with disgust. But she urged me on: 'Cut off my legs! Cut them off.'

111

This cruelly voluptuous game ended with the abrupt intrusion of female voices. The aunts and grandmothers were calling us for a snack of bread and tomatoes. Gigliola woke up from her ecstatic trance and dressed herself quickly without saying a word. Then she ran down into the kitchen making a sign for me to follow.

Now you see where the dark shadow above your lips has led me Marina – back into a sadistic memory I thought I had lost.

Dear Marina

I spent all morning sitting on the beach. There weren't many people there. Big grey clouds lay heavy on the horizon. I watched a black ship pass by along the blue line that divides the sky from the sea. I remembered a translation of a very beautiful poem:

> *My ship goes by black sails unfurled*
> *Black sails unfurled across the storm-tossed sea.*
> *My heart lies pierced*
> *Pierced as you laugh to make it bleed.*

My eyes were drawn towards a woman who was playing with her little girl. The mother was tall dark and attractive the child small fair and serious-looking already a perfectly controlled 'little woman'. Her mother was urging her to play in the sand. She was doing so – but only as if she were performing a duty. She sat there composedly with her small sensible hands and her docile eyes while her mother laughed at her daughter's clumsiness. Then the woman took the spade herself and started to build an imposing castle with towers and battlements and her daughter watched and encouraged her as if she were the mother and the other her daughter. The young woman's chestnut hair fell over her graceful neurotic face as she concentrated earnestly on her construction.

Then a man with hairy legs and the eyes of a hen arrived. The woman told the child to finish the castle by herself and went off with

112

him. The little girl carried on obediently building the castle in silence without raising her eyes from the sand.

That little girl was me. I too had to lie down and build castles so as to show my mother that I was a happy little girl while in reality I was all the time keeping a silent watch on her. I knew that the moment was bound to come when two hairy legs would appear and take her away. It was a middle-aged man whom I began to detest – a lord of the world with fierce laughing eyes and dry grasping hands and all his worldly knowledge imprisoned inside his small protruding belly. Those hairy legs which I saw from below were pillars supporting the world of grown-ups with all their bold brash ostentation and virility. They were serious portentous legs bearing weighty things that were called possessions marriage property.

Dear Marina

I think of you shut away in your large elegant bedroom. Your carnivorous plants with their thorns damp with white blood. Cactus feet firmly planted on the ground – perhaps they are bare because recently the heat has come back to torment us – your hair your bedspread your crash-helmet your screen your shutters your carpet your brown hands opening and closing that curtain of hair to disclose your round smooth shoulders too innocent for wisdom.

Between us too there has been a history of sand castles and hairy legs. You always told me off for behaving exactly like that silly mother who preferred the two muscular legs of a middle-aged man to the transparent arms of her small daughter. Her ill-fated preference was for the flashy sexual organ between those lordly legs rather than for the hidden sex that is unformed and secret and similar to her own.

Only I did not go off with the two hairy legs of a middle prick but with my dark curly-haired son who was born from my womb on that beautiful scented morning. The son with his narcissus eyes and the daughter with her curtain of hair both yelling to get back inside me.

113

And I chose the son because of my fateful guilty preference for the embrace of someone different from myself.

Chantal would say 'Now the crime is accomplished: you've loved the body of the other.' But suppose the other doesn't really exist and we're all narcissists kissing and loving our own selves and thrusting our fingers up our own arses?

During the afternoon my neighbour Basilia came in. She had left her sons at home asleep. For a few minutes she was on her own free of her two hungry appendages. She sat on my bed and asked me why I lived alone. She spoke in a low choking voice. I told her I was here to get some peace and to write a book.

'A book? What kind of book?'

'A novel.'

'A novel? You mean like those crime stories when they all kill each other and at the end find out who the real murderer is?'

'More or less.'

'So who's the murderer in your book?'

'I don't know yet.'

She was thrilled. She took my hand and squeezed it as if she were wringing out a cloth.

'Will you let me read it?'

'Of course when it's finished.'

'And when will that be?'

'I don't know. I can't tell really. Maybe in a year's time or maybe in two.'

She was disappointed. She asked me why my neck is always a bit bent to one side. I told her it hurt because a friend had bitten me there. She laughed and said she could give me a wonderful massage. She explained that her husband had taught her. He works as a masseur in a home for incurables. She slipped out like a flash and came back with a tube of ointment. She spread it on the palms of her hands. It stank of varnish.

'What kind of stuff is that?'

'It's good stuff all right,' she replied laughing. The only thing I could do was to surrender myself into her hands.

She pulled my blouse off my shoulders and started working on me as if I were a lump of dough. She worked gently at first and then more and more firmly. She has more strength than I'd ever have suspected. And a gentle intuitive knowledge. But just as she came to loosen the most painful spot she ran out leaving me in the lurch because she heard one of her boys crying. So I lost my masseuse. I was left with a sensation of warmth just where you left the sharp imprint of a daughter's teeth.

Dear Marina

This morning on my way to buy bread I thought I saw you in the distance your body shimmering under the canopy of your dark hair. It made my heart miss a beat. But it wasn't you after all. When the woman came closer I could see that her dark hair wasn't so long and thick as it had seemed but was only a few shining locks falling over her ears. And then she was much thinner and smaller than you.

How could I have mistaken her for you? Your body is so unmistakeably divided into two halves: the lower part earthy and massive the upper light and fragile. The two halves seem irreconcilable yet they go perfectly together: the polished surface of your shoulders rounded into a gesture of gentle affirmation your soft downy breasts with the tips turned upwards like question-marks your torso which evokes the memory of marble statues in a formal garden your slender supple waist – without any doubt you'd have won the figure competition at school and a volley-ball champion from Milan would have encircled your waist between her outstretched thumbs and fingers. And then below this fragile marble statue this swan's neck this wasp waist lies a solid vessel pregnant with the promise of children with its sturdy bottom and its legs set firmly on the earth. Especially that bottom so arrogant in its determination to be freely displayed and to rebel against any garment that threatens to imprison it. A bottom like an African fetish.

In the Thousand and One Nights the women of the harem – those strange creatures who eat gingerbread and drink sugared wine and bathe in swimming pools scented with rose petals – are shaped like you: delicate breasts wide welcoming hips buttocks like risen dough waists as narrow as reeds and melon-shaped breasts. And when they walk around attired in their silk fringes and veils the bracelets on their wrists and ankles tinkle delicately like the collars of pampered Persian cats.

Your body half sea-bird and half wild boar half butterfly and half mouse your body which I have loved and still do love in spite of my 'unpardonable sin' in drawing back whenever I see your clouded arcane face reflecting my own.

Though I have no wish to swallow you all up I'm attracted and repelled by your body I'm both seduced and bored by it. Sometimes my longing to caress you makes me almost melt with joy at others I only want to tear you to pieces. Like the time I went right inside you searching with my whole hand to bring out that clot of disquieting darkness which you keep hidden within your guts so that I could know it better.

Dear Marina

Today I went along to the Neptune Bar to work on the novel. Every now and again I looked up at the young man with the shining eyes as he went back and forth to the counter. I ordered a glass of milk and as he put it on the small table in front of me he gave me an inviting enigmatic smile.

I drank the milk down all in one go and he came to ask me if I wanted anything else. I caught sight of a small red mark underneath the collar of his open shirt. He realised that I had seen it and he smiled in an embarrassed way.

Towards one o'clock when the bar had emptied he came and sat down beside me. He told me a strange story of family jealousy: his mother died two years ago. His father re-married and he fell in love

116

with his step-mother. But the father became suspicious and threatened to shoot him and then sent his wife to stay with his sister-in-law way up in the Abruzzi Mountains. Now the two lovers won't see each other for three months. The little red mark on his neck is a memento of their parting.

While he was talking about his step-mother his eyes filled with tears. He asked me if I was a journalist as he'd seen me writing – but he didn't wait for an answer. He went over to the bar and came back with two small glasses of brandy.

'Shall we have a drink?'

'Yes let's drink.'

'Shall we drink a toast?'

'To what?'

'I don't know. Let's just drink.'

I am spellbound by the blue of his eyes. The mark on his neck fascinates me too. As I listen to him my attention sways back and forth while he tells me how his father spies on him and how he confiscated all his pens while he was asleep so that he can't go on writing to his step-mother.

Suddenly the owner of the bar arrived and the boy returned grudgingly to the counter to rinse coffee cups. Then he began to sing a silly love song in a high irritating voice. I left and walked home in the sunshine clasping my worksheets. I'll never finish this novel. It comes apart in my hands. I've been working on it for three years now and every paragraph has cracked open and fallen apart. Patiently I stick and paste the pieces together but I know they'll come unstuck again. The characters are like phantoms waiting their turn to come on stage.

Dear Marina

Last night I dreamed I was pinching one of your feet and I got pricked. They had thorns in them just like a cactus so fine and transparent that they were invisible. But when they stuck into my finger they were more painful than a needle. Are you a thorn I wonder? Then I found myself on a bus with windows of brown glass. It also had a sail – it was a strange vehicle half skimming the surface of the road and half hovering in the air. I was feeling fine until I suddenly realised that someone had stolen my bag. I was terrified – not on account of losing my money because I didn't have any but because of all my documents.

It's a dream I've had many times since adolescence. Somehow or other I lose my passport or my driving licence and I am in despair as if I'd broken a leg. It's the blind fear of becoming nothing and being thrown into a void.

You're not a person says the voice passed down from mother to daughter you're a crust of bread a blade of grass you're a small drinking straw you're a leaf blown by the wind you're a nutshell you're an ant who laboriously scales the side of what you take to be a mountain but in reality is only a pebble you're a melon seed you're a small bird that has fallen from the nest you're the lightest of light waves that falls in love with the prince who gallops along the seashore.

I feel nostalgic for those suppers we used to have at Alda and Bice's place for the plates with red borders for the chopped carrots for all our shared intimacy. I long to be with women chatting and looking at each other with the lightheartedness and trust that used to hold our eyes meshed together.

I wonder if I'll ever see Alda and Bice again. I was linked to them through my friendship with you. Now that tie's broken they recede into the sky above the city like two falling stars that leave no trace behind them. I'd like to phone them but they'd be bound to ask about you and so I don't.

I thought I'd overcome my shyness but every so often I find it again paralysing my hands. When I think how crippled I was as a child I'm amazed that I've been able to grow up. My shyness made me totally blind and I behaved like a dumb savage. I was fearful of crossing the street I felt ashamed of talking to people I couldn't even ask for a glass of water without blushing painfully.

One day I was at a friend's house – I would have been about seven –

and I wanted to pee but I was too ashamed to ask where the lavatory was so I stuck it out with a pain in my tummy and my mouth trembling until the evening when my mother came to collect me and take me home. During the best years in Guatemala I lived in complete ignorance about who I was. I believed I was a dog or a dahlia or a lizard. I confused the boundaries of my body with the boundaries of the world. I suffered from a naked vulnerability and everything scared me. I was so unsure of my own existence that a sharp word or an angry gesture or a look of indifference would throw me into an abyss of emptiness.

At four o'clock while her children were resting Basilia slipped silently and cautiously into the flat. She uncovered my shoulders and rested her small rough hands on my skin and began to knead me gently yet powerfully singing just like her peasant mother must have done while she prepared the bread and the pasta and the pizza dough. She sang at the top of her voice – a strange guttural song that told of a cow being milked and a son who was sick. As she sang I all at once longed to be her with her swelling breasts her melancholy dark-ringed eyes her decaying teeth and that carefree voice. She was so entirely herself. I envied her. I watched her from the sultry corner of my underground cellar. I was amazed to find her majestic and very beautiful.

Dear Marina

I've had the chain of your black tear-drop mended. I've started to wear it again and it hangs scintillating and funereal round my neck. And your ring with its minute beads of coral – I wear that on my finger all the time. In the sea it becomes opaque and almost white. So you see how I remain inside your magic space clearly defined by these marks of your possession. The green enamel serpent encircles my wrist spying on me with his one silver eye. I don't take him off even at

119

night and in the morning I find the imprint of his scaly back on my cheek.

Today Fiammetta arrived with her two dogs and her big yellow canvas bag that holds all her household possessions. She brought me some sausage made by a friend who lives in the country and *The Prisoner of Poitiers* by André Gide. Why that particular book? 'Because you're a prisoner too – imprisoned by your own self' she said laughing. 'You're a victim of the tyranny of literature just like Gide's prisoner was a victim of tyranny by the family.'

We ate mozzarella cheese and tomatoes – those small very sweet red ones full of seeds which are used to make tomato sauce: the kind your mother preserved in bottles to send you for Christmas. We used to eat them seasoned with oil salt and basil.

Fiammetta made my day explode like a ripe water-melon. I lost count of the time and of what I ought to be doing. We ate and then we talked and then we slept and then we went down to the beach. She went for a swim wearing only her pants which created a sensation among the bathers on this part of the beach. At any moment I expected a policeman to appear summoned by some zealous citizen. Fortunately we didn't stay there long. I tried to explain to her that the people who come here are mostly puritanical busybodies who aren't used to nudity. She said she couldn't care less. She plunged into the big waves thrashing joyfully through them with her great tits swinging against her slender sides.

She told me that her brother that good-looking boy Massimo is now wanted by the police. He's accused of taking part in a kidnapping to finance his political group.

'But did he really do it?'

'I don't know. But at any rate he's gone into hiding – I can't tell you where because no one's supposed to know.'

'I won't ask you. What's he going to do?'

'What do you expect him to do? He'll go on being the fearless knight-errant throwing bombs around and shooting people I suppose.'

'Doesn't it upset you?'

'Of course it upsets me – he could get killed. We grew up together and I'm very fond of him. All the same I think what he's doing is right.'

'Didn't he have a good job at the University?'

'But you can't stay watching the world rot under your very nose without doing something about it. Either you rot too or you go underground or you make war.'

'Aren't there any other ways of reacting to this rot as you call it?'

'I don't really think there are.'

'But you're a photographer. You're not a guerilla fighter.'

'I'm a coward and I'm frightened of guns and I'm terrified at the thought of prison. I don't want to kill anybody.'

Fiammetta seemed happy and self-assured. I asked her if she wanted to stay the night but she said she didn't. We had supper in the kitchen laughing and talking. We stayed up till two in the morning drinking lager and nibbling macaroons. She reminded me of the time I was acting as her go-between with Valerio. 'Go and tell him I don't love him any more' she'd said and I got into the car and rushed off into the country. It was the middle of the grape-harvest and it was raining and Valerio and his wife and sons were all in gum-boots with their shirts torn and their hands sticky from picking the grapes.

'Fiammetta says she's no longer in love with you so it's no use trying to see her.'

He looked at me with an expression of hatred as if I were the one responsible. Tears fell on to his large pink rubber gloves and the wasps flew round his tousled head. I was touched by the sight of him. I tried to console him saying that they weren't happy together and that all their friends realised this.

Fiammetta had insisted I should tell him he was a selfish coward who's used his wife as a life-raft and who had always wanted everything his own way: on the one hand the security of a wife and home and on the other a dishy young girl-friend whom he could meet secretly and spend the night with and then disappear at dawn hurriedly buttoning up his shirt. But I didn't tell him any of this because he seemed so overcome by grief. He managed to pull himself together to face his wife. She appeared with a basket full of grapes and put her awkward body between her husband and the world. She barely greeted me and then went on to say something unpleasant at the first opportunity. He was seething. His children were laughing at the smears of grapejuice all over his face.

'Tell Fiammetta that I can't live without her' he said as he propelled me towards my car. 'She can't abandon me like this from one day to the next after eight years of love between us. She must give me time to get used to the idea. I want to talk to her. Tell her that – I must talk to her.'

I drove back to Fiammetta with a box of grapes in the car-boot. I climbed the hundred and fifty steps that lead up to her flat. I rang the doorbell. She opened the door and threw her arms round me.

'What did the bastard say?'

I told her. She flung a vase against the wall – a present he'd brought her from Turkey when he'd gone on holiday there with his family. She spat on the floor.

'Just tell him what I've been suffering for the last eight years: how I've waited for him day and night outside his house spying through the windows enduring agonies of jealousy over his wife and children. Now I've had enough. I'm not giving him a thing not even a pin. I never want to see him again. He can go to hell for all I care. Tell him I've fallen in love with a girl – yes with Wanda. That'll upset him and shock him and stir up his conventional bourgeois prejudices. Tell him Wanda and I spend all night tenderly in each other's arms, the red-haired Wanda whose cunt is as red as the flames of hell.'

I went back to see Valerio but this time he made a date to meet me outside his office in town. We sat on a stone seat underneath a nest of sparrows who were chirruping at the top of their voices. He was wearing his office suit but without a tie. His handsome suntanned face stood out in contrast to his white open shirt. With his look of a mountaineer he reminded me of my father when he was a young man. I told him so and he smiled and looked pleased. Then I told him what Fiammetta had said. He took his time and offered to get me an ice-cream.

'Why do you think she hates me so much?'

'She doesn't hate you. She just doesn't want you any more and she's pissed off.'

'If she didn't hate me she wouldn't go off like this. At least she'd agree to talk to me.'

'Perhaps she still does love you and that's why she has to be so angry.'

He gave me a perplexed sideways look. We went to get a drink of water from the drinking fountain and came back to sit on the stone seat. The sparrows had ceased their clamour perhaps because their mother had arrived with food.

Valerio talked about his love for Fiammetta and about how he'd been racked with indecision.

'I couldn't have left my wife. Without me she'd die!'

'Very altruistic of you!'

He took my hand and held it with a kind of desperation. He asked me if I'd like to make love with him.

'Why?'

'Just now I want you very much.'

'But I don't want you' I said. We kissed each other on the lips. The strange thing is, that it didn't seem to upset Valerio hearing about Wanda.

'That doesn't worry me' he said. 'It's not infidelity when it's with another woman. Tell her I just want to see her.'

But they've never seen each other since.

When I got back at two o'clock after taking her and her two dogs to the car I felt completely shattered. Everything in the flat was upside-down: the sink full of dirty dishes the floor littered with cigarette-ends the wardrobe wide open and all my clothes dangling out of the drawers. At the last minute Fiammetta had asked to borrow a clean shirt and I'd told her to look for something that fitted her.

I settled down to put things straight and thought about her volcanic visit. With Fiammetta nothing is ever peaceful or predictable. When she comes into your house she turns it topsy-turvy and when she comes into your life she throws it into chaos. I can still see the crushed and mortified expression on Valerio's face when he was lying in hospital with both legs broken. Not that he intended to kill himself: he'd been sitting on the window ledge cleaning the windows. But the fact is that he fell and then had to stay in bed for five months always hoping that she'd come and visit him. Eventually he gave up all hope of seeing her again and from that time he suddenly aged. He took on a hang-dog look that was in complete contrast to his upright muscular body.

Thinking it over since there've been times when I really longed to clasp him in my arms and take hold of his prick and kiss it. But unfortunately not when he wanted it at the time of the grape harvest in August. Then I would have been embracing him out of pity and that wasn't what I wanted.

Fiammettta said she's coming to see you. She thinks you are one of the few people who can be counted on and she's going to ask you for some money for a newspaper her brother is involved with. She asked me for some as well. I gave it to her and she thanked me with a flash of understanding in her eyes. One can't say 'no' when she has that look of Bradamante clad in armour on a white horse with her bold mouth and her mind concentrated on battle all ready to set out for some far-off land to wage a desperate and unlikely crusade.

Dear Marina

Yet another tale of houses . . . I keep on dreaming of exploding houses or burning houses or underground houses full of ghostly cellars. Last night I found myself in an empty house with luminous rooms painted with white lacquer. It was a big house but somehow without dimension. Inside one of the rooms I found the statue of a woman. It looked at me with blind eyes not seeing me and yet seeing me. Then I became aware that a white fluid was gushing from her marble breast. I came closer and I collected a little of it in my cupped hand and drank it. It was milk.

When I was very small and my mother was pregnant with my sister Roberta I remember thinking that her belly must be like a house full of dark corners where something strange was lurking that was waiting to be born. Inside I imagined it was a picture by Antonello de

Messina which I'd seen reproduced in one of my father's books: a wooden platform with arched windows letting in a soft friendly light a writing desk shelves with small phials and note books a large blue peacock in the foreground and an atmosphere of calm meditation. I imagined it would be like that inside my mother's belly and I envied my sister being there surrounded by birds and rare plants.

My mother went to hospital leaving me and my brother for days and days with a friend. I don't remember this woman at all only the large glasses of sweet tepid milk she used to put in front of me to console me for my mother having temporarily abandoned me. This milk disgusted me but with my terrible shyness I couldn't refuse it. Reluctantly I drank glass after glass of it and then I'd go into the bathroom and bring it all up. At night I would dream I was drowning in a sea of mother's milk.

Teodoro was younger than me and so my mother had told me to look after him. I took her command very seriously. Not only did I wash and dress and feed him but I pestered him with peremptory orders and hit and smacked him so that he'd be good. Teodoro had round yellow eyes like an owl and he used to look up at me anxiously with his eyes full of love. During the day he never left me for a minute and at night he insisted on sleeping in my arms. Before he went to sleep I had to tell him the story of the princess and the dragon at least ten times.

That was the time when the love between us was at its height. It lasted for about three years until my sister began to walk. Then he took to going out to play in the street with his friends and I stayed at home being a 'little mother' to Roberta while my mother was at work.

As he grew older he distanced himself from me more and more. He became taller and covered in spots. He talked in a cracked voice which I hated. Then one day or rather one night he came to my room with a friend and tried to force me to make love with this horrible little youth with pebble glasses a red nose and greasy skin. Teodoro stood in front of the window holding a cigarette and watching us with a look of indifference. His friend was panting away on top of me trying to open his trousers and pull down my skirt and tear off my

125

knickers while he kept his mouth glued to my chin and his glasses squashed against my cheeks.

I couldn't utter a word and I never thought of shouting for help. I fought back with kicks and blows and finally managed to get free of this lout. Teodoro remained unmoved. He threw his cigarette end out of the window. He gave a pretended yawn and went off saying 'You're no fucking good!'

Dear Marina

This morning I went back to the Neptune Bar to do some more writing. It's too noisy at home in the mornings: women scrubbing floors with their windows wide open and their radios on full blast. And over the past few days Basilia has got into the habit of leaving the boys with me and I can't do a thing with them around. So I go out at eight o'clock to do the shopping and buy the papers and then I sit down in the bar order myself a glass of peppermint-flavoured milk and settle down to write.

I like looking up and meeting Damiano's phosphorescent gaze. Today he told me his name. When the bar was empty he came and sat beside me and talked about his stepmother who hasn't written to him not even one line the bitch and about how his father shouts insults at him when he finds him walking round the house in the nude.

I wrote for at least three hours. It is almost the first time I've felt satisfied with this dismal threadbare novel. While I was writing I felt a glow of warmth inside me. I wrote without stopping until my arm ached. I was deaf to the noise of the traffic and the sound of people walking past and all the chatter around me. I was lost in an enchanted labyrinth where the characters appeared and disappeared as if by sorcery.

Damiano wasn't smiling at me. He was watching me with a puzzled look. His eyes strayed off on their own in his calm cheeky face with its expression of mocking laughter.

Dear Marina

Yesterday the whole town was on holiday. It was the feast day of St Daniel the patron saint of this region. The streets were full of coloured lights and stalls selling nougat and almond biscuits and plastic objects.

I wandered round for a little. I bought two toy lorries for Basilia's boys and I went back home. It was too crowded for me: everybody was waiting for the arrival of Stefano Menfis a famous pop-star whose imbecile face has been plastered on every wall for the last couple of days. He sports an embroidered shirt opening down his hairy chest bright blue jeans and a silver belt with a gigantic buckle. But on his nose he wears a pair of glasses that make him look just like a mother's little darling.

The sound of his warbling prevented me getting to sleep. A powerful amplifier carried his hoarse treacly voice into every corner of the town. I closed the windows but it was useless. I started to read in order to pass the time till it was all over. And in fact it didn't last very long. I was told that for this half-hour of song he had earned fifteen million lira. The newsagent who told me this was really pissed off yet also rather admiring. He said it was a crying scandal and that if he were around he'd shoot him. But yesterday evening I saw him in front of the stage with his wife and children all dressed in white with their mouths hanging wide open.

While I was trying to get to sleep I heard what sounded like a series of explosions. I went to the window hoping it was fireworks – I've always loved fireworks as you know. But instead it was a thunderstorm. Lightning flashed like swordblades cutting through the clouds and glancing off the roof while people rushed to take cover. It lit up the sky with a display more spectacular than any fireworks. I remained glued to the window transfixed by this inferno. Suddenly there was a violent downpour of warm rain and I could smell the cooler air with its aroma of asphalt and damp earth.

Going back to bed my body felt lighter as if I'd been drained of poison that had been accumulating for months. The urge to make love rose up from my legs with little sudden fits and starts as my blood pulsed under my skin. For a brief moment I imagined Damiano beside me with his sharp blue eyes. Then I felt your breasts under my cheek. I shut my eyes and let myself be rocked by this strange androgynous fancy. And so I came hardly touching myself with my fingers. I fell asleep blessed by the rain that had washed my thoughts and softened my feelings.

Dear Marina

How interminable the mother-daughter story is!

Yesterday I read a letter by a girl who had written to the paper 'Struggle'. The girl had a schoolfriend with whom she did her homework and went to discos. One day her friend had asked her to stay the night. The girl agreed but almost as soon as she got into bed she was set upon by two obsessed women: her friend and her friend's mother. Like two furies they explored and squeezed her young virginal body and covered it with kisses. 'It wasn't that I didn't enjoy it' wrote the girl. 'I had four orgasms but I was a bit shaken by the fact they were mother and daughter.'

The 'room of incest' as Anaïs Nin called it. But she was thinking of those other incests between fathers and daughters – that dark love which bound her to her father the pianist and restless wanderer. About her mother she said little.

What do you feel about this story of the girl in 'Struggle'? At the time I thought 'It's all a fake.' Then I thought about it again and about how I used to gaze at my mother's beautiful moonsoft skin while she was having a bath. Of how much I desired her geranium mouth when she leant over me while I was pretending to be asleep and of how I'd wanted to catch hold of her breath that was like dragon-fly wings. When she left the house with her body enveloped in a long black velvet dress and her arms emerging like two soft downy serpents I could have killed her to keep her beside me. Then as my understanding grew I must have sensed that incest with the father is less terrible and less agonising than incest with the mother. Who do you want to marry? Mummy. That's not possible. Then Daddy.

I was always aware of this impending threat of incest. Fearful of rejection I held out against it by silence. But even then I could not prevent myself watching her and absorbing her perfume. She was lying stretched out on a deck-chair reading a book. I was playing at transplanting pieces of moss from one corner of the garden to the other. It was just after the war when we were in Sicily. There was no money. My father would come back from the town empty-handed. We'd rented a very small house by the sea in a poverty-stricken village where there was no electricity or running water. There were lots of children with trachoma and faces covered with flies. There were wild dogs which wandered round all night until they were killed. The fishermen were a pretty rough lot and used to stone them to death. At night the men went out in their boats and returned next morning laden with mullet and squid. The women believed in spells and curses which were handed down from mother to daughter. The Virgin was carried in procession with ten-thousand lira notes pinned to her mantle. We lived on sardines and broccoli and salads of oranges and black olives.

The house was freezing cold and we had to sleep five in a room. But there was a delicious garden where we spent our days: the persimmon tree . . . the dog Regina with her docked tail . . . the blades of scythed grass which we stretched between our thumbs to play music on . . . the neighbour's walls studded with broken bottles that the early morning sun turned into a festival of glinting lights.

My mother was reading in a deck-chair and she was so still that for a moment I was sure she was dead. Lying there with her blonde hair bent backwards dressed in her soft dress with its pattern of mauve tulips my mother was dead and I went on cynically playing.

My hands were covered in earth and I stopped and held them in mid-air with a feeling of exultation. She had died in all her beauty and I would bury her just as she was in the deck-chair throwing earth over her lovely geranium mouth and into her lap and over her swanlike neck and her temples criss-crossed by small blue serpents. I had covered her all up with earth and every night I would go and take flowers to her.

I had killed her. I was afraid of loving her too much and of becoming trapped like those men with round stomachs who visited her at home. That little dark Hercules who smiled at me from under his moustache and who lifted up my petticoat at the first opportunity 'to have a peep' as he used to say – 'just to have a peep'.

Occasionally when we were comparatively well off she and my father used to go to the cinema together in the evening. Sometimes they'd stay out late and I was convinced they'd never come back. They were lying in pieces after a fatal accident. They'd been flattened under a big lorry – she with her radiant geranium mouth and her serpent arms and he with his bewitching tuft of hair and wayward slanting eyes.

A love that is too intense becomes transformed into a bitter-sweet desire to kill. Between sleeping and waking I would imagine the scene: the shriek the heads under the bumpers of the lorry the spurts of blood my desperate uncontrollable weeping... and I'd wake sobbing and raging and pounding Roberta with my fists. Why hadn't they come back? What could have happened? Roberta rolled the sheet round her and turned her back on me. I would get out of bed and wander through the empty house calling and calling for them. Suppose they really were dead. Suppose they were never going to come back. I would roll over and over on the floor in a state of bottomless despair.

Dear Marina

Today I went again to the Neptune Bar to write. But this time it wasn't a success. The noise irritated me. The pages got blown all over the place. My head felt empty and my stomach chilled and only the sweet blue of Damiano's eyes communicated some sense of well-being.

In a quiet moment he came and sat beside me. He told me about the latest exploits of his father his rival in love. And he insisted on offering me a horrible sweet brandy which I swallowed down quickly just to please him.

I asked him if he would like to make love. He said he would and that he'd been thinking about it for days. The intense blue of his eyes seemed almost to brim over and trickle down his cheeks on to my fingers. He offered himself to me with a gentle touching innocence.

'What about your stepmother?'

'I've forgotten all about her.'

'That's not true.'

'Perhaps it isn't but I've been thinking about you for a whole week.'

'What shall we do then?'

'When I'm through with work I'll come over to your place.'

'What time?'

'Ten o'clock.'

'Do you know where I am?'

'Of course I do.'

'Where is it then?'

'At the end of the Via Garibaldi close to the Gloria Cinema.'

'So you've been following me!'

'I'll come.'

'I'll be waiting for you.'

'I really mean it. I don't want to find you've shut the door in my face.'

'Why should I do that?'

'I don't know. You might change your mind.'

'No I won't change my mind.'

'All right then I'll come.'

'I'll be waiting for you. Would you like me to get you something to eat?'

'No I'll eat at home.'

'Won't you be coming straight from work?'

'No I'll go home first.'

'Why?'

'I need to have a bath. I can't come as I am stinking of coffee and washing-up water.'

'That doesn't matter. Come as you are.'

'No I'll go home and have a shower and change and then come over.'

I went down for a swim. I felt happy and peaceful and I swam with long steady strokes. There was some yellow foam floating on the surface of the water and I tried not to let it get into my mouth. I got out and sat on a rock where there were two people fishing with a line. I dived back into the ice cold water and holding my breath went down as far as I could with my eyes open until I saw a big black rock looming towards me. It was blossoming with seaweed and beneath it I caught a glimpse of a cave dappled by long rays of sunlight a dawn of scintillating particles against the darkness. It was like the temptation of incest with the mother: a vast lake threatening yet exalting.

Later I grilled a John Dory and ate it seasoned with lemon. Then I lay stretched out on the bed and had a rest. It was already four o'clock. I slept. I read. I looked at the ceiling and listened to Rigoletto – the Duke of Mantua whose marvellous voice has waving banners in it. I waited for Damiano to arrive without any feeling of emotion or anxiety. I began to float backwards and forwards on a see-saw. '*Margherita ante porcos* – pearls before swine' said my mother's voice behind me – and two large hairy pigs were having a friendly sniff at my feet of crystal. Then suddenly I found two new-born black babies in my arms and I kissed them passionately. Only I couldn't fathom how it was they were born black. One was a boy and the other a girl and I decided to call them Margherita and Porcos.

When the doorbell rang I woke up suddenly wondering who it could be. I went bare-footed to open the door my mouth dry and my head empty. Damiano came in hastily just as I'd imagined he would: not daring to embrace me looking round with curiosity and talking in a whisper as if he were afraid someone might be there.

It was strange to be making love after almost a month without it. Our first embrace was clumsy. Then after having talked and smoked a cigarette together we grew more confident. He browsed between

132

my legs like a greedy goat. I took his round dark penis in my hand: it was encircled by fair curly hair that made it seem almost as if it belonged to someone else.

'Do you like it? Do you find it ugly?'

'No I like it.'

'You've got such gentle hands.'

'And you smell so nice.'

He kisses like a baby that's attached to its mother's breast – sucking and biting my tongue and tugging at my lips. His rough hands squeezed my back and my throat. Sweating we lay in each other's arms for a long time without love but with an overwhelming tenderness.

We fell asleep clasped together and when I woke up at eight o'clock I found myself alone. What woke me was the acrid smell of coffee coming into the flat like a flash of lightning.

I thought about the dream of the two black twins. What does it mean? I'd like to hear you explain the mystery of that vision in your most moonstruck voice: 'It's your dark-coloured duplicity – an ambiguity that has its roots in the depths of your sexuality.' Would you say something like that? 'Margherita is the daughter left behind by the advent of knowledge and innovation and travel. Do you remember that journey on the back of the winged horse with Mephistopheles when the landscape receded into the far distance growing very small and murky: and out of the darkness emerged the Goddess of Mystery? Porcos is the other – the male. He is your choice for whom you have sacrificed yourself. But he remains the innocent who will never be able to understand your woman's body. *Margherita ante Porcos* – even your mother proclaims it.' Isn't that what you'd tell me?

Every story between mother and daughter ends up in a man's womb. You reproach me for being afraid of finding myself between your legs. That's true – it scares me to see the reflection of my mouth in the secret mirror between your thighs. Each gesture reflects its mirror image every rejection reflects another rejection. But how did this stupid story of rejections begin?

The first excruciating act of incest is with ourselves – the shock

133

which overcame me when at the age of about six I was licking my own reflection in the mirror and saw my image clearly outlined only a hair's-breadth away looking so distorted and hateful that I pulled back completely horrified.

In the bath I forced myself to put my fingers between the lips of my sex searching for the pleasure that ran through my veins in an attempt to capture it in one precise but so far unidentified spot. The love that led me to myself was clinging and lifeless. I didn't feel guilty about masturbation – I did it continually. But I didn't love myself. I didn't even like myself.

I fell in love with a little boy who was smaller than me and who had a white fringe and pinkish eyes like a rabbit. He hardly ever spoke to me but he used to follow me everywhere. One day when he was ill in bed between dazzlingly white sheets I slipped my hand beneath his pyjamas and held his penis in my fingers: he was overcome with emotion and peed all over my wrist.

He was the other: different from myself. He contained all the mystery of the universe. He was not like the reflection of myself in the mirror. He was the start of a journey through the thorny paths of the world in search of the golden apple. 'But why couldn't you find the other in a woman?' asked Chantal who has been lucky enough to love women from the moment she was born searching in the warm open sex of her mother with the pallid fingers of a new-born babe.

Once upon a time there was a king who had three daughters: the first obeyed her father and chose a king for a husband. The second was amenable and chose a prince who owned many lands. The third was disobedient and so she was changed into a fox. A fox which has a bushy silver tail and used to sit at the top of a well under the moonlight gazing at the lights of the palace from which she had been excluded.

My mother told me this story and I swallowed down her words. As soon as she had finished I wanted her to begin all over again: Once upon a time there was a king who had three daughters and the first was called Balduina and the second was called Gesuina and the third Serafina and in the garden grew a beautiful tree with golden apples on it. The father had forbidden his daughter to touch the apples but

134

Serafina was a curious and obstinate girl and she was determined to try one. Hardly had she touched it when she became very small and ugly... I ate up the golden apples and with them I ate up my mother's arms and her voice and her throat.

And if the circle closed? My mother my sister my daughter and all the others? Is it certain that in this woman's world hermetically closed without a chink of light bolted barred and isolated the masculine womb with all its secrets and fascinations would never penetrate? 'Power' says Chantal 'is the power of this male womb which captures you and subjugates you.' This word 'power' in our discussions over the years... we sucked it like a sweet... the power of the devil who pierces you with his forked tail... and I cry and you laugh and we press each other's hands under the table. Do you remember when you wanted to kill me out of jealousy? How strange it was – how like a serpent you were. And then you took the oars and we rowed out to sea in a red and blue rubber canoe... your feet pressed against the rubber that was the colour of red Chinese lacquer... your fleshy earthy feet... you took off your dress and I watched you with my eyes smarting in the salty air. How can one avoid desiring the siren who slithers at one's feet and smiles so invitingly?

Marina in the marine sunshine... sitting at the bottom of the canoe glowing quietly like dough that was leavening... you slipped off your bikini and threw it away... determined to seduce me... the black curls speckled with salt the fleeting face of the Medusa... you forced me to look at you while I was rowing and you delighted in that display of yours... lazily and radiantly you played the marine game gently spreading your legs wider and wider and I was forced to look inside you and to lose myself in your black garden that invited me to become very small like a new Alice in Wonderland so as to satisfy my curiosity and venture inside.

Dear Marina

Early this morning the doorbell rang and I immediately thought it must be you. I don't know why. It's absurd – you don't know where I am and I'm sure you don't want to see me. But that thought flitted into my mind and I quickly put on my dressing-gown to go and open the door. I imagined putting my arms round you and my heart was beating fast.

I found myself face to face with a handsome dark-haired young man with smiling eyes.

'Are you Bianca?'

'Yes I am. And who are you?'

'Let me in and I'll tell you.'

'Tell me who you are first.'

'How suspicious you are!'

'I'm not suspicious but I want to know who you are. It's seven o'clock and a minute ago I was fast asleep.'

'You won't regret letting me in.'

'But why should I?'

'I need to get in.'

'I'm shutting the door. I don't appreciate jokes especially at this hour of the morning.'

'But it isn't a joke you fool. I'm Fiammetta's brother Massimo. Now will you let me in?'

He came in. He went straight into the kitchen and made himself some coffee while I got washed and dressed. I thought: 'What does this beautiful young man want from me? I bet it's either money or a bed for the night.'

This was quite correct: he wanted a place to hide because he's on the run. He'd dumped his luggage with a friend in town but he can't stay there because . . .

He never gave a thought to the possibility that I'd say no. He solemnly announced that he would pay me for the room and food and for any trouble he might cause me. He would be going out in the morning and coming back at night. He would only be staying for a couple of days.

I told him I'd come here to be alone so that I could work in peace. He smiled superciliously. 'What kind of work are you doing?'

'I write.'

'Our brothers are being slung into prison the world's going to rack and ruin we're being eaten alive by a police state – and you are "writing".'

'Why the hell have you come here to preach at me?'

'I know you've given money to Fiammetta for our paper and I'd like to thank you.'

'I gave it to her because she asked me for it and I'm incapable of saying no to her.' But I wasn't managing to say no to him either . . . 'Just thank your stars you're Fiammetta's brother or I'd send you packing.'

'Don't worry, I won't bring anything compromising into the flat I promise. And I'll be out in two days. And by the way – my name is Giorgio Paradisi. Who lives opposite?'

'A woman called Basilia whose husband is a masseur in a nursing-home for chronic patients.'

'Good. If it's necessary we can make use of them. When are you going out shopping?'

'Soon.'

'Then listen: Go round to my friend who lives in the Piazza Diaz and fetch my things. I need to change my shirt. And could you get me ten packets of Marlboroughs?'

'Look, I'm going down to the sea and I won't be back here before two.'

'That doesn't matter. I'll have a kip. I haven't slept for four days. And could you buy me a tin of coffee? Can I have a bath?'

The friend who was to give me his things was a woman with a spoilt childish expression on her face. She handed me the suitcase without a word. When she came with me to the door she only asked 'Who else is in the house with you?'

'Nobody.'

She made a face as if to say she knew exactly what would happen. I asked her if she lives on her own. She told me she doesn't: her husband is a teacher at the local lycée.

137

I lugged the suitcase up the hundred and twenty stairs cursing my new guest. I didn't have time to go down to the beach. I ate by myself while he slept. In my bed! But from now on I'll insist he sleeps on the divan in the sitting-room. That handsome sorcerer with the disdainful face won't get me breaking my back for him again. He's already made the bathroom filthy and filled the washbasin with hairs. He's left dirty footmarks on the white floor the bath-towel's wringing wet and the mirror's spattered with soap.

In the evening we had a meal together. He'd had a rest and was in a cheerful mood. He had shaved and put on a clean shirt. He never forgets how handsome he is. I could see what a kick he gets out of being a heart-throb. Some of the time he likes to appear strong and invincible at others he becomes small and helpless and craving for attention.

He talked to me at length about the political situation of the 'regime' about utopia and about war. 'Democracy is capitalism's brutal dream of maintaining its own continuous dynamic' he said his violet pupils dilating with fanaticism. 'A perverted form of capitalism which perpetuates its fascist bias under a faceless anonymity.'

While he was talking he neatly polished off the fish I had cooked for him. 'The socialism of the so-called socialist countries is quite simply a form of hyper-capitalism devised by a bunch of bureaucratic stuck-up turkeys in the name of the working class. Bianca the most devastating crimes in history are being committed today by these so-called humanitarian big-wigs who weep crocodile tears for children dying of starvation. They've declared the 'International Year of the Child' as if they weren't the primary cause of children dying ... for them life exists only when it produces a profit ...

'Only the language of violence can have any meaning today Bianca ... words are dead ... utopias have vanished ... words like democracy constitution justice are all played-out ... for anyone who's young and has a spark of sensitivity they're nothing but lies lies ... one can't help shuddering ... our rejection must be total and absolute. Some people are so sickened by it that they choose to kill themselves with the needle but that way you do capitalism a favour: you contribute by putting money into circulation and putting

138

yourself out of circulation. We've had enough of salaried employment forced on us by the myth of the growth of production. Today the only answer is the gun. New history demands a new courage and new methods and a clear-sighted vision. Love demands robbery and crime. For the new man the new love demands the burning sword of violence for the renewal of belief in a true communist liberation. Do you have a lover?'

'What the hell business is it of yours?'

'All this hostility ... I guess it means you're scared ... '

'I'm not going to listen to you.'

'It beats me what you think you're up to in this squalid place.'

'That's my business.'

He smiled maliciously. 'Like all the bourgeoisie you can't see further than your own nose. You're digging your own cabbage patch and you think you're being part of history. You aren't. You're out of history. You're nothing.'

We went off to bed like two enemies. Him on the divan in the sitting-room and me in my room. I locked the door as a precaution: he's the type who's quite capable of raping you to thrust the revolution into your belly.

Dear Marina

For three days I've done practically nothing except cook clean and quarrel with Massimo. If he hasn't gone by tomorrow I'll go away myself. I'll leave him the flat and go back to Rome.

Basilia has been round twice with her children hanging on to her coat-tails. She put her head shyly through the door and asked permission to come in. Curiosity made her round eyes even larger than usual. I told her I had a friend staying. She gave me a wink.

'No' I said. 'He's not my lover. He's just someone I know that's all. He's the brother of one of my friends actually. He's called Massimo – no I mean Giorgio.'

She looked sulky and disbelieving. She thought I was trying to hide the truth from her and in the circumstances the truth could only be a story of love and intrigue and betrayed wives and abandoned children and clandestine seduction. I was annoyed that she should think I was clasped in the arms of some blond Adonis but I couldn't convince her. She went off with a crafty smile on her face. I said: 'Will you give my shoulders a massage?' I was longing for one of those quiet afternoons listening to her frightening stories. She answered a little dryly: 'I don't think you need me just now' and shut the door behind her.

At the Neptune Bar Damiano greeted me with a sombre look: 'You said you were alone. You've been deceiving me.'

I tried to explain that this intruder had turned up out of the blue but he didn't believe me.

'How did you know about him anyway?'

'I saw him at the window while you were down by the sea.'

'What do you think you're doing spying on me?'

'I love you. Of course I want to know what you're doing.' The blue of his eyes was stuck on to his angry offended face.

'I'm not one of your belongings Damiano. You don't own me.'

'That argument's a bit thin. If two people are making love they must respect each other.'

'I've told you I'm not doing anything with Giorgio.'

'But he spends the night in your flat.'

'So what?'

'It compromises you.'

'I couldn't care a damn whether it compromises me or not. I only want you to believe me.'

'Get rid of him. I can't stand him being there with you.'

'I can't right now. He's my friend's brother.'

'If you don't get rid of him then it's all over between us.'

'You're talking as if we were engaged. If your stepmother came back wouldn't you be making love to her?'

'No I wouldn't because now I'm with you and I want you with me.'

'Can't you believe me when I tell you there's nothing between me and him?'

'No.'

'Then good-bye!'

'Good-bye!'

Back at home I found Massimo Giorgio sunbathing on the horrid little balcony that leads off the kitchen and is overflowing with dirty clothes. He didn't cover himself up when I came in.

'I want to store up a bit of sun for when I'm in prison. Let me see what fish you've bought. Do you know you're quite a good cook. If I stay with you you'll spoil me. I'm used to tiresome women who won't put a pan on the stove or iron a shirt on principle. You don't iron shirts either, but you're very together and you're a good cook. You're a born housewife and you want to be a writer. If you know how to write as well as you can cook you'll be another Virginia Woolf – though as far as I'm concerned she's wordy and boring... I'd rather have Proust. Do you know you've got beautiful breasts: they're round and juicy. Delfina hasn't got breasts nor has Giulia – just two dark dried-up nipples. Women's tits aren't all that important otherwise I'd never have got to marrying Delfina. All the same they do have some significance. I don't mean aesthetically that doesn't mean a thing. But to be able to caress them... I bet yours feel very soft... Don't worry I'm not going to touch them I'm not that common. But if you want you can come to my bed whenever you like. Do you realise it's two weeks since I made love? Always on the move with a scraggy beard and a dirty arse and sweaty armpits... I have to do it again before long. When one's fighting a war one doesn't half relish the little things of life... the touch of flesh... the taste...

'For instance have you ever read Che's diary? These men who don't give a damn about their bodies who can hack their way through the jungle who can dig up rocks with their finger-nails... they suffer just like anyone else from the lack of a bath or a hot meal... the day when at last you can light a fire wash your neck take off your shirt have a dish of beans and rice... you feel yourself reborn you feel strength and well-being coming back to you... '

I skinned and trimmed the cuttlefish and threw them into boiling water. He was talking with his eyes shut half-hidden behind the striped glass of the kitchen door sitting up on an old inflatable lilo next to the bucket of dirty floor-cloths. 'Delfina's been in prison for six months you know . . . but already we weren't getting on . . . perhaps it was my fault rather than her's . . . but she's very pig-headed and she never utters a word. Did Fiammetta tell you about her? They didn't like each other. Fiammetta found her pretentious and stand-offish. It's a fact that during the three years of our marriage we never quarrelled once. When she was angry she'd close up like a clam she'd refuse to say a word and I'd be left to deduce from the way she was looking so uptight and annoyed that she'd got it in for me.

'Then she found out about Giulia who was her best friend. It was a stupid thing on my part because I wasn't in love with Giulia. It was just something to pass the time. But Delfina took it badly. She made a big issue of it and put it to me straight: either her or Giulia. I ended up by choosing Giulia not because I really wanted her but because from then on Delfina refused me and pushed me out . . . Hell, we were teachers together our classrooms were next door to each other. I used to hear every sound when she was ticking off her boys and I was saying to my kids rather feebly "All right do what you like but don't bother me!" Another thing – she hasn't got any tits either. My life seems fated!'

'I was certain Delfina would have her revenge. She's that sort of a vindictive person. I thought – she'll make love to my brother – she'll burn the house down – she'll denounce me to the police . . . Instead she got her revenge by going to prison herself. Lots of my friends were amazed at all this: a good revolutionary doesn't get trapped into stupid love affairs . . . and then the wife's best friend – it's so much the traditional bourgeois stereotype. I'm not claiming it's all her fault though.

'What else can I tell you about her? She's the most clear-headed of us all in everything she does. She's the most courageous and the toughest in any kind of crisis. She's the sort who can go for months on end eating nothing but a sandwich a day and kipping down in a sleeping bag on bare boards. She knows how to shoot like a picked marksman she can steal like a magpie she can forge passports she can sell false money – and she does it all so well that it's impossible to match up to her... the angel of the revolution. But the trouble is angels aren't all that sexy... '

I put the squids on the table. I seasoned them with oil mustard lemon and parsley. There was a tomato and celery salad yoghurt and some strawberry tart that I'd made in a moment of boredom. He ate everything voraciously while he smiled and talked. He's the sort of person who eats with his tongue. He enjoys his food all right but he gobbles it all down in a frantic hurry.

I felt pleased that he appreciated my cooking... this vice of being the provider of nourishment this obsession with food. First I fill his belly up with my cooking then his belly will swell with a baby. It must be some sort of oral insemination. Or probably it's just the anxiety of a mother who sees her son in danger and wants to fill him with herself stuffing him with love and security. I can't get away from my feeding instinct when I have a guest – anchovies in oil zucchini marinated with paprika aubergines baked with garlic and lemon... tomorrow I'll buy some ricotta and make him spinach rissoles... I'm amazed to find myself thinking in such an idiotic way while he fixes his hungry eyes on my face. I'm resigning myself to this invasion and so I'm compelled to make him feel better and to attend to his needs by serving him like a neurotically perfect housewife.

But then I took a grip on myself and told him he's got to leave because I can't get on with my work with him in the house. He looked at me sideways to see how seriously to take me. I can't have looked very convincing because he started his chatter again:

'In the end Delfina and I were eating entirely out of tins: beans and tunny-fish... tunny-fish and beans... tinned beef gruyere cheese... I came out in spots all over my body. I said "Why the fuck is it we aren't even capable of frying an egg?" Then for a short time we bought everything in the delicatessen... riceballs... pizzas. That was a bit better than tinned beans and tunny-fish but it still wasn't all that good. In fact I used to feel quite sick sometimes. Then we started to scrounge: we'd go round to our friend Chiro who cooked like a king. We went to see him pretty well every evening taking a bottle of wine as a contribution. Then there was Delfina's cousin Elisa who used to make great dishes of spaghetti with meat sauce. But this was before all the trouble began and they started looking for us ... I don't like you ... the idea of making love with an intellectual stinks a bit ... still there must be something about you that attracts me because for the last two nights I've dreamt I was touching you: maybe it's some sort of enforced celibacy. Do you want me to help you with the washing-up?'

Dear Marina

Another three days have gone by and Massimo Giorgio is still here! I haven't managed to get rid of him. He says he's waiting for his moustache to grow so that he won't be recognised.

'I don't really care ... ' he says. 'But there comes a moment when you just can't stand being on the run any more ... when you'd almost rather have some sort of peace in prison. But the trouble is once you're inside you can't go on being an activist. And there's another problem: once they've got hold of you they never let go of you. What have you got us for supper?'

I've resorted to taking myself off for the day. I do the shopping in the market at half past eight and then I go to the Neptune Bar to write. I've made it up with Damiano. We embraced in the toilet leaning against a filthy wash-basin that drips rusty water. It was so good to smell him again to feel his rough hands on my face and to see the gleam of sky-blue that wells up from beneath his half-closed eyes.

At midday I leave my shopping bag with Damiano and go down to the beach. I swim a long way out to sea. I've discovered a rock which is out of reach of the waves where I can lie and sunbathe when the sea isn't too rough. It's coated with tar and encrusted with yellow limpets. It gives off a lukewarm smell of decaying seaweed. Deep down the rock must be full of hollows and caves: I can hear the continual eddying of the sea a slow laboured breathing like a hoarse tuneless song.

I like staying glued to that rock among the limpets and the gurgle of the water that makes me think of shadowy caves inhabited by swaying seaweed. A few drops of salty water splash on to my feet as the waves break lightly against the glassy rock-face sluicing it with little dazzles of luminous foam. Through my half-closed eyes I'm unable to distinguish the threshold between sea and sky. I'm suspended at a mysterious balancing-point where the forces of the sea and the forces of the land meet.

At two o'clock I go back home to find Massimo Giorgio lying on my bed or sunbathing naked on the little terrace. He's irritable because he's been left on his own for so long. He's hungry. He gets sarcastic: 'So that's how you work? Sunbathing naked on the beach? Christ knows who you've been having it off with. God! I'm so hungry my stomach feels like a vacuum!'

'Why haven't you eaten what was in the fridge?'

'I don't enjoy eating on my own.'

While I get lunch ready he circles round me tasting the wine tearing off pieces of coarse bread dipping his fingers into the oil from the anchovies. Sometimes he looks so handsome: his clear-cut features his large well-shaped eyes his mouth tenderly sculptured in amber-coloured marble his smooth soft hair falling down on to his neck his long muscular arms his slender legs his narrow waist his pelvis jutting forward as if he were making you an offer of his splendid virility. When he sees I'm looking at him he smiles in amusement with a flash of shyness in his eyes.

'Do you know how I met Delfina? It was at University – but not as you might guess when our noses met over the same book or because we ate a pizza together. No – she was my father's lover. As you know my father's a lecturer and she was his best student: a country girl – but who'd ever have guessed that from seeing her small delicate head and her slim fair body. She never missed a class and was so brainy that she understood everything first go. He grew so fond of her that he decided to lure her into his bed. No – I've got it wrong: it was she who decided to sleep with him. She really fancied this handsome communist who was infatuated with words and music. He had been there in '68 with the students and had joined them in their occupation of the University and had thrown himself against the police and been driven out of his job and then reinstated – a born fighter!

'So they fornicated happily under the horrified eyes of her mother who was a simple country woman smelling of garlic. But craftily he didn't let on that he had a son who was better than he was – he didn't let her into that little secret. Then one day guess what: she came to ask my mother for my father's hand – in other words she wanted to be on good terms with her "so as not to give offence to another woman like myself. I don't want her to hate me because of him." That's how she put it. My mother who is a perfect lady listened to her with an icy look and said she considered her husband free to do as he pleased but she didn't want "to confuse everything with an equivocal alliance between women." That was the word she used – "equivocal". Delfina went away disappointed. But just as she was leaving she met me the handsome young eagle straight from the nest – the fragrant up-dated edition of the father. She looked at me. She fixed my image like a photograph and in a flash she decided to grab me.'

I'm oblivious of time. Although I'm desperate to get rid of him I still go on cooking him delicious tit-bits. I listen to him fascinated for hours on end. He has an easy-going piquant way of telling stories that makes me laugh. It all pours out of him as if he hadn't talked to anyone for years. Perhaps nobody else ever does actually listen to him in the rather sleepy silent attentive way I do.

'At that time I was having it off with four other girls' he starts up again bold and confident. 'To tell the truth I've never been monogamous... I'm bewitched by hair by hands I'm somebody who needs to fantasise... I enjoy the looks the sideways glances the seductions the escapes the advances the concealments. I enjoy balancing on a tight-rope between one emotion and another without getting taken over by dramatic situations. I enjoy idling in other people's beds I enjoy killing myself with pinpricks of jealousy I get a kick out of ending up the loser. While I'm busy caressing the woman I love I'm all the time longing for another face another body. I dilute my revolutionary certainties with my amorous uncertainties. I'm as weak and indecisive over love as I am strong and decisive over politics. I enjoy sex when it's a risky game. If I'm not living on a knife-edge I fall asleep. Look how I came a cropper with Delfina! She's exactly the opposite to me. She's strongly monogamous. She's fiercely passionate she can't stand insecurity and uncertainty. Once she's made her choice she goes right to the end at the risk of breaking her neck. We saw eye to eye in politics but never in love.

'You might say I'm a bit of a shit – perhaps I am. I don't like taking things too much to heart. Intense emotions and dramas make me sick... One look is enough... a rain-coat fastened round someone's waist the glimpse of a back in a restaurant a pair of slanting eyes two fingers holding a spoon... this could be material for psycho-analysis... but that's just a load of crap. War is war and I'm fighting a war...

'In the end Delfina left my father with the excuse that he refused to be straightforward with my mother and her. He nearly had a heart-attack... That little girl over there with short-sighted eyes and narrow sloping shoulders who does she think she is?... he weeps he goes into convulsions he sweats he vomits he floods the whole house with his vomit. My mother sympathises with him and stays with him and looks after him but inside she thinks he's just a stupid old man.'

Dear Marina

Now that my life has been taken over by Massimo Giorgio and his long involved sagas I so yearn to see you. I long to hear your voice teasing and scolding me. I feel such nostalgia for all the journeys we made together for the bread rolls dipped in oil the salt ham for diving into the river plunging into the icy water for cheese sliced with a penknife the taste of apricots and the peace of being together and not needing to talk.

You got up from the ground singing to yourself and cheeky as a monkey you lifted up your skirt and peed all over my shoes. 'Do you see how steamy my piss is?' and you squatted down without any embarrassment your head bent between your legs and your pee spurting out over the pebbles. I know that if we did see each other you'd spit out a sackful of hate: 'You're a twit you're a nit you're a shit you're a tit you're a bitch a bitch. Your brain is sick with its will for prick your belly cries out for a birth your breasts cry out with milk all of you cries out for a child never mind whether it's a girl or boy. You've betrayed your sex you'd be better dead you've accepted a man-child's heavy tread you've let him invade you trample all over you cover you smother you you bitch oh you bitch.' That's what you'd say.

For two whole years it was always the same among the women in our group: we all felt guilty over our dependence on the umbilical cords that bind us navel to navel to our lovers our fathers our husbands our sons ... Annangela with her pearly cheeks and her ovarian cysts and so much gentleness ... we went fishing together with both hands in the river of our shared memories quite terrified by all we were bringing out into the light of day: the groping ivy which lays waste the father's garden ... the knife that a woman's hand will strike into the back ... the desire to meet oneself to look at one's thighs legs feet breasts armpits ears ... intuitively perceiving and tasting for the first time the purity and ambiguity of a sex that has a thousand forms and never ceases to astonish smashing the blown egg-shell of the family which has kept relationships between woman and woman secret and separate as if they were unhealthy perversions.

For months and months we talked of the mother but without seeing how every woman longs for motherhood and is never fulfilled with another woman – an insatiable search that has always to begin again ... in the hatchets of ancestral taboos.

How beautiful you were with your black hair falling like a curtain and that billowing blouse slipping down over your shoulders and your breasts. Even now I can't give up these tokens of your magic; the serpent bracelet imprisoning my wrist the ring with drops of blood encircling my finger and the long black tear-drop which hangs round my throat. With these amulets of yours I can confront the fiery fumes of any angry dragon – I am invincible!

Dear Marina

Last night I dreamed I was taking a big apple tart out of the oven with my hands still covered in flour and eggs. I cut the tart open and inside...there you were! I recognised your cactus feet and your curtain of hair immediately. Like in the children's nursery rhyme when the tart is opened and huge black birds fly out and circle round. So you rose upwards – you had two small wings and two hands attached to your shoulders like a little flying seal. I don't know whether you were a thalidomide child or whether your wings were natural. I must love you very much to find you everywhere even in an apple pie!

Last night Massimo Giorgio heard me opening and shutting the window and realised I couldn't sleep so he got up and brought me some camomile tea. He sat down on my bed and talked at length about Giulia. He isn't sure whether he loves her or not – perhaps he does perhaps he doesn't – but he has a deep longing for her. Then he told me about the wife of his friend where I went to pick up his suitcase. She fell so much in love with him that she wanted to leave her husband and her two children. But what hope was there of him for a moment wanting to turn an enjoyable game into a sacred family pledge? So he left her in the lurch and came to stay with me.

He was kind and tender and he tried to make me laugh. He didn't speak any more about making love. We chatted until three in the morning although it was really him who did most of the talking. Eventually I fell asleep. He kissed me on the cheek and went back to bed.

This morning I found the kitchen in turmoil. He'd used three saucepans to make the camomile tea. He'd flooded the table and dropped a dozen matches on the floor and spilled sugar all over the cooker. He'd left the jar of sugar open and it was black with ants. I was all ready to wake him up and give him a good telling off but I knew so exactly how he'd react: he'd laugh and look me up and down as if I were preaching a boring sermon. So I went out. What upsets him most of all is to be left without an audience. He doesn't read many books they soon bore him. But he's a compulsive reader of newspapers; he can read them from beginning to end gulping down every article from finance to book reviews and even the sports column.

Today I called in on Basilia. I wanted to see her and listen to her musky voice. But she was busy: this evening she has relations coming and she was preparing supper for eight people while her children tugged at her demanding unabated love and attention.

I drank a glass of lukewarm white wine while helping her to peel tomatoes. She told me about her husband who wants to make love to her from behind 'like a sheep' but she doesn't fancy the idea and they argue about it all night until she pitches her voice in a way that she knows will wake the children and start them screaming so that she has an excuse to get away from him.

Dear Marina

Massimo Giorgio has gone. I feel nothing but relief even though lately we'd both learned to put up with each other. He'd given up trying to seduce me and he'd been less demanding over food. He'd spend long hours on the telephone playing with the flex and twisting it between his toes. He ate so much over the last few days he acquired quite a tummy and he scolded me about it gently before he left. With some effort he'd managed to grow a rather wispy moustache. His face looked less handsome and cheerful – the little strip of black hair makes him look surly and taciturn.

While he jokingly thanked me for services rendered to the revolutionary cause I glanced at the kit-bag he was packing: two pistols and a sizeable supply of bullets. I said: 'But you told me you hadn't got any arms.'

'It was much safer for you not to know. Don't let's spoil everything at the last minute. Damn it all Bianca have I put you in any danger? I've been a good well-behaved boy and I haven't been seen by anybody. Now they've called for me. My moustache is ready so I can go. My time's up and it's back to the front line for me!'

So off he went looking suntanned and very smart in a white open-necked shirt a linen jacket slung casually over one shoulder and light blue jeans with large faded patches over his crotch and thighs as if to call attention to his shapely body.

I cleaned the house. I unblocked the bath-plug. I emptied out the fridge. I burned my hands cleaning the floor with bleach. I was all alone and the sole possessor of my time and my flat. I realised that what I had objected to most about him was the smell of his after-shave lotion which lingered all day in the bathroom with its sweetish cloying scent.

Over the past few days Damiano and I have been making love in the most nerve-racking places: in the room behind the bar on top of an old wine cask inside his ramshackle little Fiat with seats that won't push back – an acrobatic feat of neck-twisting with our legs clamped between the gear lever the seat and the window-winder. Another time in the early evening we went to the park and hid ourselves behind a flowering acacia that gave off a strong spicy scent. We didn't undress because we felt too scared of being seen. However it wasn't unpleasant.

Afterwards while we sat on a bench he treated me to a long discourse on jealousy. He says he isn't jealous but he obviously believes in the stupid notion that one should be faithful in the eyes of society. By this he means that a husband shouldn't announce publicly that his wife is involved with another man. I tell him that's rubbish. He laughs and gives me a long lingering kiss. His tongue tastes of dried figs and his lips are very soft. Then we return to talking about jealousy dissecting and examining it with minute care.

I've begun to write again. The flat seems so big. I begin to sing. I make myself a really festive supper to celebrate the recovery of my solitude. I put *Norma* on the record-player and settle down to eat with an enjoyment that I thought I had lost.

At half-past six Basilia came round. She was pleased to find me on my own. She uncovered my shoulders and spread some ointment on her hands and began to knead me with an amazing dexterity and

151

gentleness. I waited for her to start recounting one of her murky and bloodthirsty stories. She seems disturbed by some conflict with her husband but I don't know what it is. On the surface she appears resigned to her self-immolation but in actuality she rebels against it even if her rebellion takes devious underground paths. She never contradicts him and she devotedly obeys his every wish. She's physically terrified of men's violence. But at the same time without giving anything away she carefully prepares a defensive strategy.

Suddenly she stopped muttering about herself and began to tell me about a woman in the park who used to lift up her skirt whenever she saw a man pass by. 'A shameless woman... She never wore any knickers underneath. She stayed as naked as the day she was born. She used to seat herself on a bench half-hidden by the trees and then she would open out her private parts with her fingers. If any man came near she'd chase him away with a kick in the balls. She'd only let herself be seen from a distance. She liked having strangers stare at her with astonished wide-open eyes. But others she'd send packing. Sometimes she'd make a sign to a man to sit down on a bench in front of her and then she'd do a long piss squirting it right over on to the flower beds and if the man got roused she'd smile like a siren and signal for him to stay. Then she opens herself wider with her fingers and from inside right in front of the dumbfounded man she pulls out a small bright red handkerchief and then a blue one and then a black one and then a yellow one and while she's fluttering them she has an orgasm because she gets such a thrill out of it. She's kinky that's what!'

As she massages me Basilia sews me together with the thread of her erotic fantasies. She makes hems down my shoulders stretching and squeezing me as her hard rough fingers thrust into my flesh.

'One day when she was there in the park with her legs wide open as usual the crazy old fool saw a man approaching. It was evening and he was by himself. She was just about to beckon to him when she saw another man arrive. This second man was the biggest bastard in town a person who was involved in all sorts of swindles and shady deals and dirty business: he pushes drugs to young people and he's hand in glove with the chief of police. She saw the two men talking to each other quite unaware of her watching them. Then the drug dealer pulls out a knife and sticks it into the other one. He kills him just like that. The man fell to the ground and the bastard went off but just as he was leaving the garden he caught sight of the woman because there were two dogs always sniffing round her. So he walked over and said to her: "Tomorrow you must come and see me at the builder's yard where I work. I want to talk to you."'

'And did she go?'

'Of course. What could the poor thing do? If she hadn't gone he'd have found her all the same. Before she went she washed and powdered herself and put on perfume because she knew she was going to her death. So she made herself look her best and she called on the priest to make her confession. Then she went to the builder's yard: he strangled her and buried her behind a concrete wall all beautiful and perfumed as she was with her hair washed and without any knickers on.'

In the evening Basilia invited me over to her place to eat marrow-flower fritters. Ape-like and affable her husband offered me a chair. He poured me out a glass of marsala while his wife got the supper ready. One can see how he loves her with a blind possessive love. The television was on permanently and the children played on the floor in front of it until they fell asleep with their mouths flattened against the carpet.

Basilia picked them up one at a time and carried them off to bed. Her husband picked at his teeth with a small toothpick and told me about the director of the old people's home where he works. 'He's always dressed in white even down to his shoes. You should see his shoes – his wife whitens them every morning. He's punctual when it comes to paying wages that's one good thing. Yes he's reliable and fair but as cold as an icicle. He never fails to greet his mother every morning as soon as she gets up. She's a little old woman all twisted with arthritis and he keeps her in the home for free. He stands behind a window in the top room and if he sees an old person fall down he blows a whistle to call one of us to go and pick him up. When two of them quarrel he orders us to tie them to the water-pipes and we have to leave them there till the next day. Last month one of them died and he said it was because he was over eighty and had a weak heart.

'But that's a lie: if he hadn't been strung up there for three days he'd have been all right. But that man – he doesn't give a damn about the old people. Nor do their relations. They never come near the place unless there's something to inherit even if it's only an old blanket. Otherwise they let them rot. And we steal from them . . . it's just too easy when they're senile. Some of the staff have been there for years and they've become so crafty . . . they're the most hard-boiled of the lot. To start with I was kind-hearted and considerate. I gave them a lot of attention but then I came to see things as they are. I realised that if I didn't learn to adapt I'd just get ripped off. You see the wages are pathetic and if you don't look after yourself you're kicked up the arse. One of these days I'll take that man and knock his head against a wall . . . that goat face he has . . . but that's only talk. When it comes to it I wouldn't hurt a fly . . . '

Dear Marina

Yesterday I phoned Giorgia for news of you. So as you see I can't live far away from you without wanting to know what you're doing and who you're meeting. Giorgia told me she doesn't see much of you. She said you've been ill and that you've met a girl with the strange name of Guiomar a refugee from the Argentine who does painting and decorating for a living. I couldn't find out whether you still see Alda and Bice or whether you have decided to drop them as well as me in your pig-headed determination to have absolutely nothing more to do with me. And is Guiomar in love with you?

I can't get out of my mind the rapier in your eyes when you're angry the child-like laugh with which you shake things off with such indifference and how when you're asleep between the flowered sheets a sinuous thread comes into being which links your sleeping body to

154

the window – the window to the wall and the wall to the bedhead and the bedhead to your neck a tenuous line suspended in the air and crystallised within the boundaries of your closed room.

'Fair is foul and foul is fair' sing the witches in Macbeth. 'Hover through the fog and filthy air'.

You and Alda and Bice and me in that herb-scented kitchen... those plates with the red borders and the jugs filled with a dark sparkling wine might be the blood of a baby or even the blood of the devil. I don't know if we shall ever see each other again or if we shall ever have a meal together set out on those heavy china plates looking at each other with the absolute naturalness and total trust that only women can have for each other.

I long to see you again to hear you laugh even if you do kick my pale aching chest with your cactus feet. I imagine you kissing Guiomar coming close up to her to slip your tongue into her ear. I imagine you taking off your clothes for her and making her touch your sex with its soft black curls. Am I jealous? Yes I am: of how you snuggle close against her how you make her feel she is your mother and your daughter how you eat her up with the fire of your brazen love.

I've always been attracted by the lovers of my lovers. Just as I was always fascinated by my father's girl-friends. Less so with the men around my mother or rather not at all – probably because they always ended up by thrusting their hands under my skirt.

The women my father had were mysterious and unattainable. They had long legs and sumptuous mouths and sultry eyes and fair hair that came down to their shoulders like a perfumed head-dress.

There was one girl who had a bandaged head. Her image haunts me still. I must have been scarcely four years old when I met her. I don't remember anything beyond a journey on a motorcycle with my father to get a green lizard – that's a sort of ice-cream. For me an ice-cream and a green lizard were one and the same – two strange green objects that were both cold and slippery and which I mixed up in my mind.

We skidded down a muddy track and the wheels of the motorbike sank and slipped and spurted up mud. My father was dressed in white

155

but he wasn't a bit bothered by the splashes of mud which were spoiling his white trousers. To worry about that would have been small-minded: if there was mud around one could only get muddy and laugh at it. So he went skidding to right and left without ever toppling over because he was so skilful. Lurching and floundering we came to a small town with the endearing name of Amatitlan. It lay under a shroud of low muffled clouds between two wings of an impenetrable forest. It was there that we were going to have our green-lizard ice-cream.

I never suspected that the journey had any other purpose than the green lizard. But instead we went to visit the house of this girl with a bandaged head. I saw her talking to someone behind the faded green slats of a Venetian blind. She was young – she couldn't have been more than seventeen – she might almost have been my elder sister. She was standing inside the room in the half-light. Her calm far-away eyes stood out in her pale wan face. From the way my father looked at her and held her hand as he talked intimately into her ear in a low voice I realised that he must be madly in love with her. I was overcome by longing and devoured by curiosity but I daren't say a word. I did not want to disturb their heart-to-heart talk and the way they entered into each other with words and looks and sighs.

Stirred by my father's love for her I immediately fell in love with her too. I wished I could be her with my head bandaged because of some terrible calamity that had brought me to the edge of death. I wanted to enter right into her so that I could experience her secret flavours. I wanted to kiss her until I had consumed her.

Since then I have never felt hatred for any of my rivals only a persistent curiosity. I told you about Bruna who was Marco's lover. If I felt any sense of diffidence or anxiety it was not from her it was in confronting him.

So now with your Guiomar: I long to see her soon. With such a lovely name I think of her as being tall and fascinating and very beautiful and as dark as a mulberry tree.

Dear Marina

It's ten o'clock in the evening. I've been working all day oblivious to everything. I didn't even go down to the sea. Tonight I'm waiting for Damiano to come.

Today I telephoned my brother Teodoro. Recently he's become quite loving just like he was when he was little. He rings me up to tell me all about himself and his problems. I am conscious that I've grown very fond of him though since the day of that attempted rape I've never been able to really trust him.

He says he's in love with two people at the same time: Lucy an American girl who teaches at the Shenkar Institute and Adriano who is a young friend of hers.

'Do you think it's possible to love two people at once?' he asked me.

'Yes I do.'

'A man and a woman?'

'Why not?'

'How enigmatic you're being.'

'But what's happened to Michela?'

'We've broken up or rather she's left me. I suppose I'm a bit difficult to put up with.'

'Cynic!'

'No I'm not being cynical. I just feel anxious and worried.'

'I think you're quite a brute.'

'No Bianca I've never been a brute.'

'You have with me.'

'You're always harping on about that silly escapade. It happened years and years ago. Do you realise how old I was then? Thirteen! You can't pass judgement on the stupid prank of a boy who's only just started to shave.'

'What's Lucy like?'

'She's not pretty. She's small and bony with fair faded hair and she wears glasses. But I love her.'

'And Adriano?'

'Adriano is me when I was fifteen – before I became brutal as you call it – and without my cynicism. He's into heroin so he's always broke. He's got eyes like a cow that's just about to be butchered. He's so beautiful that he stirs up all my sadistic instincts.'

'Have you heard anything of father?'

'He's married Consuelo in Guatemala.'

'When is he coming back?'

'Who knows?'

'And mother?'

'I had lunch with her yesterday. She drinks too much and looks all puffy. She doesn't look after her teeth either. Yet in spite of it all she still manages to keep something of her old glamour.'

'Did you give her any money?'

'I introduced Adriano to her. She looked at him and said: "Darling what a pity your boy-friend is in such a hurry to die."'

'What does she say about Lucy?'

'She says I should marry her.'

'And are you going to?'

'Are you really suggesting I should get married again after having tried it twice? You're being a bit thick!'

'And Roberta?'

'I think she's better. She asked me for a loan.'

'Did you give her one?'

'Are you kidding? I'm absolutely broke, Bianca. You know that.'

'Does Lucy know about Adriano?'

'I'm going to tell her – but not just yet.'

I don't think he's altered much. And I spy on him just like I did when I was little and I used to watch him in the garden digging patiently for worms. Then one day I saw him in front of the bathroom mirror smoothing down his hair with spit. Four reflections of him all flaxen and shimmering. We used to go together to look for tadpoles in the river for hours on end our legs immersed in water the tropical forest breathing over us. Once we went to sleep with our arms round each other and when we woke up I saw a saucepan beside his head. I said: 'What on earth is a saucepan doing in the middle of the forest?' It was a snake lying curled up. We fled on tiptoe so as not to wake it up. We went on explorations hacking our way through low branches with hatchets like we had seen in films. Roberta used to follow us

158

toddling along behind. We would stop open-mouthed in front of some Maya ruin buried under a tree root. One day while we were playing among the moss-covered stones the sky suddenly grew dark and the atmosphere became veiled and livid. We lay down under a huge plant that gave off a spicy scent. Suddenly the wind died down. Not a leaf moved. A magnetic stillness surrounded us. We were seized with terror and we waited holding each other by the hand. Fortunately Roberta had stayed behind.

All at once the cyclone exploded knocking us sideways with gusts of wind so violent that in a moment we were dragged over a distance of twenty yards without ever knowing what was happening. It only lasted a few minutes but afterwards we felt totally annihilated covered in scratches and bruises and shaking with fear. At home they had given us up for lost. And we actually were lost going round and round in circles for hours before we could find the road home. At that time we loved each other very much – that's to say not a sentimental love but one that grew out of our shared enjoyments.

Dear Marina

Guiomar... that name flung at me by Giorgia... it jangles my thoughts. What is she like? What colour are her eyes? Is her mouth small or large? Are her lips soft or full or thin? And her feet? You know how I have this curious obsession with feet: the feet of a statue in my childhood which I couldn't take my eyes off in case they rose up and flew away to heaven... your feet like succulents or cactuses... Marco's long shapely feet... the white ice-cold feet of my mother. What are Guiomar's feet like?

Once I knew a girl who came from the Argentine like your Guiomar. She was called Benedicion and her greatest mania was to go to the supermarket and fill her bag with cheap make-up. We met each other at a friend's house where there was a fair lanky boy whom we both found attractive. The boy responded to the amorous looks we

159

were giving him and at the end of the evening he suggested we should go for a drink in the nearest bar. Afterwards we ended up at his place. We went up the stairs all holding hands with him in the middle and us on each side.

We drank and smoked and kissed each other tenderly: first him and me and then Benedicion and him and then all three of us together. Eventually he said 'wait a minute' and disappeared into the bathroom. After a little while he came back with a yellow towel wrapped round his waist.

Then we undressed too. We lay down on the bed. We began to caress each other. But from that moment all the tenderness vanished and the game became transformed into something predictably brutal: he started to order us about – 'now kiss each other – now touch each other – now say something worth listening to.' And all the time he was busy masturbating. The delicacy of the gazelle had disappeared and his graceful body had become miserable and obscene. In his blind hungry gestures there was only the hateful desire for rape. He was no longer looking at us as he flung himself impetuously on our bodies to penetrate and ravage them. All of a sudden I was overcome by a violent hatred for him. I said 'I'm getting out of here.' I was about to get off the bed when groping blindly he seized my arm and twisted it behind my back. He crushed me with the weight of his body and held my chest in a vice-like grip between his legs so that I couldn't escape.

At the same time Benedicion was crying because she had suddenly noticed her legs were all bloodstained. She was talking in Spanish and sobbing with a kind of childish rage which made her black eyes look very big. 'You bastard' I said. 'You fucking bastard' and he suddenly lost his nerve. He let me slip away from underneath him while he stayed there lying face downwards with a comical look of disgust on his face.

I was just getting up and dressing when I caught sight of a hairbrush on the chest of drawers. I grabbed hold of it without even thinking what I might do with it. Of its own volition my hand reached out towards his fair-skinned bulging bottom. He didn't move. He just lay still and let it happen. And while I gouged the

160

brush into his flesh I experienced a strange whiplash in my guts that I'd never experienced before: I'd got my satisfaction – I'd got the better of him – I'd got my revenge – and my only feeling was a sort of cheerless melancholy.

He was squirming about and shouting 'For God's sake you're hurting me!' He was about to roll over when I saw Benedicion sit on top of him and imprison his arms with her legs. I thrust the brush harder into his bottom seized with a frenzied desire to hurt him. I wanted him to surrender. I wanted him to be at the complete mercy of my hand which could either thrust into him deeper and deeper and make him scream or if I wished I could draw back and free him. He was completely in our power – I knew without even looking at her that at that moment Benedicion was my accomplice and wanted the same as I did.

In the end he managed to free himself and for an instant we were afraid he would beat us up. Instead we watched him flee into the bathroom holding his hand against his bottom. He washed himself for a long time without saying a word.

Benedicion and I got dressed quickly so that we could get away. We went hand in hand to have an ice-cream. Later on she left to go back to the Argentine and I never saw her again. I heard from friends that she got married and had two children.

Dear Marina

'Without solitude my life would be more lonely' said Emily. 'And when I want I shut myself inside a cellar and the walls talk. To make me visible the world seems none other than a great crack.'

A crack through which she emerges as if she were emerging from her mother's sex. Emily . . . her eyelashes a dazzling filmy whiteness . . . displaying her purity like a divine grace . . . in love with her sister-in-law Sue or with Kate? Or with her father?

'Where is he? I cannot find him' she cried out when he died. 'I have not had a mother because I think of a mother as someone to run to when one is afraid.' Emily seeking protection from that mediocre man of letters who throughout her whole life denied her the least whisper of appreciation or sympathy. Every little word of praise measured and weighed.

'Your poems are those of a child dear Emily.' With what condescension does this pedantic literary man write about the two women poets his sister Louisa Higginson and Emily. It was she who abased herself thanking him and seeking his advice.

'I had a terror – since September – I could tell to none and so I sing, as the Boy does by the Burying Ground – because I was afraid – '

'The women chatter and the men stay silent. For this reason people are afraid of women.' So Emily wrote in 1870. That chatter is so disturbing because of the explosive force that smoulders in the corners of the eyes and the violence which underlies things unspoken and undreamed of in that world of wash-tubs soapy water felted woollen dresses whalebone collars and heavy plaits coiled at the nape of the neck.

Yesterday evening Basilia came shyly in and inclined her head inquisitively to one side of her wrinkled neck. She made me uncover my shoulders and slip off the sleeves of the kimono I was wearing and then she began to massage me vigorously. I've reached the stage where I can't do without this energetic kneader of dough – without her kneading I can't seem to feel myself. For a time she talked about her children: not in a sentimental way but with a lucidity that was sometimes quite brutal. Although she knows they are selfish to the point of murder in their desire to suck her life-blood and trample on her she loves them passionately and she is willing to let herself be eaten up without uttering a word of complaint.

Indeed it's almost as if she gets a kind of morbid pleasure out of it. Yesterday evening Maruccio threw a bottle at her and almost broke her teeth – 'Look how that one's chipped – he's got such strength that little boy – even more than his father.'

I told her I was reading a book about the mother-goddesses of antiquity who peopled the earth over four thousand years ago: fierce yet gentle mothers who knew how to caress their sons but also how to kill them who brought love but also plague and murder who kindled admiration and also terror and who turned every son into a soldier and a virgin lover of the mother. Later the Erinneans transformed themselves into housewives with coloured housecoats dirty overalls old slippers and their hair in curlers. Basilia listened with curiosity and commented that it must have been very strange in those days.

'Basilia what I'd like is for you to tell me one of your stories.' She was pleased to be asked and I waited for her to begin . . . Once upon a time there was a king who had three daughters . . . but it is my mother's voice I hear lilting in my ear. Basilia's stories are more down-to-earth – a mixture of the crime page a strip cartoon and witches' spells. 'How about it then Basilia?'

'I'll tell you about Sabina who really adored her Aunt Aminta. They lived on the outskirts of the town up towards the mountains – you know where the municipal drinking trough is near where that vine called the bitter plum grows? Not far from there Aunt Aminta lived with her niece and they earned a living by working spells together and telling cards for money. Sabina was eighteen and her Aunt was fifty. Sabina did the washing and ironing and cooking while the other slept. It was she who possessed the secret knowledge and if she didn't sleep all day she couldn't work her spells. She needed all her strength for that sort of thing and so she rested night and day. She was paid good money because she was so skilled. She could cure sick animals she could bring back love when it was on the wane and she could bring on the dreaded cancer when someone had suffered a wrong.

'Then one day Aminta was found dead. She wasn't old. She hadn't been ill. And anyway her body had been butchered it had really been hacked to bits. And so they set about questioning everyone in the place. Who could it be? Was it this person or that one? Who had been asking for spells or medicines? But no one had a clue who it might be. Poor little Sabina was crying her eyes out until she had no more tears to shed because she was left all on her own without a cent and without her aunt and she didn't know what to do. Everyone rallied round to comfort her as best they could.

'The house was turned upside down and the police sergeant said

163

that there must have been at least five people concerned: half of them must have been holding her down while the others butchered her and chopped her up. That day Sabina had gone to the market at Sant 'Orsola to buy some new saucepans which are still there in the house and when she got back that's what she found and her legs gave way under her.

'They put one fellow in prison – a man called Ciccio who had been to see the old woman that day to ask her for a spell. Then it turned out that at the time of her death he'd been in the local inn and twenty people had seen him there. Then they arrested someone else – Castagnolo a poor homeless creature who used to sleep wherever he happened to be and was dressed all in rags. His jacket was all holes and under it he stuffed newspapers so that he looked quite fat instead of which it was nothing but the newspapers and when he walked the paper made a noise like the wings of fluttering birds.

'But everyone had seen Castagnolo that day because he had been pestering Maria at the baker's shop for some bread and Isolina at the butcher's for a few scraps of bacon rind. In her haste Isolina gave him six eggs which she thought were bad though it turned out they were quite all right – you know how long eggs last from those hens that are fed on artificial poultry food.

'Well – if it wan't Castagnolo who could it have been?'

Basilia's voice grows deep and portentous. It is like a rock rolling downhill taking with it earth and grass and small pebbles rolling with inexorable power propelled by those profound forces which harmonize time and space past and future!

'So who was it?' I ask while Basilia's knowing fingers delicately prod my neck. She takes her time and she delights in the suspense as she provokes my curiosity. She plucks my skin as if it were a toneless guitar with loose strings. For a while she works in silence patiently relaxing the nodes that constrict my neck. Then eventually she takes up the story again with the sure touch of a born story-teller.

'The police-sergeant says "The case is closed. It's a total mystery for Christ's sake." "Oh yes," the peasants keep saying "Someone must have done it!" but no one will ever find out the truth because there's no evidence. No one admits to knowing a thing about it. Oh they'll be coming out from Naples I daresay but they won't find anything either. It's all a waste of time.

'Then it happened one day that Giacomino noticed Aminta's kitchen-garden was all withered and dried up and he said to himself "I'll give that poor Sabina a surprise I'll dig up the potatoes that are ready for lifting and I'll clear it all up and weed it and tie up her little tomato plants." So he starts work and while he's busy working away with his hands in the earth he feels something hard. He digs down and what does he find? A skull bone – and then an entire skull that has been gnawed by rats and then lo and behold he unearths a shoulder blade and then – well, to cut a long story short, Aminta's garden has been secretly suckling a new-born baby. Giacomo dug it out and was so amazed and flustered he left it lying there while he popped along to the priest to tell him about it. Don Ghezzi went to see the police and in less than an hour the whole village gathered there to look at this strange fruit from Aminta's kitchen garden.

'When Sabina got back home from work – she was now working as a maid for a lawyer in the Communist Party who has the big house up on the hill – she immediately burst into tears and everyone guessed that the child was hers.

'"But Sabina why did you do it? Why? Why?" and the women seized hold of her and tried to strangle her.

'The police sergeant said "No no no you can't do that. You must abide by the law and strangling is not permitted." But from then on suspicion against Sabina grew. "So it was you who killed Aunt Aminta?" "No no I swear it wasn't." But no one believed her any more and in the end it all came out: It was Sabina who'd done it because her Aunt Aminta had snatched the unborn child from her belly and dragged it out by its feet. Then she'd finished it off by giving it a blow on the head with a spade so that the infant had a great dent in its skull. But the question was why had Aunt Aminta dragged the baby from Sabina's belly?'

Again Basilia stopped talking and rested her hands palms down on my shoulder. She paused for breath making the most of the silence to keep me in suspense. Drops of sweat ran down her arms smelling of acid like withered parsley stalks when they've been left in water. The big round rock has not yet reached the bottom of the valley. Now it is rolling down slower and slower held back by all the dry sticks and twigs it carries with it but it will not come finally to rest until it has reached the very bottom.

'Aunt Aminta was insanely jealous of Sabina because she loved her so much and when Sabina began having it off with a man from San' Angelo her aunt put a spell on her so that he would die. But instead he went off to Germany where he found work in a steel foundry and Sabina was left with a full belly. Aunt Aminta said she must get rid of this child of the Evil One but Sabina didn't want that. So her Aunt forced her to take something to kill the child inside her and then she pulled it out by its feet and cleaned out her belly. She slit it open and then sewed it up again with a needle and thread and put on an ointment she knew of to protect her from infection.

'They buried the child in the kitchen-garden among the potatoes. But Sabina never forgave her Aunt – who wasn't really her Aunt at all but someone who had brought her up and used to kiss her all night long. So Sabina told the whole story to the sergeant – how her aunt had wanted her just like a man and how when she was lying asleep Aminta used to uncover her and kiss her first on her breasts and then on her belly and then between her legs opening them just a little but without ever forcing her or waking her up. Then she used to turn over and kiss her again on her neck and her shoulders and all down her back right down to her feet and how she never grew tired of gazing and gazing at her.

'"But why didn't you drive her away?" the sergeant asked and then he told the whole story to the priest who told his mother the old baker woman who in her turn told my cousin who then told me. And Sabina answered "because my Aunt put a spell on me." "How did she put a spell on you Sabina?" "She did it by giving me a black sticky drink every night before I went to bed so that I couldn't move. I felt her touch me but I couldn't move a limb or wake up. I would sleep like the dead and then she could turn me over and kiss me." "But why didn't you come out with all this when she was alive?" "I was frightened" said Sabina. "My Aunt knew everything and saw everything and if I'd talked she'd have cut out my tongue." "But why did you kill her and why did you cut her up in pieces?" "Because that's what she used to do with the photographs of people she wanted to hurt: she cut them up and then she buried the pieces. She didn't do that with my boy-friend who went to Germany and that's why the spell didn't work. She didn't do it with my baby either so when he died she scraped everything away from my inside and she was crying because she was so upset that I was ill. I could feel her tears on my breast and on my bottom and she was kissing and biting me but I couldn't move an inch because I was paralysed." "Poor Sabina" said the sergeant. "Now you'll have to spend the rest of your life in prison." "It doesn't matter" she replied. "Now that Aunt Aminta is dead nothing matters any more."'

Dear Marina

Last night I dreamed we were on a train together but I don't know where we were going. Red hot sparks were flying in through the carriage window. I was balancing a cup of milk in my hands and I saw some of the sparks fall into it and go out sputtering. You were laughing. Your laughter irritated me – I don't know why exactly. It was night-time and the sky was dark and starless. You showed me a wicker basket with small birds imprisoned inside it. They were chirrupping away happily.

I know where that dream comes from: I once read in the *Malleus Maleficarum* how witches caused male organs to vanish collecting about twenty or thirty at a time and shutting them inside a cage where they were held captive eating corn and maize.

Do you remember last year when I was writing about Zena the witch and you lent me some books? And all those accounts of trials I was forever reading and re-reading in the library when I was so caught up with the subject? I've continued to ask myself why it is that there always came a time when the witches confessed. It was well-known that a confession was essential before the death sentence could be carried out. They were subjected to torture but in the end they also took a perverse pride in confessing things they had never done though perhaps would have liked to do – vaunting their power in the face of the judges.

In my play Zena is like you – her hair a black curtain her cactus feet cramped inside home-made leather boots tied with long dirty laces. They're not really boots they are more a kind of small sandal: a piece of thick rough hide covering the sole of the foot and another piece of hide with all its hairs stretching over the top both bound together with strips of rolled gut. She wears a pair of red stockings made out of hand-woven sheep's wool – a long skirt of coarse wool which she never takes off not even on Sundays – a cotton bodice once white but now grey with age and a dirty knotted shawl the colour of faded lilac. She lives in a hovel made out of old wooden planks stacked loosely together and her only possession is a fat white goose who runs backwards and forwards in front of it hissing angrily and acting as a savage watchdog.

Her next-door neighbour accuses her of having taken away her breast milk out of spite because her husband has not paid for the treatment of his rheumatism. He testifies that Zena did indeed cure him with a stinking black infusion she brought inside an eggshell.

Zena denies everything before the ecclesiastical tribunal. But they bring more witnesses forward:

'Is it not a fact that one day you caused the Bishop to fall off his horse by looking at him out of the window?'

'No it is not true.'

'Is it not a fact that on another occasion you went to the Sabbath with all the other women and that you danced till dawn and copulated with the Devil?'

'No it is not true.'

'Is it not a fact that you ate the heart and spleen of a child and replaced it with a heart of straw and sent the child home and that as a result it died of consumption three months later?'

'No it is not true.'

'But all the others have confessed Zena. Only you are left. Where do you have the marks of the devil?'

168

'I do not have them.'

The doctor makes her take off her clothes and pricks her with needles all over her body to find where the skin is numb – that is the sign that the Devil has left his mark there.

On Zena's body they only found two places: one inside her thighs and the other behind her ear where one evening the Devil had come in the guise of a handsome young man dressed in darkest blue and kissed her.

'Is it not a fact that at your meetings you worshipped the Lady of the Night a woman clad all in black with a thousand devils at her command?'

'No my Lord it is not a fact.'

And she stuck to this in spite of being bound and hung from the rack – one of the commonest instruments of torture at that time a kind of acrobatic flying see-saw to which the woman was bound with her arms bent and then forced upwards so that after a time her wrists were dislocated and the pain became unbearable. All the others had confessed but not Zena. She was trying to draw it out because she knew that as soon as she confessed she would be burned to death.

'Zena your parents are saying you must confess because they're not willing to pay out any longer for keeping you in prison.' The bill included the straw she slept on the irons they used to torture her the food they gave her in prison and even the refreshments for the judges during their breaks.

After seven days Zena finally gave in. Both her arms were broken her feet were bleeding from the lashes and she was unable to eat or drink.

'Anything to end this torture. After all death can't be worse than this' – and Zena told all her sins to the ecclesiastical judge and seeing that anyway she was now condemned to die she had a field day inventing every sort of fantasy to astonish him a never-ending saga of strange sorceries and obsessive killings of carnal intercourse with the devil of voluptuous pleasures that no one would ever experience in heaven or earth.

Thus it was that Zena whose grandmother had placed her inside a circle marked out in chalk when she was ten years old and had made

169

her take down her knickers and piss on a crucifix – whose mother had been burnt alive for witchcraft when she was fifteen – was now sent to her death with her arms dislocated and her feet swollen and putrescent together with ten other women all witches who had confessed to having eaten children procured abortions castrated strong men by their thoughts alone filled the bodies of Christians with straw made asses fly and drunk the blood of corpses.

Nine million witches were burned between 1484 and 1782 the year in which the last two witches were burned in Switzerland. But in 1816 there was still a report of a woman drowned in Germany for witchcraft. Now the Lady of the Night has been vanquished. No one remembers her any more. The gentle blue Madonna with her submissive countenance is the only woman who can be loved as the symbol of life after death.

Dear Marina

This morning work went badly. I felt at the end of my tether. The novel that had seemed to be happily under way has ground to a halt and settled down to die. I think this is the end. I shall give up writing. I shall go back to Rome and live off dry bread and peaches ready to rush to the phone every time it rings.

For lunch I ate bread and grilled peppers all on my own and kept myself company with a little white wine that tasted of walnuts. In the afternoon I went to the Neptune Bar. Damiano wasn't there. In his place was the fat owner looking meek and coarse-featured. I hurriedly drank a glass of peppermint milk and went back home.

For the last few days Basilia has not come because Mauro is ill and she daren't leave him for a minute. Today has been very hot. I couldn't bear to stay indoors so I went out. I passed in front of the Neptune Bar again and peered stealthily inside in search of Damiano's blue eyes. But he still wasn't there. I bought a stack of papers and went to read them up on the mountain they call The

Cows Horn amidst the dry broom and wild mint and thistles. Hundreds of little flies whirled round my face. I sat under a pine tree overlooking the sea which today is a greenish colour frayed with yellow streaks.

After an hour I came down. Even up there it was too hot and I was being driven mad by flies and ants. Once again I passed in front of the Neptune Bar - still no sign of Damiano. I bought a pistachio ice-cream. I don't know why green fascinates me. When I was a child I dreamed of a doll (who would be born from my mysterious and potent womb) with long green hair and a blue-green heart and eyes the colour of a green lizard.

For the first time since I have been here I felt very much alone. My throat contracted with a sense of indefinable loss. Perhaps now is the moment to bring this self-imposed exile to an end and return to the city and see my friends.

In bed I couldn't get to sleep. Instead I am here writing to you. These letters raise my spirits more than anything else in this stagnant seaside holiday. In front of me I've got a glass with gin with ice and lemon.

Marina I want you to know how much I long to see you and to hear your voice as carefree as those glowing sparks I dreamed of. I imagine seeing you arrive with your baskets your Moroccan bags your frilled blouse your long fringed skirts and of course your graceful body set so firmly on those sturdy legs of yours that tonight are surely riding a broomstick above the roofs of Rome.

Dear Marina

This morning I was down by the sea when Damiano appeared. He was pale and unshaven.

I said 'What on earth has happened to you?'

'My stepmother has come back. Bianca - I know I'm a stupid bastard but the fact is I've discovered that she's the one I love.'

'That's all right' I said. 'Don't worry about it. You're the one who used to act jealous.'

He took me in his arms and burst into tears. 'I can't bear to leave you because I like you so much. But I love her I love her and she won't let me see anyone else' he said clinging to me desperately. We parted with a sad kiss standing in front of the dairy on the road that leads up to the mountains.

I started to walk on. I told myself that it was really better this way. But I felt my inside contract. That tight brittle masculine womb the blue ever-flowing fluidity of his laughing eyes his rough but gentle hands came suddenly into my vision. I told myself it wasn't serious: I'm not in love with him, I'll soon get used to it. But I felt wounded all the same.

As for my novel I seem to be completely stuck with it. The trouble is I'm not in a mood for writing. Every other minute I get up with some excuse or other – to make myself a cup of tea or to have a shower or to file my nails or to clean the kitchen. As soon as I can I go out and I always end up going past the Neptune Bar if only to catch a glimpse of him from a distance. 'Absence' says Chantal. 'Yes – one loves the absent one' and she would look at me maliciously flinging a lock of her black hair behind her like a nocturnal bird extending its black wings and uttering the ancient Sybil's voice of warning.

It is absence that extends us and holds us spellbound. I have put my toes into hot water and it seems as if all my strength and emotions have dissolved in that soapy liquid. I have lost all desire for food.

Sunk into an old armchair with broken springs lying on the mattress that stinks of mould sitting in front of the kitchen window I am alone with myself in a long unconsummated incest. I have begun to hate myself in a stupid sort of way.

Basilia came round. Her eyes are red because she's had no sleep for three nights. 'The boy has a high fever' she whispers dismally but her eyes flash with a hint of exaltation. I sense that deep down inside her breathless body in some suppressed part of her maternal feelings she longs for the death of this boy who is so rapacious and has so much power over her.

She uncovers my shoulders. She presses her calloused thumbs into

172

my flesh. There is a faint smell of garlic and washing-up water. 'When I was pregnant with Mauriccio I thought he was going to be born at seven months and then instead he didn't come out till nine and a half months poor little love. In fact he weighed all of eleven pounds and he split me in half. I was in so many pieces they never managed to sew me up properly. His uncle died of cancer when he was twenty six and so did his cousin at thirteen. I'm so afraid... because with his cousin it started with a fever just the same and then the illness followed.'

Her chill tears trickled on to my shoulders. Her hands are slack and uncertain today. I tell her not to bother with the massage we'll have a glass of wine together and we'll talk. But she insists that she doesn't want to stop. She kneads me tenderly making movements with her fingers just as her mother and her grandmother would have done. She dries her tears. She starts to talk about Mauriccio. But then she gets bored and she slips into one of her disquieting stories and in a moment she has recaptured the robust magic of the story-teller.

Dear Marina

Last night I dreamed I was walking round in bare feet trying to get hold of some telephone tokens but there were none to be had. I went into a telephone box. All I found was a notice saying 'out of order'. I went into a bar and bought a token but the slot was jammed. I went straight to another café where the telephone gulped down tokens but remained mute. The more I tried the more frantic I became. Can you guess who I wanted to talk to? You! I had something urgent to tell you but I hadn't a clue what it was and at one point I was crying with rage.

I woke with a feeling of anguish. I got dressed. I went down to the sea. I wanted to go for a long swim. Then on the beach there was a large official notice which said that bathing was prohibited.

The sea was actually a strange muddy colour with violet foam

173

floating on the surface. All along the shore the waves were bringing in dead fish ringed with yellow scum. A bathing attendant said they'd come out of the sewers. Someone else mentioned that a factory had flushed out its reservoirs and discharged it all into the sea. Another person said it was all to do with an oil tanker that lost its cargo of crude oil yesterday in a rough sea – and today the strong wind has blown it inshore. What is indisputable is that the entire town is permeated by such a stench of rotten fish excrement putrifying seaweed chemicals and oil that it makes one retch.

On the empty beach I came across some children playing with the corpse of a dog. They were shoving twigs into its eye sockets and pushing its mouth open with sticks. It was smothered with buzzing flies.

I walked up and down along the beach my feet sinking into the dirty sand. It's not the loss of Damiano's body ... but I do miss his kisses the timid yet cheeky way he used to rub his full lips against mine to warm them the way he used to suck my tongue with his eyes closed as if he were tasting the juice that came out of it the gentle hesitant way he used to press his face against me like a son who is starving with hunger.

'Your stupid sons ... each time you let them escape from your womb ... and then all you can do is to lick them like a milch cow.' I can still hear your insistent voice. You've tried to kill me so often with needles with a knife with a spoon even with a key. I know you'd have torn me to pieces and let me bleed to death ... you'd have fondled my temples while my life blood ebbed away over your skirt and over your shoes. You would have laid my body out like a holy object with a hollow prayer on those funny lips of yours shadowed by black down. You'd have laid me out and buried me in one of the flower pots on your terrace next to the basil the gentians the sweet peas the begonias and the pansies.

I didn't feel a bit like eating. I cooked a piece of liver and then threw it into the rubbish bin. I put some dressing on a salad and then left it where it was. I drank a glass of gin with sugar and lemon and cubes of ice which I pressed against the roof of my mouth. I relaxed. I experienced a mild feeling of euphoria.

174

Sitting down in front of the typewriter I managed to type a whole page. But then I tore it up. I would like to write a novel about love not these stories of make-believe.

I lay down on the bed. I shut my eyes. Damiano's face bent over me. But I told myself he isn't all that attractive: his teeth are broken his lips are too full his mouth is too big his forehead bulges his eyes are too sharply blue. I tried to keep my distance and look at him objectively without emotion... his small dark penis tinged with violet his feet that are so gross and calloused with their dirty broken toenails. (Damiano plays football and he can't afford to buy a decent pair of boots) and his thin long arms and in reality he is so incredibly good-looking and attractive and there he is sprawling with his step-mother in damp forbidden beds....

Is this woman who stands between his body and mine dark or fair? Is she small or is she tall? I don't even know her name. I would like to talk to her I would like to lift up her skirt and slip in beside her. I would like to kiss the corner of her mouth. I would suck in her saliva and brush her eyelids with my tongue and I would lay bare her sex. I would open it with two fingers I would enter into her and I would let myself drown in the black waves of her womb.

Dear Marina

How boring the last few days have been! Basilia remains incarcerated inside her flat with her sick Mauriccio. Damiano has vanished engulfed by Neptune who has carried him away into I don't know what far-away Sargasso Sea of flowers and blossoms. I even miss the presence of Massimo Giorgio and his idle chatter.

Last night I dreamed I touched Damiano's dark penis. But as soon as I took it in my hand it was transformed into a crow that opened its wings and flew away. I was dressed as a soldier with a cartridge-belt across my shoulders but I didn't have a gun. I wanted to shoot the crow which was nibbling at some fruit but then I found myself in an

175

orchard where I was gorging on stolen strawberries. 'You're a thief too' cried out the crow.

Children can be boys or girls. I would have dragged you from my womb and breathed on you like a milch-cow. But I left you where you were and enveloped you in layer upon layer of my saliva. You became as hard as a pearl. I wanted to hurt you to penetrate you. I would have liked to force my fist up your vagina to stick my fingers up your anus. You would have accepted it all. That was your destiny – to suffer through me and to make me suffer so as to create between us a violent tension of pain and pleasure. Like when you were sitting on the table while I was writing and you stripped off and sat on top of the typewriter offering me your open sex and it was obvious that you would never abandon your unending attempts to seduce me. You gripped my temples between your knees and said 'Now let's see which of us is born out of the other – me out of you or you out of me – am I sucking your honey or are you sucking mine?'

I long to get away from this place. All the enchantment is over. The sea is sick – it smells of death. The flat has been invaded by mice. The streets are clogged with gleaming cars emitting a stench of petrol fumes. Each day the sky becomes paler and heavier. It hasn't rained for weeks and the fields are all burnt up by the sun. The grapes are withering on the vines. The figs hang empty and shrivelled on the branches: they have no pulp only dry reddish seeds. The mountain is yellow as straw and it gives off a smell of burnt grass and shit.

But I know I can't get away until my novel is finished. All I can do is to pin my longing for escape on to these white walls. I must get some poison for these damned mice. I must force myself to eat some good red steak and drink good strong coffee. I must get down to writing because that is the sanest and most profound aim of my life. It's not a duty – duty is as sterile as the colour of a banana – it's a sense of fulfilment that grows with use. Damiano leaving me has paralysed my imagination. I have lost all desire. All that's left for me is to write to you and that's what I go on doing.

In the evening around seven o'clock I went out for an ice-cream. I came back to the flat. I wrote a few lines. Then I went out again to buy a light bulb. The owner of the shop was sitting at the back with

176

her legs apart fanning herself with an envelope. She gave me a friendly smile. 'A bulb? How many watts?' She lifted her two naked arms which were as hefty as a boxer's and looked at me with her small genial eyes.

'It's hot in this shop. Why don't you keep the door open?'

'And what would people be saying?'

'How do you mean?'

'That I'm making a spectacle of myself.'

'But you're working. That's not showing off.'

'Work. There isn't much of that.'

'Not much?'

'Very little.'

'Do you run the shop on your own?'

'No. There's my husband too. But he's ill just now.'

'Is it serious?'

'He's been in bed for two months and who knows if he'll ever walk again.... Are you on holiday?'

'Yes I'm on holiday.'

'If only it would rain. The air's full of dust.'

'Do you have a vineyard?'

'No. A kitchen-garden.'

'And is it all dried up?'

'We water it. It doesn't need much. But my brother-in-law has vines and everything's burned dry with the drought.'

So we went on chatting away as if we were old friends. As always I was tempted to let myself fall inside her. These lonely women with hearts as dry as an empty well. I knew how her sensuality was trapped between her teeth and her throat. Her words said little her body revealed everything: how she had become bored with her limbs when she was still very young even before she menstruated and how she had grown fat out of laziness and indifference. She'd let herself go to seed without lifting a finger – gnarled bottom bursting from underneath a check skirt breasts and belly united in a solid mountain. Only her arms are still active. They are strong and muscular. They've been used to lift heavy weights. She leaves them bare without bracelets or ornaments.

177

From her black eyes darted small needles of very sharp thoughts. Beneath her surface kindliness lay a mixture of curiosity and resentment. I knew exactly what she was thinking of me: that I was an idle tourist poking my nose into other people's business a bit simple and probably a whore as well. But at the same time she was glad to have me there because it was better than being all by herself in the sultry darkness. She looked persistently at my breasts as if she wanted to touch them. She scrutinised my face as if she were searching to know how old I was and whether I had children and why at an age not so very different from hers I had a single chin and an agile body. She was wondering whether I wore a bra or not. Anyway she didn't approve of women without bras whom she dismissed as feckless bitches who hang around half naked with their tits on show . . . she would have liked to touch mine to examine them and to lay me out on the bench and undress me so that she could peer inside my mouth and my vagina and up my anus. Then she would have got bored and flung me out.

I asked her if she would like a coffee. She looked at me in astonishment – 'What does she want? She's already paid for what she's bought and there's no discount for light bulbs . . . she's a bit soft or perhaps . . . could she be checking the place out for a burglary? I must be on my guard. I mustn't take my eyes off her one never knows.' She looked at me suspiciously but she didn't have the strength to say 'no' because after all she did fancy having a cup of coffee and gossiping with me would help to pass away the evening.

I went out to a bar and asked for two coffees and some cakes. I chose nice big ones filled with cream and covered in pink and white liqueur-flavoured icing. I returned to the shop and sat down on a stool in front of her. I asked her about her husband and her work. She answered me grudgingly without enthusiasm – too suspicious to let herself go. But she wasn't at all displeased that my curiosity had been roused. When the boy from the café arrived with the coffee and cakes she smiled like a child taken by surprise. She watched me with her piggy eyes glassed over with boredom as she wolfed down the cakes.

Dear Marina

Here I am sitting at the table looking out beyond the gasometer to the mountain called 'Cows Horn' and a little slip of glistening sea shadowed from time to time by the grey belly of a petrol tanker. I have got the tape-recorder on full blast so as to drown the voices of people quarrelling on the floor above. I feel quiet and calm as I listen to the beautiful voice of Fischer-Dieskau – do you remember those Schubert songs we used to listen to down by the sea?

But now it is the Duke of Mantua resplendent in red velvet and thigh-boots with an ostrich-feather in his cap and wide-open seductive eyes and the legs of a deer. He sings of his delight in the beauty of women and brags of his conquests:

'Questo o quello per me pari sono
A quant'altre d'intorno mi vedo . . . '

As my father flies through the window from one of his lovers the same banners are flashing in his eyes and there is that swelling between his legs beneath his skin-tight trousers. A hundred women with bruised eyes and clasped hands and tense necks and naked breasts call him to them. Radiant and care-free he is flying on his black horse towards a child with a pinched face who watches him with her mouth wide open not knowing whether to laugh or cry.

You don't like opera Rigoletto least of all. Every time I used to put it on the record-player you'd force me to change it. But now you can't say no and I'm going to tell you the story. It has fascinated me for many many years and still does. I've begun it a thousand times and you always refused to hear it. It's about a father and a daughter and their crazy love for each other. I know that's why you hate this opera – because of my obsession with it – because I too am a daughter tormented by her love for a father who flies and flies away.

In the opera the daughter Gilda is a born loser a trembling and tearful sweetheart with her silken hair and her embroidered bodice and those long chaste skirts and hands like a nun's: an abandoned bride destined for sacrifice. Rigoletto warns her against the Duke of Mantua. She declares her love. *'Io l'amo'* she sings.

179

'But I've given you plenty of time to forget him' her father argues.
'*Io l'amo*' she insists obstinately as the trombones murmur beneath the violas.

'*Povero cuor di donna!*' cries Rigoletto and he prevails on his daughter to spy on the Duke from behind the tavern door. So father and daughter connive to witness the lover's deceitfulness. The handsome young Duke arrives. He asks for a room and some wine. He embraces the servant-girl as he strides around the tavern. Outside the storm gets up the trees are tossed by the wind and the sky is torn by flashes of lightning. Then comes the merest nuance from the orchestra like a small stream barely rippling and he throws himself into the famous aria:

'*La donna è mobile*
Qual piuma al vento
Muta d'accento... '

Rum ta ta tiddeley. Rum ta ta tiddeley. The tempo of the hurdy-gurdy. 'Ever unfaithful' – what a legalistic expression – but the brilliance of the music makes you catch your breath.

The Duke and the servant-girl flirt together while Gilda watches in desperation from behind the door. Her body is on fire her heart is broken in two a flaming serpent reaches up to the most vulnerable part of her being and insinuates itself between the lips of her sex. My father and I spying on the lover who is also my father or rather a youthful replica of him when he was twenty-six and I was only six. We spied on the two of them and watched them kissing and we were overcome by the enchantment and the cruelty of it.

The Duke proclaims his 'heart-felt adoration' for Maddelena the servant-girl:

'... *sol per te quest'alma amora*'

but she does not take '*il signorino da vero libertino*' too seriously. She knows a thing or two and she's not going to let herself be taken in by his talk of love. All she's after is the money. She lifts her red skirt a little showing her black stocking and lets herself be kissed on the neck. He is so bursting with self-confidence so full of love for himself:

'Oh yes I'm bad' he laughs '*Sono un mostro.*' He begs her to let him

180

love her *'nel gaudio e nell'amore'*. 'Kiss me' he cries and then breaks into another flawless aria:

'La bella mano candida . . . '

the flight of sugared birds forever crystallised inside a wave that will never break.

Gilda and her father are still spying secretly from behind the door. To him it seems that this must be enough to convince the girl: the betrayal must disgust her the man must seem petty and fatuous. But Rigoletto has failed to take account of Gilda's tender heart and he doesn't know about that small flaming serpent that lies coiled in her belly and how pleasure and pain are a unique and boundless delight that melts her innocent heart.

'Bella figlia dell'amore . . . ' the Duke is singing. What bad taste – 'My beautiful enchantress . . . ' how banal! But then it isn't the words you are listening to it is the echoing voice of Carlo Bergonzi that has taken you over. The aria expresses all the treacherous excitement of unrequited love – a love that watches in secret that cannot sleep while the other dreams that dies while the other prospers. Cruel and fickle the voice rings out:

'Vieni e senti del mio core
Il frequente palpitar . . . '

Maddelena for all her dashing airs and red stockings and peasant acuteness can't prevent herself falling under his spell. The Duke of Mantua who is disguised as a poor young student fascinates and captivates her. Not that she believes in his promises of marriage . . . but perhaps a night with him . . . to experience those irresistible arms clasping her body . . . to caress that fair silky moustache and those heavy eyelids with the tips of her fingers – and this is the person she and her brother are under contract to kill!

'Why is it him we have to kill? Why not the hunchback instead?' she suggests to her brother Sparafucile. He's been paid for the job he must stand by his contract. He is shocked. He's given his word – it's a matter of honour. So it seems that according to Verdi even a professional hit-man has his moral code!

In the end they reach a compromise: they decide to kill the first unfortunate traveller who arrives at the inn that night – but then who is likely to be out in this weather when the night is so pitch-dark that one can't see an inch in front of one's face? Who indeed?

The trap is set. The sacrificial lamb will submit to the slaughter. Her rapture will be consummated. The singer Renata Scotto has chosen not to make Gilda too passive. She accepts her destiny proudly – 'I'm willing to die so that he can be spared.'

From now on the tasteless vulgarities of the librettist are unleashed. Gilda returns to the inn dressed as a traveller all booted and spurred with cloak and dagger. The crucial moment draws near. Her dark intent is about to be accomplished. Her arrival in the night is the arrival of every woman who respects herself every woman who has swallowed history to the last dregs and has learned to rejoice in her own downfall. The soft arms of death the eternal mother will welcome her tenderly.

With the firm tread of a warrior Gilda approaches the inn. As she enters she is stabbed by Sparafucile in place of the man she loves.

Maddelena is overjoyed to have saved her 'Apollo'. Sparafucile thinks only of the money (but of course with due respect and honour).

And so as the strokes of midnight are heard through the raging of the storm the pathetic hunchback Rigoletto arrives convinced that he has outwitted the arrogant Duke by means of his secret plot. But the limitations of his warped servant mentality blind him to the reality of his folly.

With the imperturbable innocence of the guilty the Duke of Mantua sleeps serenely on. Then at the very moment when Rigoletto is in the act of throwing the sack which he believes contains the body of his enemy into the churning waters of the river he hears that hateful voice in the distance:

'La donna è mobile,
Qual piuma al vento,
Muta d'accento,
e di pensiero... '

He is singing to himself of his own beauty and his own fickleness. It is he who is the feather in the wind ever fickle in speech and thought. His spell-binding voice pierces the darkness expressing man's archetypal fear of castration.

Rigoletto makes the shattering discovery of his daughter's dead body – there just where he expects to find his hated master he finds the jewel of his heart.

> *'Oh fanciulla a me rispondi ... non morire tesoro, mia colomba lasciarmi non devi ... '*

> *'Mio padre ... addio.'*

The honeyed flow of Renata Scotto's voice goes round and round in my head and trickles down inside me. Father and daughter struggling desperately in vain. Defeated by too much love and too little vision. They embrace and bid farewell finding and losing each other in the futility of sacrifice. My father and I in a last mortal embrace which carries off his fated youth his legs of gold his beautiful mouth and the delicate disquieting swelling between his legs that reveals his unmentionable otherness.

Dear Marina

Damiano and his step-mother. Yesterday evening at about six o'clock I met them for a moment face to face when I was least expecting it. They were at the far end of the promenade from the Neptune Bar. He was bending over her a little his glancing eyes more of a clear rinsed blue than ever. She – small round dark wearing a fresh dress of white organdie with red polka dots.

They didn't see me either until the last minute. I don't know if he had told her about me. But I guessed he probably had because when he said to her 'This is Bianca' she had a moment of panic. She stared at me with a mixture of curiosity and dismay – but not with any sign of antipathy or dislike. She has round clear black eyes and everything about her is neat and tidy in contrast to him with his blurred outline and the watery blue of his eyes.

I went back home to the flat singing. The mystery is resolved. I've seen her face to face – the other woman – my rival – and I experienced a sense of euphoria and peace. I really love that woman. I like the way she's so round and neat and I'm glad she is so different from me and I wish I could have talked to her. And who knows – perhaps she'd have liked it too – at least that's the impression I got. But Damiano was on tenterhooks his eyes ran with faded blue ink as if he were weeping inconsolably.

I put on *Rigoletto*. I wrote till late in the evening completely oblivious of the time. At one moment there was a knock at the door. Perhaps it was Basilia but I didn't go to open it. I wrote as I haven't been able to do for a long time with the sails of my imagination unfurled with excitement.

Marina if I am ever able to finish this bloody novel I shall owe it to you: to your provocation and prickliness to your cactus feet that have led me along the path of understanding and gaiety.

The Missing All – prevented Me
From Missing minor Things –
If nothing larger than a World's
Departure from a Hinge –
Or Sun's extinction, be observed –
'Twas not so large that I
Could lift my Forehead from my work
For Curiosity.

That poem was written in 1865. Emily is wearing a new skirt of white muslin with two lace frills at the bottom a belt of ivory-coloured leather a close-fitting bodice of white satin and two or three red bracelets encircling her wrists like Saturn's rings. Behind the head of brown hair caught in a silvery white net is a big casement window. That window contains a picture: a vase of irises and beyond it three larch trees a line of oaks and blue periwinkle flowers at the fringe of a dark wood.

184

A narrow Fellow in the Grass
Occasionally rides –
You may have met Him – did you not
His notice sudden is –

A minute bloodless phantom walks where I walk and follows me between the walls of an empty house. As a child I believed it was my conscience watching me. Its shoulders were weighed down by two great jagged wings. It would appear suddenly on my shoulders and tell me how stupid I was and how hopelessly guilty. Its feet were like lead and its body was made of air. It needed no food to sustain it but whenever I sat down at table to eat it used to perch right behind me. Sometimes it would thrust its feathers on to my plate. At others it remained roosting on top of the cupboard in my bedroom from where it watched me with a fixed stare that radiated astonishment and hostility. It sat up there like a lemur monkey restricting my freedom and throttling my breath. Whenever I masturbated I tried to hide under the sheet but the phantom was there imperturbably beating her wings as a sign of disapproval. If I got angry her eyes would go red and to punish me she would paralyse my legs stifle my breath and bring cramps in my belly.

For sixty years Emily always looked out of the same window staring at the same larches the same oaks the same irises. Her sex was hidden under frothy muslin dresses billowing organdie skirts satin bodices and starched petticoats with whalebone collars. A mature virgin secreting herself behind bunches of lilies or hydrangeas with giant petals hiding beneath the protection of her younger sister in a deliberate ignorance that was also an ironic challenge to God.

We outgrow love, like other things
And put it in the Drawer –
Till it an Antique fashion shows –
Like Costumes Grandsires wore...

Like my love for my father that stays embalmed in those photographs I pull out of the drawer it has something old-fashioned about it fossilized in the garments of a former age. But I could never discard those photographs: he and I by the river almost underneath a waterfall in the shelter of the forest. I little more than five and he in his early twenties standing up on a rock blond and naked his body poised like a marble caryatid the prow of a ship ready to break through the roughest waves and emerge victoriously through every storm. I was standing with my head turned in his direction watching him. Two of my front teeth missing my fair hair falling down to my shoulders and my arms and legs so thin I am almost a skeleton. I am asking for love but without much conviction as if I know that all he will give me is permission to worship him in silence...

He and I together in the garden of our house both out of breath from having just been on a bicycle ride. He wearing white gym shoes and a guilty smile on his face – probably having only just got back from a secret assignation with some lover – his hair in disorder and his trousers tied round his ankles with shoe laces and me with my dress gathered round my waist with what my mother used to call 'honeycomb' smocking. I can still remember the cheerful noise this dress made as if I were wearing a whole rustling bee-hive beneath my throat...

The two of us in the mountains sitting on the snow our eyes narrowed in the dazzling light. He wearing a big sweater with an arrow design down the back and a pair of large shaggy gloves. He is holding my head so tight between the gloves that it seems as if he is trying to pull it off and he is laughing with that bewitching smile that made me love him so...

And the photograph he took of me in a bar in Rome. I was eighteen by now with red lipstick slashed across my mouth and I was swallowing down my drink with the look of a malicious child. It is the morning of my birthday and I am wearing a white transparent blouse and high-heeled shoes. I must have been most dislikeable in my get-up of a suburban vamp. But he is gazing at me with a look of admiration almost as if he were a little in love.

There are many snapshots dating from that time which catch the carefree feelings I had when I was eighteen. There's one of me with a blonde pigtail hanging down my shoulder another of me poised on a staircase my hair thrown to one side like Veronica Lake one where

I'm in a bathing dress stretched out on the terrace of the house my cheeks covered in freckles and one of me in a nightdress with a silly smile on my face and despair in my eyes.

That was a time when I most hated our poverty. I couldn't stand going around in shoes that had been re-soled and coats that had been re-lined. I couldn't stand having no money to go to the cinema and restaurants and I used to get myself invited out by middle-aged glamour boys who having paid for dinner demanded bed. I made love lovelessly and with a bad grace. I liked night-clubs swinging through the early hours of the morning lying low in wine-bars drinking whisky listening to jazz flirting with men and getting back home at three in the morning. At that time I was living in Rome with my father. My mother had stayed in Sicily. I didn't look after myself. I wanted to die. I went out with hateful people. I wore a mask of cynicism. I smoked and drank like an imbecile. I painted my nails with bright pink nail varnish.

But luckily all that didn't last long perhaps only for a year or eighteen months. Then I fell in love. I gave up all that rotten life so that I could tackle something new and exciting – living as a couple. The only thing I never gave up even in the most difficult moments was my writing. Even if I only had a few hours now and again I would get down to the typewriter and write.

Dear Marina

Yesterday evening I drank half a bottle of gin to help me try to get to sleep. Then I subsided into restless dreams.

I dreamt that my grandmother had shot me in the head and I was bleeding to death. It was a horrible experience to know that I was dying that slow death. I kept very still waiting for life to ebb away gently and leave me cold and empty.

All this was because during the afternoon my mother rang me up to ask me for money to pay the rent and the phone bill. Then she told me about my grandmother who has gambled away half a million lira. Beforehand she had bought herself a life annuity and 'then she played the tables using us for stakes and the result is here I am living off boiled potatoes. I can't afford anything else.'

My grandmother lives all alone in the country with a gun beside her bed. She has sold what little remains of the family estate (one house and two small fields) in order to live off the fat of the land until the time comes when she has to live off charity. She never gives a damn about her children or her nephews.

I've never told you about this rather delinquent grandmother of mine who came over from Guatemala when she was only twenty to marry a handsome Sicilian Duke. She had eight children of whom five are dead. After my grandfather's death she took up with a Middle-Eastern arms dealer a shiftless creature who committed suicide at the age of fifty. Then she got hooked on a good-for-nothing Englishman who drank away twenty hectares of lemon trees which belonged to her and died of cirrhosis of the liver.

Now she lives alone with a bull-mastiff and a gun which she keeps permanently loaded. She paints her hair with burnt cork and keeps her skin soft with a lemon dipped in olive oil. She spends all day in bed doing crossword puzzles and every evening she gets dressed makes herself up dabs on scent puts on high heels and goes out to play cards. She's over eighty and she still drives a car. She can't bear people under her feet and she calls her daughters 'those two whores' and openly describes her nephews as 'half-wits'. She trusts no one in the world except Poncho the mastiff.

When I was little I used to sleep in her bed. I was terrified of those giant close-ups in which each of her eyelashes was as big as a thumb and her teeth shone so threateningly and her eyes were like two big lakes in the middle of a landscape of dark smoked flesh.

My mother says she has Indian blood but doesn't like to admit it. She's as black as a crow but what makes her so terrifying is that she's as proud as Lucifer. At school I was ashamed to talk about her.

'My granny gets my sandwiches ready and brings me to school' said the girl who sat next to me. 'She gave me a toy train too.'

'Mine gets me washed and dressed and mends my clothes – what does yours do?' asked Ina.

How could I explain that my grandmother not only couldn't care less about me but threatened me with a gun if I as much as ventured near the henhouse where she kept four pathetic half-starved hens who produced very small pink eggs? How could I say that the moment I came near her she'd shout 'Get out of here you fool!' and that once a week she'd do me what she regarded as a great favour: she'd have me sleep in her bed. She used to undress me telling me all the time how ugly I was: 'At your age I was like a flower. You haven't got any breasts you're all skin and bone. You haven't even got a bottom!' and in the morning she'd boot me out of bed with kicks and thumps.

She used to show me photographs of herself when she was thirteen. She did indeed look as if she were already a woman with her big head her black glistening hair her plump breasts and her shapely arms. I was thin and stringy and tow-coloured and witless and terrified and I used to hide at the bottom of her bed admiring her strong powerful beauty.

Yes I was scared of her – but I was also fascinated by her stories of Guatemala and her childhood in the country. She used to recount how her rich parents had baths of marble and massive door-handles made of gold and ate nothing but pheasants sent over specially from Paris.

'Don't believe a word she says' said my mother. 'She's out of her mind. She's a congenital liar and all her stories are rubbish. Her father was a drunkard who lost every job he ever had and as for her mother – she was an Indian peasant who married the old man for his money. In fact her parents sold her to him when he still had some left before he drank it all away.'

I enjoyed listening to my grandmother talking about herself and for the sake of that I was willing to face her fits of temper and her bad moods.

'Granny tell me about that time you were in Guatemala city and you rode in a carriage along the Gran Paseo.'

'Go to hell Bianca. I've got a headache. Leave me alone. It won't be long before I'm dead and forced to leave everything to those half-

189

witted children. They'll chuck all my photographs down the lavatory and chop up all my furniture. But you wait – I'll see they don't get a thing. I'll spend every penny before I die – and in any case I'll live to be a hundred like my grandmother Consuelo and my great-grandmother Maria.'

Seeing my scared expression she smiled. 'You're a pathetic little thing aren't you! You're just too thin-skinned for this world. You'll never go places. You're a born loser. You've got arms as thin as a rabbit – they really upset me. But there's nothing to be done about it – either one's born strong or one's born weak. My husbands were weak and they died like squashed flies. I'm strong and I intend to stay that way till the end. I was born of strong stock I'm the daughter of conquistadores... when my grandfather went out on his well-fed stallion – it never had less than twenty kilos of oats a day you know – everyone bowed down in front of him and he'd give the Indians a flick of his whip for their trouble. He wore spotlessly clean cotton gloves – he was always immaculate and the peasants were more scared of him than they were of thunder and lightning. I don't know how it ever entered my head to marry a stupid weakling like your grandfather but the fact is he was fair and handsome and ever so polite and well-behaved and I was a well-brought-up girl dressed all in white with flat-heeled shoes and silk stockings straight from Paris and plaits so long I could sit on them. Your grandfather fell in love with me the moment he saw me and every day he used to send me a bunch of roses as white as snow... He was so gallant – no wonder I was attracted to him. I didn't know he was the last flicker of a family that had gone to seed and was so degenerate it could no longer stand on its own feet, I never twigged that he didn't know how to do anything and that he spent the nights looking at the stars through a telescope. What a fool he was!'

'Don't take any notice of a word she says. She's quite mad' my mother used to tell me. 'Everything she says is lies. She used to have a job in a laundry and she only married Papa in desperation after having had two kids by him. She's always had a screw loose and she's got a nasty character...'

Lying in the double bed in the dark before we went to sleep she and

190

I would become friends for a moment. I knew she enjoyed telling stories and it didn't matter if they weren't true. She knew I was spellbound listening to her and she let her imagination race on. Sometimes when she told me about savage wars and bloodthirsty battles and people having their heads chopped off and being buried alive I used to start trembling. I would feel for her hand and would press it in mine but after a few seconds she would push me away like she pushed away everything with the fury of a lioness.

The world of her imagination was ferocious and cruel yet it had an exquisite sweetness... the white arcades of her 'patio' with its red bougainvilleas and the scent of orange blossom... the brightly coloured mantillas... the little cakes flavoured with cinnamon and ginger... the amorous kisses exchanged under a sky laden with stars... the dances by firelight... the exercises on the piano brought over from Berlin especially for her... the elegant men who fell in love with her and stood beneath her window every night to pay court to her. At dawn she would set out on horseback to ride over the estate weaving between banana trees and nut trees and fig trees and magnolia trees and palm trees that were as tall as great pillars. With her gun she would pick off a wild boar from a distance of a hundred metres... a virgin clad in white with her long hair reaching down to her ankles and pigskin boots and a fan of Chinese satin hanging from her waist...

Dear Marina

This morning I slipped out of a dream of radiant sunshine filtering through sea water and got up with such a feeling of freshness...

I felt as if I had been deep inside the storeroom of your thoughts a marine seascape of byegone times... an empty horizon... some unknown land dense with trees that had never been trodden by human feet. It was a morning like I have sometimes experienced in South America after walking for miles along the coast. A seascape before the Spanish conquest with something secret and menacing suspended in the limpid atmosphere.

I woke up with these sensations and I thought of you. I made myself some coffee and then I settled down to write. I couldn't wait to get on with my writing and I didn't even go down to buy a paper. I put on the tape of Rigoletto to drown the noise of voices in the flats. I like to be able to raise my head and visualise the Duke of Mantua arriving with his dark eyes and his black curls and his long legs clad in red stockings and the mauve ostrich feather dangling from his hat. The Duke of Mantua... almost a child... barely twenty and he comes like Don Juan from my womb singing with that happy look on his face like my own son and suddenly I am overwhelmed with love for him.

In contrast to my beautiful dream the sea here is sick. The water is polluted and bathing is forbidden. More and more dead fish float on the surface. It seems that some factory has emptied poisonous effluent into the sea though no one really knows for certain. The newspapers keep quiet about it. The beach is deserted. An atmosphere of doom hangs over the whole town.

I must go down and do some shopping. The fridge is empty. Yesterday I ate bits of dry bread dipped in olive oil. But it was the bottom of the bottle and it came out dark and bitter. I don't feel like going out - every minute I don't give to the novel seems wasted. I am nailed to my typewriter and I daren't leave it for fear that this fecundity will slip away from me.

Dear Marina

I think my love for you is like that seascape in my dream - something delicate and timeless something enclosed and entirely remote from sex and the drudgery of daily existence.

Today I went out shopping after three days of starvation. I finished the last bit of dry bread yesterday. Tonight when I went into the kitchen to snatch a bite of food before going to bed I watched a charming scene: mother mouse balancing on top of the bottle of oil dangling her long black tail into it and then pulling it out to let her daughter mouse lick it. The daughter was underneath standing upright on her two back paws to reach it. As soon as she heard me the mother lost her balance and fell plop into the half empty bottle. The daughter ran off squeaking. I took the bottle and went out on to the communal terrace where I let the mother go free. I went back to bed but I couldn't get to sleep – I kept thinking I could hear the daughter's plaintive squeals for her mother.

Basilia came to tell me that her son is a little better. I put my arms round her to try to communicate my feeling of tenderness and affection for her but then I told her I had to work and I sent her away. I don't know whether she believed me – she is always so afraid of being unwanted.

'How's your back? Wouldn't you like a massage?'

'Not now Basilia I've got too much to do.'

'Aren't your shoulders still hurting?'

'Yes they are but I've got to finish something urgent and if I don't seize the moment it'll slip through my fingers.'

I didn't want to appear impatient but I gave her a peck on the cheek and almost pushed her through the door. She looked mortified. Tomorrow I'll go and see her and take her a present.

I've been trying to sort out the construction of this bloody Chinese puzzle. In front of me I've assembled a mountain of little chunks of cardboard of every conceivable shape which I've somehow got to put together to make a recognisable design. All the pieces look alike and it seems impossible to make them fit and you sit there with your head in your hands discouraged and helpless. Then one day the solution comes to you out of the blue. Your eyes alight decisively on the right pieces and fit them together and slowly the puzzle takes shape and makes sense and you watch it emerging out of chaos. It is a picture made up of flat surfaces in the foreground and distant planes of objects people houses all arranged according to some mysterious configuration. Views merge gently into each other the sky grows misty and cloudy. The earth is carpeted with flowers. We are in a sleepy town in China in the seventh century.

Women are carrying water jars suspended from big yokes on their shoulders. Two ropes hang from the yokes and from the ropes swing two earthenware jars brimful with water. One of the women is just about to go into a wooden house with a small front door painted red. Another goes down a narrow lane that disappears into the fields. On the left of the house are other houses which also have small painted front doors and orange or peacock-blue glazed tiles.

Children are playing on the ground with stones. In the distance a red and gold palanquin carried by two youths with bare legs and big straw hats is travelling towards the open countryside. From between the curtains of the palanquin a small gloved hand emerges but one can't tell whether it's a man's or a woman's. Beyond the fields on the far side of the main road is a landscape of tall grey rocks spiky with blue grasses.

So here I am sitting in front of my puzzle as if I were ten years old in the room in Sicily just after the war. I have discovered the secret of its composition. I am just on the point of assembling the last pieces and bringing together the fractured image of a fascinating old Chinese woodcut. I haven't time to eat or drink. Just like I was then I am in a frenzy to finish it determined not to lose a single piece in the excitement of contemplating the image which my fingers have created out of the confusion with so much effort and patience.

Dear Marina

A fortnight has gone by since I last wrote to you. I have been up to my neck in the novel. For twelve days I wrote for ten hours a day until I ended up in a state of intoxication. Then I stopped and for three days I've done nothing but sleep. Now I wake up feeling tired and slightly sick with my stomach tense and a mist in front of my eyes. I've almost no desire for food but there's some kind of inner hunger boring into me.

Basilia took me under her wing as if I were an invalid or more accurately someone suffering from an obsession. She brings me boiled herbs. I haven't a clue what they are but I swallow them down and they stimulate me like coffee.

My shoulders were really tense and painful and she came back at night when she heard the bath water running before I went to bed and gave me a quick massage.

She would go and buy fish and cook it for me. She'd bring it along already boned and leave it on a small plate on top of the writing desk as if I were a kitten. But I wouldn't touch it. By evening it would be covered in flies and would end up in the rubbish bin. The only things I enjoyed were her aromatic herbs and her infusions which can be drunk in a second and which bring the cool freshness of a wood to my palate. Afterwards I was overcome by a slightly drunk feeling and I wrote till nightfall oblivious to the passing of time.

One morning the front doorbell rang. I didn't go to open it. It rang again. After a few minutes of this I couldn't bear to hear it ringing and ringing in my ears so I went to open the door feeling like a sleep-walker.

Can you guess who it was? Damiano's step-mother! Her small powdered face was dark and serious-looking. She sat down without waiting for me to say a word and began to tell me about Damiano and the way he's being unfaithful to her. He's carrying on with his aunt – who's the sister of his dead mother and who has two sons as old as he is!

'I found it out by chance and I immediately challenged him with it and threatened that it was either me or her. But he swore that I'm the only one he loves and that with the aunt it's not serious – it's just a game.' She says she thought it was all over but now she realises it's not. She focuses her sparkling eyes on me and says 'I just don't know what to do.'

Bewildered and stupefied I had missed half of what she was saying. I was also amused by the absurd story of the aunt. I thought of Damiano's overflowing eyes his large gentle hands and his desperate love for his mothers. I wanted to kiss her. But she was so serious and unhappy and trusting that I didn't dare break the spell of her confession. But why on earth does she come to me about it? Did she register some empathy in my eyes that time we met by the sea? Had she recognised my desire to know her to open her to enter inside her clear dark skin?

I advised her to go and talk to the aunt. She looked at me suspiciously. I can't have seemed very persuasive – the trouble was I was desperate to extricate myself. A few days earlier I would have kept her talking for hours about Damiano. But now she was keeping me from my most pressing commitment and I felt vexed. I was thinking 'when I get back to work shall I have lost the thread as has happened so many times in the past?'

But she was in no hurry at all and she had no intention of going. She talked about him with the candour and openness of a hurt child. I watched her gesturing with her small suntanned hands. Her wrists tinkled with metal bangles. He had probably given her these perfectly circular bracelets to be fastened on her like handcuffs. She wore the same closed circles round her neck and on her ears like a sign of ownership.

'But how can he love her and me at the same time?' she asked frowning. And that was exactly what I had asked myself over Marco and with the same stunned hopelessness. How can one love two people at the same time?

I took her hand – the soft silky paw of a kitten. I had a strange temptation: to move that hand on to my sex and press it. I didn't want to talk. I was bored by this story of double and triple loves. The only way I could use that moment to reassure her was through a gesture of love. But I also knew that she would have repulsed me.

I don't know how long she stayed there talking. I'd ceased listening to her any longer. I stared at her with a stupid fuddled look as if she were a ghost. I pressed her hand and fixed my gaze on her mouth furrowed by a small criss-cross of wrinkles. The scent of her cheap make-up rose insistently in my nostrils.

Finally she got up to go. At the front door I embraced her in an effort to communicate affection and solidarity but I was so lacking in energy that I think I must have seemed cold and brusque.

Dear Marina

I had decided to leave right away but now I can't do that. I'm basking in the limbo of this convalescence. I haven't the will to do anything. I put off all decisions. The mere idea of packing up my luggage and putting everything in the flat to rights makes my head spin.

Basilia treats me as if I were an invalid. She brings me milk and vegetables. She fills little plates and leaves them for me beside the bed on top of the chest-of-drawers. Like the little altars I used to build with flowers sugar and chocolate behind my desk at boarding school.

Towards three o'clock when the children are asleep she comes to give my shoulders a massage. And every time she comes she tells me some horrifying story. I listen to her but the words come from a distance and I lose the thread. She realises that I am not following her and her voice grows less assured. It becomes weaker and loses its impetus.

Now and again the desire to see Damiano grips me so strongly that somehow I gather up the strength to get dressed and go out. But as soon as I am within twenty paces of the Neptune Bar I change direction. I'd like to ask him to make love with me again but I know that to go begging for love only brings poison. I know that because I've been through it before. So instead I go down to the beach and swim out to sea alone swallowing small mouthfuls of cold water. I return home exhausted and dazed.

I want to telephone Giorgia but I don't do it. Even lifting the telephone receiver is an effort. I am letting myself be fed by Basilia as if I were a domestic pet with dishes of milk overcooked rice hunks of cheese boiled eggs and pears.

Looking out of the window makes me feel queasy. Sitting at my work table makes me vomit. Eating bores me to tears. Having to sleep irritates me. I no longer have any sexual desire. Even the idea of masturbating fills me with profound boredom.

Once or twice I've tried to take up the novel but the business of reading it seems beyond me. I'm convinced that what I've done is bad and ridiculous and yet every now and then I wake up in the night terrified that the 'precious thing' on the table has vanished or been spirited away by enemy hands. I get up trembling all over and go and check it is still there.

Even Verdi no longer gives me any pleasure – only boredom. I put on the tape recorder and listen to it in a distracted sort of way but I am antagonised by his theatricality – all those obscene emotions just blurted out meaninglessly on the stage.

I would so enjoy talking to you. I long to hear your voice – but the telephone lies there within reach of my hand inert and mute. I would like to see you even more but without the effort of looking for you. I shut my eyes and imagine hearing you arrive: you open the door. You come in. You are wearing a blue skirt and flat sandals and one of your gathered blouses which is slipping off your shoulders. Your hair falls down to your waist like a blanket. You approach my bed. You look at me mockingly. You bend down. Very lightly you touch my lips. I open my eyes and the enchanted dream house starts to come to life and I long to play in it once more.

Dear Marina

I have had a high fever for two days. Basilia called in a local doctor called Doctor Cipolla who's got a stomach like the Dome of St Peters and wears bi-focal glasses. He took my pulse and listened to my chest and stared at me blinking his nervous piggy eyes. But he was considerate and pleasant and I quite liked him. Then he opened his mouth and spouted out such banalities: that I'd got a chill and had an inflamed throat and must swallow down sulphanamides. A hundred years ago he would have presented me with leeches to stick on my neck. He charged me twenty thousand lira and as he went off he added pompously:

'You should have someone with you. Solitude isn't good for the nerves.'

Today I'm better in spite of Cipolla and his sulphanamides which needless to say I haven't taken. I managed to swallow some mozzarella cheese with a small piece of bread. Basilia is worried about me and she runs backwards and forwards through the flat. Tonight she is going to have supper with her sister-in-law so her hair is rolled up in curlers and she has a red handkerchief tied over it. She must be very worn out after Mauriccio's long illness what with everything she has to do in her own place and the care she gives me. But I can't stop her doing as much as she can. It seems that in the end all this effort keeps her healthy: she is happy and stimulated and she laughs about nothing even if she does feel ashamed of her two missing front teeth and always clamps her mouth shut in a reserved kind of way.

I don't know whether I need her or not. She doesn't give me time to react to her absences. But certainly she needs my need. It doesn't take much to revive her shrivelled puny body. For once it isn't me who's being the mother: I am settling down egotistically into the role of the sick daughter.

Dear Marina

Last night I dreamed I was on a train. Instead of going forwards or backwards it went directly downwards beneath the ground towards some unknown destination. To begin with I was scared but then I experienced a feeling of exultation. I abandoned myself to the overwhelming forces drawing me towards the centre of the earth. I held your hand between my hands – though I'm not sure whether it was yours or Basilia's. But anyway I clasped that hand and held my breath – it was like when I went on the big dipper and my stomach rose up into my throat and my eyes stretched wide open in the face of a black emptiness.

Today I have been able to listen to the Duke of Mantua without feeling worn out. There is a sharpness in the honeyed voice of Renata Scotto – something hard and crystal clear that lit up my senses.

I am better. I've just eaten some fish followed by water melon.

Basilia brought some huge ice-cold slices on a wooden platter. We ate them together with the red juice dripping down our chins. We were laughing helplessly but we didn't know what at.

I shall be sad to be separated from her from the gentle yet powerful sapience in her hands from her laughter from her deep throaty voice from her need to be swallowed up. That's the reason she makes herself small and ugly: so that someone can eat her up without feeling too much guilt. Her sons gnaw at her from morning till night and she gazes at them with infinite love. But also with hatred. I have detected the hate that flashes from those dark laughing eyes. I have glimpsed the cruelty which suddenly leaps out like a little demon with a forked tail. Sometimes I've even had the uneasy suspicion that she is very quietly poisoning her family with her brews of secret herbs so that she can weep over their deaths for the rest of her life. Every day her husband becomes more angry and free with his fists. Her sons grow heftier. And Basilia watches them incuriously with half-closed eyes. She is worn out from giving in to every one of their fads but also from harbouring the mysterious strength of women that makes her terrible in her fragility.

Dear Marina

This morning I was woken up by a phone call from Giorgia who gave me your latest news. She told me you had begun a love affair with a 'student from Padua called Gerardo'. I jumped up in bed. What Gerardo? And what of Guiomar? And all your theories about the phallus – the natural enemy!

As usual Giorgia has no money and no job. She told me she has decided to go and pick grapes somewhere near Macerata where food and lodging are provided free. Her voice sounded cheerful down the phone.

'A friend of mine made 800,000 liras in a month.'

'But how many hours do you have to work?'

'Twelve hours a day.'

I rang Roberta to find out how she is. She's not well. Her whole body aches and she suffers from insomnia. She's no longer able to walk. She asked me for money in a guilty tone of voice that I find hurtful. Suddenly she attacked me:

'All you know is how to give me money. You never come and see me. You're always away always in some other place when I need you.' She was crying. 'You square your conscience with your shitty money and you don't give a damn about me.' She's right. I didn't know know to reply.

'If you aren't earning anything and you're ill it's natural I should help you' I say. 'I'm earning more money than you and I help you because I love you. You know that.' But it doesn't ring true.

I have always watched her from windows and secret places: like the time she stole that piece of apple tart and started to crumble to pieces . . . that long distant island afternoon when her beauty flooded my heart. As with my mother there is a shadow separating us: the age-old temptation of incest . . . the terrible fear of finding myself with the flesh of my flesh between my lips. It is for this reason that I close the doors and put chairs and carpets and tables and dishes of food between her and myself. It is because of this that I prefer to watch her clandestinely from outside the window and to transform love into money and the safe haven of maternal generosity.

I don't accept her aging and crumbling into ruin. Like with my mother I feel inexplicably guilty for everything that has gone wrong since those times together that were so perfect and fulfilled. There's something inhuman about my obstinate rejection of her. I accept myself growing old and my own death but I don't accept them in the case of my sister. I don't accept her suffering from this illness which is eating away her bones. It seems so horrible that when I see her I lose all sense of gaiety and joie de vivre. As a result I avoid her and this makes me cruel and insensitive.

Marina I would like to know more about your Gerardo. How does he live? What does he do? Giorgia only told me he is a student – but a student of what? Tomorrow I'll ring her again for more details. But I already know what she'll say:

201

'You're only ringing up about Marina.'

And of course that's the truth. But in order to demonstrate that it's not the truth we will chatter endlessly about her and all sorts of irrelevant things I know already.

Dear Marina

Today Damiano's stepmother came round again. Her name is Margherita and she's nicknamed Rituccia. She told me this as she sat stiffly on the edge of the chair twisting a ribbon that hung from her hair. She wanted to know what Damiano was like when he was with me.

'Supposing he'd said "I want you but I want Margherita too" what would you have done?' she asked me.

'I don't know. He never did say that.'

'But if he had?'

'But he didn't.'

'He thought it though.'

'How do you know?'

'He told me so.'

'Why didn't he tell me then?'

'He felt sure you'd say "no".'

'I'm not sure whether I would have or not.'

'You see he likes having two women.'

'Can you accept that?'

'I don't know. Maybe I do accept it because although he swears he's not seeing his aunt any more I know they're still involved.'

'But does his aunt know he's having an affair with you?'

'I don't know. I haven't had the nerve to go and talk to her.'

'Perhaps if you went to see her you'd stop worrying.'

'I'm married to his father. I can't give myself away to his aunt. Supposing she told him about me?'

'And does your husband know what's going on with his son?'

202

'I don't think so. But he must guess something because every now and then he threatens to kill him.'

'And if you left your husband would Damiano want to live with you?'

'Perhaps he would. I don't know. He's never talked about it. I'm ten years older than him and he might feel ashamed.'

'But he isn't ashamed to make love with you?'

'No.'

'Nor with his aunt – and she's eighteen years older than him.'

'No.'

'So what are you going to do?'

'Nothing. I can't leave him and I can't feel any peace of mind.'

'Do you love him?'

'I think about him all the time. Without him it seems like I'm not myself.'

'Do you sleep together at night?'

'How can we when I'm sleeping with my husband and he's in the next-door room? We make love up on the mountains or in the woods or in a friend's house.'

'Do you like the way he makes love?'

'I like the way he kisses.'

'Me too.'

'It's as if his lips turn my soul right upside down.'

'I felt that too.'

'Do you still think about him?'

'Yes I do.'

'Do you long for him?'

'Yes.'

'Did you feel bad when he left you for me?'

'Yes I did.'

'The first time it happened I was in the kitchen making sauce' Margherita told me impetuously as she leaned forward. 'Damiano came in and put his arm round my waist. Only for a minute as a joke but my legs went all limp. I'd never felt anything like that before . . . Afterwards in the evening I was waiting in the kitchen when he came back from the bar. He didn't really embrace me – just a kiss on the ear. "Hello mother" he said. That's what his father wanted him to call me. He sat down at the table to eat his supper and then off he went to bed. I was like a zombie all next day waiting for that stolen kiss. In the morning when I got up I thought – shall I look beautiful enough? Shall I smell nice? Every day while I was cooking and cleaning that thought was always with me and then one day my husband wasn't there and he held me a moment longer and I kissed him on the mouth... '

It was nice talking with her. I enjoyed having her there sitting so quiet and composed in front of me her eyes sparkling and her voice full of excitement. We went on talking about love for three hours and when she left I felt quite lost.

I stole Basilia away from her children and took her to the fair. Heaven knows why but as soon as we got to the merry-go-round we started to behave like two excited children smearing our mouths with a ball of spun sugar. For two days I've watched the big wheel with its lights going round and round in front of my window. They always put on the same pop record that goes '... tomorrow I shan't see you-oo-oo-oo and if you're tired of me-ee-ee-ee...'

Every so often Basilia got worried about her children whom she had left with a neighbour. But I dragged her through the booths forcing her to play at fishing for prizes shooting at targets and making her climb up the slippery slope and go down the slide with me.

We ate fried squid torrone and almonds and we drank a horrendous orange juice that tasted of bleach. When we were sliding down the rails inside the tunnel of death she held on to me so tightly I couldn't get my breath.

We went back home with our hair all tousled and feeling exhilarated. Of course the children started to tell her off and like a fool she fell for their amorous snares and burst into tears. Her husband attacked her as soon as he got back from work. I heard them shouting at each other. Perhaps he was hitting her too. Now it is I who feel guilty for having dragged her out of the house. But I don't believe she'll regret it. She has talked about the fair so nostalgically saying she hasn't gone to it since she was thirteen. In fact for years she's never gone out at all except to do the shopping.

Dear Marina

I've decided to leave tomorrow. I shall go and see Fiammetta in Sicily where she's rented a house on top of a cliff. 'There are three hundred steps to get to it' she told me triumphantly. 'There's no electricity or running water but it's a marvellous place. The water's clean and clear and you can catch fish weighing five kilos so why don't you come? But you must arrange it because I've no more money to put in the phone' – and she laughed exultantly as only she can not giving a shit about anyone or anything. I said 'yes' and I felt more light-hearted. I want to leave this place that's over-run with mice and I want to swim in a sea where the water's clean and I want to be touched by Fiammetta's gaiety.

I said good-bye to Margherita who has become miserable and silent. She wished me a good holiday. She made me promise to write to her and in return she will write to me about Damiano. Then she told me the latest about his double and triple love affairs. She kissed me demurely on the cheek and went off tapping her high heels on the pavement.

As it's my last evening Basilia has asked me to go out with her. She seemed anxious about it.

'Aren't you afraid of your husband?'

'He's on night shift.'

'And the children?'

'Once they're asleep they don't wake up not even for an earthquake.'

Sparkling lights... red tablecloths... flowers... candles. It was a good restaurant I took her to. She hadn't been to a restaurant since her wedding-day. She was thrilled and delighted and kept running her hands over her dress.

'Do I look all right?'

'You look lovely.'

'You're joking. I'm old.'

'Old at thirty-six? You must be crazy! Now – what would you like to eat?'

'I don't know. You tell me.'

'What takes your fancy?'

'What I'd really like is cannelloni with cream.'

'And after that?'

'A cocktail of scampi with a spicey sauce.'

'And then?'

'What about duck with orange? I've never had it. It's on the menu and I'd like to try it.'

We both gorged ourselves. Waiters with white gloves bending over us discreet and sly ... music from the little orchestra mawkish and sentimental ... wine on ice that had to be taken out of a little silver bucket each time ... flambé bananas ... ice-cream with brandy. In a moment of euphoria Basilia confessed that it reminded her of the latest photo-comic with Fabio Testi. And just like the people in the comic we were playing our parts – eating and drinking and behaving like ladies. We even danced in the sugary darkness on a floor of blue and yellow glass. Only the dashing young engineer or the elegant grey-haired air pilot was missing and this gave a slightly bitter flavour to our comic strip.

Basilia was dreamy and entranced for a while even forgetting her sons back at home. She half closed her eyes and drank her wine gracefully without getting drunk. By the end of the evening she was laughing like a woman who feels beautiful and confident of herself. And in some way she really had become beautiful: her eyes were shining her cheeks flushed and she moved with slow langorous gestures.

We went home just before midnight. Her husband was due back at two o'clock in the morning. She went in to the flat softly carrying her shoes so as not to make a noise. She hugged me dramatically in an anguished farewell in which tears were mixed with suppressed laughter. I breathed in the scent of her hair that was usually impregnated with frying oil but tonight smelled of Parma violets. I promised her I would come and see her from time to time.

I went and had a shower. I slipped into bed. But I'd eaten and drunk too much. I couldn't get to sleep. I decided to go for a walk. I got dressed and went out. The town was deserted. Without exactly meaning to I went straight to the Neptune Bar. I sat on the edge of a big tub of oleanders in front of the closed shutters.

Then I went down to the sea. It looked dark and peaceful and emanated a sickly smell of oil. I walked along the beach my feet sinking into the dry seaweed stumbling over the rinds of water-melons and empty plastic cans. A broken bottle cut my heel. I turned up the Via Garibaldi and stooped in front of the closed newspaper kiosk. The black outline of a woman with high heels and a skirt split up to her thighs confronted me from a poster: 'Femininity is fashionable again'.

Further on I came across a cat with five new-born kittens. They were suckling her hairy stomach. I bent down to look at them. The mother showed me her teeth but without much conviction. She returned to licking her kittens still watching me but without moving. The kittens sucked greedily pushing their paws against their mother's swollen belly and waggling their deaf heads.

In Sicily I shall be even further away from you Marina. What difference will it make though? A hundred kilometres or five hundred are the same distance when we are not seeing each other any more. Yet it seems as if I am distancing myself dangerously from the zone of your love.

Back in the flat I read part of the novel. It seems awful. I drank some wine. I thought 'I'm drinking to a colossal failure'. I sat down to write this last letter to you before leaving. Then I shall read them all on the train.

In the end I've decided not to go back to bed. I can't stand the smell of the old matrimonial bed and I can't endure yet again the thought of the quarrelling voices of the neighbours. And the prospect of being enveloped by that scorching trail of coffee at dawn turns my stomach. I shall take the train to Sicily at five in the morning.